In the
Electric
Eden

In the Electric Eden

stories

Nick Arvin

AN IMPRINT OF BOWER HOUSE

DENVER

Design and illustration by Margaret McCullough

Featuring three new stories: "The Accident", "Location", and "Armistice Day".
"Commemorating" first appeared in *The Black Warrior Review.*
"The Accident" and "Location" first appeared in *The Normal School.*
"Armistice Day" first appeared in *The Rocky Mountain News.*

Library of Congress Number:
2018937273

ISBN 978-1-942280-55-2

10 9 8 7 6 5 4 3 2 1

For my parents

Contents

Introduction

We mark the eras of human history by our technologies—Stone Age, Iron Age, Information Age—and we often mark the eras of our own lives by our technologies as well. I place a memory in context by recalling the car that I drove at the time, and a life-changing phone call is remembered, in part, by the shape of the phone that I gripped. An important aspect of my memory of 9/11—an event made possible by the intersection of some specific technologies—is hearing about it on the radio, and then searching for a television where I could see the news, and finally of watching the towers fall on a tiny, silent cathode ray TV set on the counter at a diner.

We assume that the progress of time turns technologies into history, but perhaps it is the other way around, and without the progress of technology we would have no history. In the film *Cave of Forgotten Dreams*, Werner Herzog shows two Neolithic paintings that are located on the same cave wall and appear so identical in style they might have been painted by a single artist. But carbon dating has shown that they were painted 5000 years apart. Herzog, in a voiceover, observes that the paintings indicate a people who lived "outside of history." Time was a circle, until the rapid evolution of our machines pulled it straight, and if our technologies define the line of the past, then we assume that they will do the same in the future. In 1999, I was in a writing workshop where another student, Antoine Wilson, submitted a short story titled "It Is the Business of the Future To Be Dangerous." I particularly envied that title. Later, I learned that the phrase comes from the writings of the philosopher Alfred North Whitehead. "It is the business of the future to be dangerous," Whitehead wrote, "and it is among the merits of science that it equips the future for its duties."

The future seems more dangerous than the past because we cannot imagine what we will soon invent, or even the consequences of the things we have recently invented—whether the effects of social media, the emissions of our engines, or the ramifications of artificial intelligence. But the only solutions we consider involve different technologies, new technologies, more technologies. To go backward is impossible, for a thousand reasons. The rush of progress is larger than any one of us, a dumb behemoth; where it will lurch next, we can only guess, and even the engineers, scientists, and programmers who feed it are helpless to stop it, can only hope to give it the slightest of nudges.

I wrote the stories collected in *In the Electric Eden* during the years 1998 to 2001, and the book was first published in 2003. At the time I intended for only two of the stories in the collection to be considered historical fiction, but looking at it now I see that time makes all fiction into historical fiction. The stories that were contemporary when I wrote them rely on technologies and devices that now seem quaint, or soon will. They record a world where many of us didn't own a cell phone; voicemail was a relative novelty; YouTube, Facebook, and Twitter didn't exist; and Amazon was a website that sold books. I remember I was sitting at a desktop computer searching the internet when I stumbled across a video of Thomas Edison's 1903 film of Topsy the elephant's electrocution—featured in the title story of *In the Electric Eden*—and the fact that I could watch a video on an internet website still seemed remarkable to me.

By that time I had studied engineering in college, and I had worked for a couple of years in product development at Ford. Engineering was a career I had stumbled into, based on a knack for math and science and a vague attraction to the idea of building things like rockets and airplanes. But I'd grown up in a little Midwestern town where I didn't know any actual engineers, and I had no practical experience with what they did day-to-day. Becoming an engineer was like parachuting into a strange tribe with its own language, customs, and habits of thinking. It was interesting to observe these people, and to consider the effects of the things we were creating, how the things we make in turn remake our lives, our feelings, our souls.

Fiction has always been my means, or mechanism, for grappling with the world, asking questions, trying to find patterns and threads of sense. It is in our nature to understand ourselves and our world through our stories, and as we shape our stories, our stories in turn shape us, in a restless cycle. Stories and technologies are similar in this way, two feedback loops between creators and creations, two conversations we are having with ourselves.

Engineers who write fiction are relatively rare, and many of the engineers who do write fiction favor science fiction, which often reflects on the same themes I've mentioned here. My own stories are set in the past or the present, but it is all of a continuum: the present is the science fiction of the past, and fiction describing tomorrow is the historical fiction of tomorrow's tomorrow.

In one of the stories in this collection, a character in the eighteenth century marvels at a new technology that allows a man to fly. He observes, "The hard shell of the impossible had been cracked, and who could say what might appear next?" I believe that, whether we are noticing it or not, the hard shell of the impossible is cracking every day; these stories are an attempt to notice.

—Nick Arvin
2018

"Progress, therefore, is not an accident but a necessity. . . .
It is a part of nature."

—*Herbert Spencer*

"I, though interested in diesel engines, did not take my
eyes off the girl."

—*Max Frisch*

In the Electric Eden

My grandfather Henry kept an unusual umbrella stand beside his front door. Encased in seamless gray leather, it appeared coarse-grained and lusterless in the shadowed corner where it stood. Beneath my fingers it felt rough and slightly bumpy. Generally cylindrical, it widened at the bottom, like a tree trunk, or an elephant's foot—which it was. Topsy had been the elephant's name.

Recently, I received an e-mail that started me thinking about the umbrella stand again, and I began to do some research, in the library, on the Web.

One central fact can be agreed upon: they Westinghoused Topsy on the grounds of Luna Park, Coney Island, on Sunday, January 4, 1903. But the histories and novels tend to depict the event with bright lights and blazing colors, offering in it a symbol for all the excesses of Coney's heyday. We see an elaborate stage, a giant switch labeled 100,000 Volts, bleachers filled with cheering spectators at ten cents a head. Thomas Alva Edison, the Wizard of Menlo Park himself, presides. A score of men strain against ropes as big around as their arms to bring Topsy into position. For a warm-up she eats bushels of cyanide-laced carrots and shakes them off. In the background Luna Park's quarter million electric bulbs burn against a dark sky, transforming night into noon and providing the park with its advertising sobriquet: The Electric Eden. The execution switch is thrown and two hundred and fifty thousand filaments flicker and dim.

The scene my grandfather described to me, however, seemed much more flatly horrifying.

The trouble all began when another animal, a dog named Marie, was lost.

Henry was just a boy at the time and Marie belonged to his Uncle Fielding. Fielding was fun, the sort of man who knew instinctively where a dog wanted to be scratched and who could pull a boy onto his knee and chatter happily—whispering one minute, then booming into a shout and shaking and tickling—until the child was silly with giggles. Fielding was a drinker, however, and when he drank his face became red, his eyes bloodshot. He would go on binges, and then he no longer scratched dogs or told stories. Instead he smoked ferociously. His wife, Emma, referred to this, angrily, as Fielding's "bibulous state," and she avoided him at such times. She would come over alone to visit with Henry's mother and father or she would disappear into her bedroom and claim illness until her husband sobered. On the occasions when Uncle Fielding—actually Henry's mother's cousin—came over in his bibulous state, Henry was sent outside to play.

Everyone acknowledged that Emma, Fielding's wife, was pretty and quite a catch for Fielding. She was charming—this was the word that always came up, "charming," although Henry had once overheard his mother mutter "arrogant." Emma did tend to hold herself at a distance from others, and she had impeccable posture, her chin raised a few degrees above level. Before Fielding met her and they married she had been a teacher and she never entirely lost that teacherly air. Henry, however, did not find her arrogant. Emma often brought him candies or slipped a nickel into his palm when his mother wasn't looking. She always asked how his schoolwork was going. She said the world was making rapid, wonderful progress and a good education would make Henry successful in it. She once took him to see a moving picture show about the attractions at the 1901 Pan-American Exposition in Buffalo and Henry nearly fell off his seat watching the immense images that moved like life upon the silvered screen. They depicted in silent detail the Exposition's crowds and marvels: the Infant Incubators, the Aerio-Cycle, the Electric Tower capped by the Lady of Light. Afterward, he thanked Aunt Emma repeatedly. "It was beautiful," he said.

"I only hope it was educational." She smiled. She spoke to the theater manager and took Henry to the booth upstairs to examine the projector, an Edison Company Projectoscope with a hundred intricate, silvery, simultaneously spinning parts. Emma admired Edison, his work ethic and his products, and she had recently given Henry's family an Edison phonograph for Christmas. Sometimes when Fielding and Emma came over they would dance waltzes or two-steps together while Henry turned the phonograph crank.

Despite Fielding's drinking binges it was evident that Emma loved him very much and he her. They sometimes held hands like children do, and Fielding never made decisions without Emma's consent. The two of them exchanged at certain moments a complex, secret look that Henry never saw either of them offer to anyone else. They had no children of their own, but they did have Marie. She was a collie-shepherd mix with dark eyes that bore a permanent expression of wide curiosity. Fielding had taught her a number of clever stunts including one where she stood on her hind legs and balanced a small steak on the end of her nose for as long as a minute, until Fielding gave an order and she flipped it, caught it in her jaws, and swallowed it in a gulp. Even Emma, normally above putting her hands on furry creatures, sometimes consented to rub Marie's belly, to the dog's squirming delight. Marie accompanied Fielding everywhere—except to work, and she passed his workdays slumped morosely by the door waiting for Fielding to return. She was not allowed to stray off, and Fielding kept her leashed whenever they went out on the town. He claimed that the immigrants crowding into the Lower East Side would happily steal a dog like Marie and make her into sausages. Everyone laughed at this.

But late in the spring of 1902 Marie did vanish into the streets of New York. Her disappearance set off a series of tiffs and quarrels because it occurred while Fielding was at work and Emma was at home—she had opened the door to let in some air, and she had not noticed Marie was gone until Fielding came home.

Some days later Fielding came over to the apartment where Henry and his parents lived, still upset about the dog. He complained to Henry's parents in tones not so much bitter as despairing. Henry's mother tried to comfort him; Henry's father said Fielding would just have to forget about the animal. Fielding sighed. After a minute he wondered aloud if Henry would be interested in going to see the circus. It might cheer them both, he said.

Henry was eleven years old at the time: of course he wanted to go. His mother gave him a few dimes and sent him out. Fielding folded a newspaper into a boat and Henry pushed this up and down through the gladdening spring air, narrating aloud a series of adventures, shuddering the boat side-to-side with each explosion of its imagined cannons. The day was warm and the streets were filled with people. Carriages and pushcarts rumbled on the flagstones. Men doffed their hats to ladies with parasols. Vendors in long gabardines sold fruits, tobacco, crockery, eyeglasses, stationery, fabrics, and other sundries. They took a ferry from Thirty-fourth Street to Queens, and looking back Henry could see all along Manhattan the unfinished buildings that punctured the skyline with skeletons of steel I-beams. In Queens the buildings were not so tall and the streets seemed wider. They passed hotels and saloons and boardinghouses, and there was a sharp, unpleasant smell that Uncle Fielding said was the kerosene refinery. He strode ahead and Henry followed, playing with the paper boat and calling to Fielding now and again to see some surprising thing, and the distractions were such that Henry did not notice until they were waiting in line at the entrance to the circus that Fielding had begun steadily rolling cigarettes and tippling from a flask in his pocket.

For ten cents they saw Jolly Trixy, the Fat Lady, with Princess Wee Wee, thirty-four inches tall, and Zip, the What-is-it? They watched a man put a series of longer and longer swords down his throat, then, finally, a live snake. Henry thought these things were wonderful, but Fielding was smoking cigarettes as fast as he could roll them, and after the sword-swallowing he led Henry on a long silent ramble that moved between several tents without going into any.

From the big tent came the noise of a brass band playing a tune that started slowly and then went faster and faster. Henry thought they might go inside, but his uncle led him around behind. A knife thrower was perched on a stool over a bucket of water, shaving with a blade shaped like a letter from a foreign alphabet. When he glanced up there was a nick of blood on his cheek. In circled cages, tigers and lions rested their great heads on heavy paws, and in a fenced area nearby stood several show horses, their manes woven into intricate braids. A half-dozen elephants idled in another pen. Fielding walked over, set his elbows on the fence above the water trough, and watched as an elephant put her trunk in and sucked, then curled the trunk into her mouth and drank the water down. "Know why elephants drink so much?" Fielding said. "To forget." He laughed.

Henry put his hands on the fence. He felt uncomfortable with his uncle in this state and began to wonder how he could start him back toward home. The elephant gazed at them with one eye. The creature was huge and ponderous and gray like something more mineral than animal. Fielding's laugh, meanwhile, ended with a hacking cough, and he broke out his tobacco and rolled another cigarette. He lit up and puffed. The elephant raised her trunk to eye level and poked toward Fielding. Fielding grunted. "Here." He held out the cigarette.

The elephant grabbed it, as she might a peanut. The knife thrower from his seat across the pen called, "Topsy! Stop!" but the elephant opened her mouth, revealing wide flat teeth and an enormous muscular tongue, and deposited the cigarette there. She closed her mouth, then seemed to pause a moment. Henry pulled his hands away from the fence and backed up a step. "Uncle," he said. Fielding sniggered drunkenly.

The elephant stamped the earth abruptly with one foot—Henry felt the shock travel sharply along his spine—then screamed in a rending, hissing trumpet's wailing. Her trunk lashed like an enraged serpent. Henry began to stumble back and his uncle grabbed his shoulder painfully. The elephant reared, and the creased and flabby gray flesh of her vast belly hung before Henry. Fielding was pulling him backward. Henry's thoughts were rushing and without sense and already there were tears in his eyes making everything more confused. Suddenly the elephant came down, splintering the fence and knocking over the water trough. Henry's shoes were soaked and he wondered—even as the elephant charged—if his father would be angry about the ruined leather. The serpent trunk seized Fielding and in lifting him pulled Henry upward also, until Henry cried out and suddenly Fielding let go. Henry landed on his back, the air knocked from his lungs, and now, above him, Fielding's feet kicked and one of his shoes had come off and he beat with his fists against the trunk curled round his neck. The elephant shook him testily. Henry pushed against the ground with his elbows and slid a little away, still gasping, air like sand in his throat. The elephant stopped shaking Fielding, lowered him slightly; she seemed to be calming somewhat. The knife thrower was shouting, but Henry had no sense of where the man was, near or far. Then the elephant brought her head back, turned Fielding upside down, and, with a casual gesture, as a man might beat a mud-caked shoe against a stone, swung Henry's uncle against the packed earth of the fairgrounds.

He fell limply when she released him. She ran forward, trampling the body. Bones cracked. Henry rolled away and covered his head with his arms. He heard the elephant's heavy steps receding, then she seemed to be gone. Henry raised himself to his knees. The elephant was trotting past some of the smaller tents of the circus from which men emerged and fled or shouted and gave chase.

A line of spittle leaked from the corner of Fielding's mouth. He lay twisted and misshapen, his neck crooked strangely, blood leaching into his shirt in several places. The first people to gather and stoop over Fielding's body ignored Henry. In their cages several of the African cats roared and paced. Henry sat among some barrels near the big tent, and curled himself tightly so his knees pressed into his eyes and he saw white-hot stars of pain.

After a time someone tapped Henry on the shoulder. The knife thrower peered down, the shaving nick on his cheek still raw. "Weren't you with him?" he said, inclining his head toward Fielding's body, now covered by a multicolored tent canvas. Henry nodded. A police officer, silently gripping his arm, escorted him back across the East River. When they reached the apartment on Fifteenth Street, the officer stood in the parlor, clutching his hat in his hands, and attempted to explain to Henry's parents what had happened. Henry sat to one side, silent and small.

Aunt Emma did not emerge from her home for a couple of days after Fielding's death. But she came to the funeral, and with her tall proud posture she looked splendid dressed in black. Fielding had been well liked and a crowd of neighbors and friends and coworkers gathered at the grave. This seemed to please Emma and she accepted their condolences with grace and calm.

After the funeral she began to get out again. She had some money left, but she talked about finding work to support herself—perhaps she could return to teaching. She came over for dinner at Henry's mother's invitation. Henry watched her quietly and she seemed a little more distant than usual—she did not have any sweets or coins for him, did not ask him about his schoolwork—but otherwise she seemed fine.

She didn't ask him about the elephant until a couple of weeks after Fielding had died. What had happened to the animal? Henry didn't know. The last he had seen, it was running away. She asked if Henry might accompany her to the circus and although it was not clear what she planned to do there—she said only that she wanted to talk with the manager—Henry's parents consented.

For the trip Emma wore a new dress with ruffles down the sleeves and skirt. She tied a red silk ribbon around the collar and wore a wide-brimmed hat with a matching red ribbon around the crown. She even bought a new hat for Henry, a bowler that was too large and settled just above his eyebrows. "You'll grow into it," she assured him confidently, as though she expected he might well grow into it that very afternoon. At the circus they were taken to a heavyset man with quick black eyes named Grieling. He spoke to them inside a small, lime-green tent with a straw-scattered floor, a few crates filled with papers, and a desk of boards laid over two sawhorses. Emma explained who she was and inquired after the criminal elephant, Topsy. She said that, in her opinion, the most severe justice should be brought down on the animal. This boy—she indicated Henry—had witnessed the most horrible and unwarranted murder of his own uncle. Something ought to be done.

Grieling sat behind his makeshift desk with steepled fingers. He glanced at Henry, then stared at Emma, allowing the silence to grow obvious and discomforting. "I would like to help," he said. "However, the animal in question is no longer here."

Emma tapped her foot. "What do you mean? I don't suppose she just flew away?"

"No, ma'am. We sold Topsy along with a couple older elephants to"—he riffled through some papers, then held one up—"Messrs. Thompson and Dundy. Seems they're building a new amusement park in Coney Island, adjacent to Steeplechase, and they've retained some elephants for the heavy lifting."

"You let the beast go?"

"Certainly. That seemed like a good place for her." He smiled. "After all, it's well away from where passing drunks might attempt to feed her lighted cigarettes."

He allowed another of his pauses, and Emma drew herself up. "My husband loved animals. If that beast got a cigarette from him, she must have snatched it from him, stole it right from his lips, I expect."

"My knife thrower said he saw your husband offer the cigarette to her."

"Your knife thrower is a liar."

Grieling shrugged and looked at Henry. "You were there, son, right? How was it?"

Henry looked at the man a second, then stared at the ground. He felt the two adults gazing at him. Their silence seemed to exert an enormous pressure, forcing words from him that he did not want to speak. As he opened his mouth, however, Emma interrupted: "Let the child be. He has nothing to do with it. The indisputable fact is that your animal murdered my husband. It's a matter of justice."

Grieling shrugged. "Regardless, on Coney Island the elephant will be strictly employed as a beast of burden, for lifting and carrying and such. The only people she might hurt would be the men working with her, professionals." He flipped through some of the papers on his desk, glanced up. "I'm sorry. I cannot help you with the elephant. Was there anything else?"

Emma strode out so quickly that Henry had to run to catch her. He was sweating and breathing heavily by the time they arrived at home, but his aunt appeared still fresh and unbent, as if she had merely crossed to the other side of the room and back. Henry's mother asked what had happened and Emma said, "Tomorrow I'm going to Coney Island," and she stepped outside again, leaving Henry to explain, which he did, slowly, laboring through a growing sense of inadequacy. And later, alone in his room, listening to the endless, battling cries of the newspaper boys in the street below, he sat wondering—if Emma had not interrupted, how should he have answered what Grieling had asked him? He did not know himself what he had been about to say.

The next day Emma went alone to Coney Island. She returned greatly agitated. She said she had found Thompson and Dundy on the site where they planned to build Luna Park, in a small office crowded with blueprints and documents waterfalling from cabinets, off shelves and desks. Dundy greeted her graciously and cleared a chair for her, nodded and sighed with empathy while she spoke. Thompson, working at a sketch on his desk, did not appear to be listening. But when she finished, Thompson looked up, Dundy glanced over, and Emma could see between the two men, without words, a decision being formed. Thompson returned to his work, and Dundy said, softly, "You have to understand, we paid a considerable sum for that elephant."

She protested that the elephant was a man-killer, a murderer. Dundy said Topsy was only hauling lumber now. She was a very useful animal. He began to touch Emma's arm in a most inappropriate manner, and he made his points with perfect, infuriating unctuousness. Emma, to her own aggravation, grew shrill. Thompson finally broke in from his desk, loudly, "I understand, ma'am, that your husband fed old Topsy as lighted cigarette. Seems like you would expect an animal to react in some way or another to that, wouldn't you?" Emma said she was so upset she nearly cried. Dundy took her by the elbow, led her to the door, and gave her a pat on the behind as she went out.

Emma decided to write appeals to the editors of the New York dailies, to the mayor's office, to the police commissioner, to lawyers and local officials and state politicians. She asked Henry's mother to proofread these for her, and together they stuffed and stamped the envelopes. They mailed the flurry of letters in a single day, and Emma seemed pleased with the accomplishment. That evening she stopped in Henry's room and said to him, "Tell me, Henry, what's the truth? About the cigarette?"

Henry was relieved by the question, relieved by Emma's casualness and to be able to say what he knew. He said, "I think Uncle Fielding thought the elephant wanted to smoke."

"Ah." Emma looked away. "Well, that would be like him, wouldn't it?" She seemed to intend this as a small joke, but her voice didn't quite manage the joking lilt.

Henry understood, suddenly, that he should have lied. He said, "I mean—"

"Well!" his aunt said, but then she did not seem to have anything more to add. She said, again, "Well," and turned away.

The replies to her letters trickled in slowly, or not at all. No one was interested; her problem was too odd and morbid. One official, the only correspondent who seemed to have gone to the trouble of looking into the matter at all, brought up the issue of the lighted cigarette. Emma's efforts to locate work were also unsuccessful, in large part because her health began to fail—she complained of dizziness, shortness of breath, weak limbs. She took to bed. Henry's mother started delivering soups and jarred fruits to her, did her housecleaning, and after a month decided to simply move Emma into their apartment and save all the walking back and forth.

Henry slept on a cot in the front room while Emma took his bedroom. Sometimes in the night he heard a moaning so soft that he was not certain if the sound was only a delusion of the late, restless hours. Frightened, he never did get up to go and check. A doctor came once a week and peered at Emma through a pince-nez. His reports were terse. He said, "The main thing appears to be grief. Give her time."

The Edison phonograph Emma and Fielding had once danced to was moved into her room and Henry was often given the task of sitting beside it and turning the crank. They had a number of cylinders and he went through each of these, one after the next, Emma insisting he should not skip any. When he changed cylinders he could hear through the curtained window the rattle of hooves and the general call and babble of conversation from stoop to stoop and window to window. He imagined his school friends playing in the sunshine while he labored in this grim room. He turned the phonograph crank, and with a sick feeling he recalled the accelerating music from the big tent at the circus.

One day Emma beckoned him to her side. She was feeling particularly poorly at the time, and he stood awkwardly while, as if to verify his presence, she probed with her fingers at his belly. Then she gripped his arm and shook it weakly. "Tell me," she said, peering at him. Her eyes seemed glossy with fever. "Really. Did he feed her that cigarette?"

Henry stared at her. Had she forgotten she had already asked? He stepped back. "No," he said.

She turned away. "Yes," she said. "That's what I thought."

Emma had not been out of bed for weeks and a gossamer of snow lay in the streets when a letter arrived from Thompson and Dundy. Without explanation they announced they had decided the man-killer elephant should be executed and a large gallows would be built to hang her. They extended to Emma and any other immediate family members an invitation to attend and witness. The day's papers carried the same news. All of them mentioned Fielding "who had fed the elephant a lighted cigarette." They noted that Topsy had recently threatened a group of Italian workmen involved in the construction of Luna Park. The elephant was beaten off with two-by-fours and no one was hurt but this, apparently, now provided the impetus for killing Topsy.

"Ugly showmanship," Emma said. She seemed caught between her hatred for the animal that had killed her husband and her newer but equally powerful hatred for Thompson and Dundy. They were executing the elephant, she said, only to get their new amusement park in the news. "I can't possibly go," she said at last. "I'm much too weak."

In the papers, letters appeared from members of the ASPCA protesting that among civilized peoples death by hanging was now recognized as an inhumane form of execution. Surely it was equally cruel as a method of execution for elephants. Thompson and Dundy ignored their pleas initially, then abruptly conceded the point and announced that the Edison Company would electrocute Topsy on the same scaffolding where they had originally intended to hang her.

This roused some interest from Emma. "Henry should go," she said. "It will be very educational."

On the day Topsy was to be executed the weather had turned harshly cold. Luna Park still would not open for several months and it presented a bleak, unfinished landscape; the towers, pagodas, and minarets of its rococo fantasyland were only half-built and the park's electric lights in their hundreds of thousands had not been installed. In attendance were just a few reporters, three men from the Edison Company, and a handful of interested persons, Henry among them.

The electrocution, scheduled for 1:30, was delayed when Topsy balked at mounting the ramp to the execution platform. She stood with her legs stiff, leaning slightly backward against the pull of her trainer's rope. She ignored coaxing and offers of food. No one was willing to apply much force.

Henry was both cold and sweating. He stood some distance behind the other observers. Their breaths puffed and swirled and partially obscured the elephant. She looked smaller than he remembered her to be, yet still massive.

The electrocution apparatus was very simple—two flat-plate electrodes for Topsy to stand on, one for her right front foot and other for her left hind foot—so finally the Edison men simply moved the equipment to an open yard and the trainer walked Topsy over. They fed her two cyanide-laced carrots to make her death certain. A technician with a high-pitched voice called, "I'm going to turn the switch now." Then he did. Topsy lifted her trunk briefly. Smoke billowed from under her feet. She sagged and keeled rightward. The only sounds were the heavy impact of the elephant against the frozen ground, then a smatter of applause—gloved hands clapping. The smoke and the smell of burned elephant flesh dissipated quickly in the open air.

Henry found he felt neither joy nor relief. He understood this to be justice and important, but, shaking in the cold, he was not certain what justice was supposed to feel like. It seemed wrong of him to feel so cold and miserable, to feel so sorry for the elephant and somehow guilty.

One of the men from the Edison Company recorded the entire sequence with a moving picture camera. He stopped filming as soon as Topsy was down and began packing the camera away. The other two Edison men retrieved the electrodes. The reporters jotted notes, then chatted a moment or set off for someplace to warm against the chill. A gentleman who had paid for the elephant's remains sent in a couple of skinners to strip the hide. He announced to the reporters that Topsy's head would be preserved for mounting, her organs sent to a professor of biology at Princeton. My grandfather walked alone to the ferry that would carry him back around Brooklyn toward home. He stood at the rail in the stinging cold, looking down at the white scrim of the boat's wake, at the gray peak and trough of the water. It seemed he saw there, again and again, the elephant's quiet death and collapse.

His aunt wanted him to describe the event in detail. He told her how the elephant's feet had smoked, described the noise of it hitting the ground. "Oh, I wish I could have seen it," Emma said. "I wish I could have."

It was a relief when she started to emerge from her bed more often. She ate more and the color returned to her face. She began to talk again of finding work, of getting an apartment of her own again. It made Henry happy to see his aunt improving. Tending to his aunt's illness forced him to ponder endlessly his uncle's death, and the death of the elephant as well, all of which caused him an anguish that he would have liked to have been able to forget. He had never spoken about it with anyone, for he knew his father would only scoff and his mother would tell him, kindly, that he must drive such thoughts from his mind. Now he had more time to go out on his own to play, and his aunt also pointedly drew his attention back to his schoolwork, and with these distractions, and the passage of time, the images of the deaths of his uncle and the elephant lingered less before him.

Then one day Henry was out on the streets and he noticed a handbill advertising a public lecture and demonstration by the Edison Company. It said: SEE FOR YOURSELF: THE MORTAL PERILS OF WESTINGHOUSE CORPORATION'S HAZARDOUS ALTERNATING CURRENT! Among other features, the handbill promised a presentation of the moving picture of Topsy's electrocution. Henry remembered what his aunt had said—that she wished she could have seen it—and, struck by the thought that this might further hasten her recovery, he ran to tell her.

The day of the demonstration she wore one of her best outfits and told Henry to retrieve his new bowler. They walked several blocks to a small auditorium and got seats near the back, behind well-dressed ladies and gentlemen who whispered quietly and gripped pens and notebooks. Henry felt very young, and Emma had to remind him to remove his hat. The stage curtain rose and silence followed. Near the front of the stage was a table sprouting various straps and thick wires that ran offstage. A silvered screen for the moving picture hung at the back of the stage and beneath this were three animals in cages—a cat, a dog, and an orangutan. The cat sat and stared at the crowd while the orangutan hunched in a corner of his cage and picked meditatively at his fur. The dog looked familiar. "Marie?" whispered Emma.

A man in a dark tie and coat strode onstage and introduced himself as a personal friend and assistant of Mr. Edison. He explained that the Edison Company and its competitor, Westinghouse, were engaged in a national debate about whose technology was superior for supplying electricity to the home—Edison's direct current or Westinghouse's alternating current. The Edison Company wanted the public to be fully informed regarding the dangers of AC. "As you will see," he said, "even the slightest exposure to Westinghouse's AC can lead to instantaneous death."

Henry was straining forward, trying to make out the dog's features. He saw Emma glance at him. "No," he whispered to Emma. "That can't be your dog. It doesn't even look like Marie." This was a lie, however. Whether it was Marie or not, this dog looked very much like her, with her black and tan coloration, with her dark, curious eyes.

The man on stage grimly noted that the new electric chairs William Kemmler and Martha Place had been electrocuted in were AC-powered. "However," he said, "to give proper credit to the public service of our competitor, we prefer to say that the criminals were 'Westinghoused.'" He pointed to the animals behind him. These were strays, he said, wild animals on the city streets that had become dangerous. Despite all its problems, Westinghousing did provide a quick and humane form of execution. Two men in white coats came on stage and began strapping the cat into the tabletop electrodes.

"It's Marie," Henry whispered, shaking his head. "Right, Aunt Emma?"

"Stop squirming, Henry," Emma said abruptly. "Listen to the presentation."

The man with the tie picked up a switch and held it casually in his left hand while describing how the present methodology had been empirically derived through controlled scientific experiments on dozens of animals, using electrodes in different places and with and without the use of saline water, which proved to be unnecessary because the natural fluids inside the animal were sufficient to pass current through. The ASPCA, he said, approved of this methodology as an efficient and painless means for the disposal of the hundreds of stray animals collected by the city each year. He threw the switch. The cat died quickly and silently, crumpling onto the table.

A woman in the audience raised a white-gloved hand. "How many volts were used?"

The Edison representative checked a dial. "Just 234 volts."

While they strapped in the dog Henry hunched in his seat, in dread. The dog stood meekly, the switch was thrown, and the dog, like the cat, collapsed without sound. Emma did not flinch, did not move at all that Henry could see. Nor did she react when the room darkened and they showed the silent film of Topsy's execution, nor even when the orangutan was put on the table, the switch was thrown, and with a crackling noise its fur burst into yellow flames excreting coils of stinking black smoke. Fortunately the Edison men had buckets of water nearby, which they hurriedly emptied on the burning orangutan. The audience set down their notepads and applauded.

Emma was stern and silent during the walk home. Then she went to bed, and in the days that followed her illness and weak limbs returned, her posture fell. When Henry was sent in one day to tend to the phonograph, the heavy curtains were drawn so that only a thin, vertical line of light illuminated the room, leaving all the corners in darkness and lending yellow edges to those objects that could be seen. Emma waved him away from the phonograph. She did not want the noise. Henry watched her shape in the dark a minute. Sometimes at night now, when he could not sleep, his brain seemed to surge erratically around the images of all he had seen. At other times he would seem able to see and feel nothing but the bedsheets against his skin, and these he felt intensely, as though they were heavy, made of rusted and pitted iron. He wondered if the surge of electricity that killed the elephant had touched him through the earth or air. He wondered if he had caught the same strange illness his aunt had. Suddenly wanting to reassure her, he said, "That wasn't Marie. I'm sure it was not."

"Don't you like dogs?" Emma said. Henry was the only other person in the room, yet he wasn't sure if she was speaking to him. "Don't you like animals?"

"It wasn't Marie, Aunt Emma."

"Oh, but Henry—" she turned and stared at him, glassy-eyed. Then, her features suddenly contracted, and she snarled, "You're the one."

Henry retreated to the door. He hesitated with his hand on the knob. Emma looked around slowly. When her gaze lit on him again she said, "Henry," and her voice was filled with sudden strength and clarity. "My husband is gone. Don't you understand? Fielding is dead." But she turned her head from side to side on her pillow as if to deny her own statement.

Henry opened the door and fled to find his mother. She listened to him, then she went into Emma's room and shut the door behind her, and thereafter his mother alone tended to Emma. But Henry still lingered nearby, uncertain what he was waiting for, or hoping for, or guilty of. *"You're the one,"* she had said. He sat in the next room or paced along the hallway and his emotions alternated between simple ennui and strange feelings of pain and uncertainty—and years later, when my grandfather sat in his armchair relating all this to me one late evening, he said perhaps—perhaps it was merely, exquisitely, a confused kind of love. At the time, however, he did not know how to name it or how to respond.

The next week Emma began to cough violently in spasms that brought up blood. One day when Henry came home from school his aunt's bags stood beside the front door. His mother was bustling about. She said, "Your aunt is going to stay at her cousin's farm in Missouri. The doctor feels fresh air will do her good. A change of scene. There are too many reminders here." Behind her Emma was coughing painfully, and Henry wondered if he was himself a reminder.

Emma, when she emerged, was dressed as finely as ever but moved with a terrible languor. Her flesh had grown pale, slightly gray, her dress hung limply from the bones of her shoulders. Her thinned neck had a snakelike appearance and blue veins were visible in the flesh at her temples and in the backs of her hands. Henry's father escorted her with a hand at her elbow. She embraced Henry without strength. Still, it seemed to Henry that she gazed at him with a full intelligence. She patted him on the shoulder, then she was gone, and it was the last Henry saw of her.

That evening his mother helped him move his things back into his bedroom. "You must be pleased to have your bed again," she said. And he said, "It's my fault."

"No, Henry," she said. "You'll feel better when you're not sleeping on that old cot."

"It's my fault that Aunt Emma is sick."

"No, dear, that's not true. Don't bother yourself with such silly notions."

"It is true."

"Henry, how can that be?"

"It is," he said. It did not entirely make sense even in his own head, and he could not explain. But he felt it, and he remembered that Aunt Emma had told him so, he was the one.

"Forget that thought," his mother said. "I don't want your father to hear you saying that. Try to forget that idea. Promise to try?" she asked him, and he did.

For a time Emma sent letters fortnightly from Missouri. "The sky here is so large and the air is so clean," she wrote, "I feel it must be doing me good. The people are kind, but I miss all of you . . . Tell little Henry to be industrious and persevering in his studies." This was pleasant and positive, but it seemed mechanical when the same formula was repeated with minor variations in letter after letter. Then her correspondence stopped. About a year after she had left New York, word came that she had passed away. The cousin in Missouri wrote, "I have seen her here with the hand of grief around her heart, squeezing slowly. She struggled for a long time, but found no escape." And for this too, my grandfather Henry told me, he had felt responsible.

Quietly, I asked my grandfather, "What about the umbrella stand?"

It arrived just a couple of weeks after Emma departed for Missouri. An attached letter gave the warm regards of Thompson and Dundy and inside were several free passes to the rides at Luna Park. A letter was sent to Missouri, asking if she would like the umbrella stand. *"No,"* she wrote.

Henry's mother wanted to simply be rid of it, but his father, practical-minded in all things, saw no reason to throw away such fine and unique piece. He set it in the entryway, placed a couple of umbrellas in it, and whenever a new guest came in he made a point of showing it off. Generally, people were impressed.

Henry hated the thing: he told me this while we sat looking at it in his own doorway. For a long time, whenever he went out the door he thought about taking the umbrella stand with him and giving it to some street urchin or burning it in a garbage can. But his father would be furious, so Henry left it. Then, somehow, over the passage of time he came to be accustomed to the thing; it seemed like a part of life, irreducible. He passed by it every day. He stowed umbrellas in it. When eventually his parents died he took the umbrella stand home and put it into his own doorway, thinking he would probably soon throw it out or sell it.

Henry was my father's father, a kindly, small old man with purple lips and watery eyes, and I have always remembered how even when I was a boy he shook my hand exactly like I was a man. When he passed away, I wept.

He has been dead a long time now, and the umbrella stand has resided for many years in my own doorway. For some time I had been walking past it without seeing it when that e-mail drifted in, another random piece among all the random Internet flotsam that arrives every day in my electronic mailbox. Someone I hardly know had forwarded it to me and a dozen other people. The subject line said, "Edison vs. Elephant: World's First Snuff Film?" and it contained nothing but a blue underlined link to a website where anyone can watch the film Edison made of an elephant's execution.

Topsy pops up in a little box on the screen. The image is black and white, pixelated and blurry, but an elephant-shape can be made out, standing. Then smoke rises from her feet and the elephant-shape falls over. It happens quickly, and it appears just as my grandfather described it. Except that I always imagined Topsy raised her trunk up and forward, as if to trumpet, angry. Instead she curled it in, toward herself, pained.

Every morning I Westinghouse my toast, like anyone else. AC courses through all the walls of my home. My workday is spent at a computer fed a steady diet of alternating current through an appalling tangle of power cords. I create virtual documents, send e-mail, browse the electronic spaces of the World Wide Web.

I look at the feet, the digitized image of feet from a film made a hundred years ago, and I try to pick out the one that now stands in my doorway. Left front? Right rear?

My grandfather Westinghoused his toast too—as I recall he liked it charred nearly black.

My grandfather went once to Luna Park. His pragmatic father felt they might as well use the tickets they had been given. As they rode the ferry to Coney Island, Henry was determined not to have fun, but Luna Park. . . . With his mother and father he rode the ferry to Coney Island. He arrived determined not to have fun. But Luna Park was resplendent, fraught with diversions, utterly different from the forsaken landscape where he had seen the elephant die. Here were joyous crowds and bright colors and flashing lights and the happy tumult of children screaming, bells ringing and bands playing, criers crying, barkers barking, touts touting, and a skyline cluttered with baroque turrets, campaniles, and domes. Henry slid down the Shoot-the-Chutes, saw the War of the Worlds, visited the head-hunting Igorots and the Eskimo village, rode the camels, ate at Feltman's, and took

the Trip to the Moon where gamboling moon-men sere-
naded him with moon-songs and gave away pieces of green
cheese. At twilight Luna Park flared building by building
into dazzling spires of electric lights.

I asked my grandfather—because at that time I was young
and he was old and I was concerned for the child that he had
been—I asked him, "Were you able to forget?"

"Only to be distracted," he told me. "But I was glad for
it—just then it was enough."

I was fourteen or fifteen then—not a child and not much
of an adult either, but able at least to listen respectfully while
he told the story. And I remember walking with him that
evening, his pace and step still sure although his shoulders
drooped now within his overcoat and his white hair wisped
lightly in the wind. We stopped at a certain point where we
could see much of the city, containing its millions of unknown lives, all of it as brilliantly alight as the great old Coney
Island parks once were, yet these buildings ten times taller
and more massive. And none of it provided distraction for my
grandfather anymore, I believe, for silently he wept, brushing
his cheeks with trembling fingers while in his eyes all the un-
told lights caught and burned.

What They Teach You
in Engineering School

A s he turned out of the driveway, the old man had already forgotten where he needed to go. Behind him someone shouted, "You're going the wrong way!" which was just like these damn poker players, always handing out more advice than anyone wanted. And, well, so what if he was? What of it? He, after all, had won twelve dollars *and* the Glass Lady today. He proceeded ahead and powered up his window for good measure. He was old. He had earned the discretion to go any way he wanted, wrong, right, left, up, down, through. He had a phone. He could call someone if he got lost.

He stomped the accelerator. He had never gone this way before, and now he would. An adventure. He remembered his youth, before he married, before his two sons—the ladies, the army, the sit-downs and wildcat strikes when the union was strong. The memories were a scatter of images, then a rushing, rapid multitude, and his hands trembled on the steering wheel. But his hands always trembled now.

And now where was he exactly? He had turned left then right. Or had he? Memories had recently begun rising in tides that floated him for minutes, even hours, while matters of the present fell from sight. He drove sometimes for miles and miles, made stops and turns, all without seeing a thing.

He concentrated. Here lay the road, its white lines and yellow dashes and its smudges of black where potholes had been repaired with shovelfuls of hot asphalt. Trees lined the road, which was nice. The few stands of trees that remained these days were mostly getting torn out so they could build all those houses that looked the same and bunched together like toadstools. "Developments" they called them. Ha!

The Glass Lady—a blown glass figure, she actually looked something like a deranged chipmunk—teetered precariously on the dashboard, and the old man grabbed her and put her in his pocket. He didn't want to lose her. Winning the Glass Lady for the week from that crew of cheats and rapscallions was no small thing. The trees along the road thinned, then were gone, and he drove between long fields of corn. He was lost. This could be anywhere in the state. Way up ahead some kid was driving a go-cart along the shoulder, pulling a plume of dust behind. He passed a single, small house surrounded on three sides by the corn, its front window looking across the road at more corn. With aluminum siding, black shutters, and a gray roof it was a little smaller but otherwise not much different from his own house, which gazed across a similar road to a similar field.

He had raised his family in that house; his wife had died in that house. He had now lived there for forty-five years. When Duke, his older son, was small (and even when he was pretty big) he liked to go off into the corn and disappear for hours. The corn was well over seven feet tall at its peak, and it was possible to get completely lost in there, except you only needed to pick a single row to follow and it would eventually lead you to the edge of the field. Even Duke could figure it out.

Duke, Duke, Duke. Something to remember about Duke. (The memory came like a fish hooked but struggling hard, so that just when he saw the glimmer of its scales it plunged again into the dark. But he worked it carefully, taking in line when he could, letting it out when he had to, until, finally, he could reach down, grab it—) Duke! He was supposed to meet Duke, today, this very afternoon, back at the house. Duke wanted to take him out to dinner.

He passed through the dusty wake of the go-cart, then stopped and honked. He opened a window. A small girl was driving the go-cart—a sorry-looking machine patched together with duct tape. "Hello, girl!" he shouted. "Hello!"

She stopped and stood and peered at him. She wore a soil-smeared T-shirt under a pair of outsize denim overalls. Her hair, greasy, was cut in an uneven pageboy around two narrow eyes and a smudge of a nose.

"I'm lost," he said. "Do you know what road this is?"

She nodded.

He waited, blinked. "Well? What is it?"

"Gleason Road."

"Gleason. And which way is that?" He pointed. "Is that north?"

The girl frowned and looked into the rows of corn. After a moment she shrugged. But, peeking at the sun, and with a little thinking, he supposed that was indeed north, which meant he was headed about 180 degrees in the wrong direction. He said, "Crap." Then, "Please excuse my language, miss. My thanks to you." He pulled ahead and set about turning the car around. He twisted the steering wheel hard left and pulled forward. He turned the wheel all the way right, reversed. The three-point turn became a five, and then a seven-point herky-jerky slow dance, because the road was narrow and bordered by deep ditches and because he had a big car and his cataracts made gauging the distance between the rear bumper and the cattails in the ditch troublesome. He did not want to get stuck in a roadside ditch in the boondocks, so he was cautious.

Duke gripped the steering wheel of his little subcompact like a race-car driver—neither too tensely nor too lightly. At stop signs he slowed with linear precision, then accelerated smoothly away. He felt the hum of the tires in his body. It seemed possible that if he pulled back just right on the steering wheel he could lift the car into the sky.

In two months, Duke would receive his degree in engineering. In three months, he would begin working as an engineer. In ten minutes, he would pick up his old man and take him out to dinner and tell him about the degree (which his old man knew about already) and the new job (which was the big surprise). He stopped at a light, waited for green, then spun the wheel and aimed the car exactly ninety degrees leftward.

It was good to be in control. Much of his life had been a matter of blundering through, getting by. He had graduated high school a year late, then went to work in a donut shop, spent miserable days getting up at 4 a.m., laboring under the weight of a pastel-yellow paper hat, and coming home stinking of powdered sugar and deep-fried dough. He started getting big. Meanwhile his brother, Kevin, two years younger, became valedictorian of his class, brought home pretty girls to meet his mom and his old man, got into Cornell, and became a lawyer. Kevin managed his life with an ease that seemed supernatural to Duke.

Eventually his old man, with undisguised annoyance, made use of his thirty years of accumulated connections at the plant to pull Duke in, got him assigned to operate a press that pushed nine-inch ring gears onto heavy steel transfer cases for pickup truck axles. The work was no less dull than donuts, but the pay was about four times better. His old man soon retired, but Duke stayed on the midnight shift for six years, then the day shift for two, loading the press, pushing the two palm buttons that caused a ring gear to be crushed into a transfer case, removing the two pieces made one, loading again, pushing buttons, removing, loading, pushing, removing. It awed Duke to think of all the ring gears he'd pressed onto transfer cases now propelling thousands and thousands of pickup trucks down the highways of America.

He jiggled his steering wheel a little, pleased by how smoothly the car swayed within the lane. The surroundings were brightly familiar. Hardly a stone or an ear of corn had changed since high school when he had been up and down these roads endlessly, killing time while he should have been studying. The road began a long curve ahead and he slowed to enter it, then remembered his confidence and accelerated.

While he was working at the plant he had noticed the engineers in white shirts and polished shoes who occasionally walked up and down the assembly line. They would get together and stand pointing at the various machines, gesturing, talking. They seemed to be into endless pointing and talking, and they had offices stocked with coffee machines and computers. The offices could be entered only with special electronic ID badges the engineers wore clipped to their belts, and Duke had envied, first of all, those badges, like passkeys to some hoity-toity club. Then, thinking about it, he envied their jobs altogether. He imagined wandering the line, pointing and chatting, retreating now and again to an air-conditioned office. Oh, he knew it was more complicated than that; he saw what they did. An engineer needed to know how to bolt a machine into the floor, how to diagnose a torque testing station with a burnt-out clutch, how to fix leaky half-shaft seals by experimenting with different kinds of rubber gasket. But it looked much more interesting, more rewarding, than running a stamping press relentlessly, endlessly, forever—load, press, remove.

One day a circuit box blew and the entire line was down. An engineer happened to be nearby, watching the electricians work. He was young, his smile quick and confident. Duke asked him, "How does someone get a job like yours?" And the engineer said, "Go to Ann Arbor. That's the best place; that's where I went."

It took most of a year for Duke to mull the idea and become firm in his decision. When he announced one day that he wanted to go to college, his old man said, "It's about time." But when he mentioned engineering, his old man was incredulous. He said in a mock-gentle tone, "But, Duke, how can you be an engineer when you're always breaking things?" Which was true, Duke had a well-earned reputation for mechanical ineptitude. As a child his brother's things had been off-limits to him, because in Duke's hands toys quickly began missing eyes and wings and wheels, or their little battery-powered motors would not run, or they merely fell to pieces, completely destroyed. Later, as a teen-ager, Duke ruined a wall in the rec room while attempting to build a set of wall-mounted bookcases. He exploded a vacuum cleaner while trying to repair it, giving everyone in the family sneezing fits for a week. He nearly took his old man's head off when he accidentally sent the lawn mower blade flying. Yet, he argued to himself, didn't those mistakes only indicate he had the interest and inclination, that he merely lacked the proper skills? Skills could be learned, surely, by anyone with enough determination. He had begun to feel more comfortable with machines, perhaps because of the years spent working a press eight to twelve hours a day, five to seven days a week. Things broke down from time to time at the plant, and not as a result of anything Duke had done. Many of the tools were upwards of forty years old and fell apart under simple fatigue. When the line was stopped, Duke sat and watched the skilled tradesmen and the engineers work—disassembling, repairing, reassem-bling—and some of the mystery was removed. The machines were actually, in many ways, rather simple, products of mere human minds and hands. He could do this.

When he had made it clear he was adamant about becom-ing an engineer, his old man finally said, "OK, fine, and how are you going to pay for this?"

"I have money saved."

"Oh, right. Because you live at home and never go out."

"Dad, kiss my ass," Duke wanted to say. But he said only, "I've been saving."

"Saving," his old man said. "OK, well—" he shrugged "—good luck."

Duke took community college classes in math and phys-ics, prepped two hours a day for six months for the SAT, wrote twelve drafts of his statement of purpose, and it still shocked him when he was admitted to the School of Engineering.

His old man's response was a slightly skeptical, less-than-encouraging nod. There always seemed to be some mitigating incident. Days later, Duke, lit with confidence, volunteered to change the windshield wipers on his old man's Buick. He'd taken one of the wipers off its arm and then, accidentally, let the arm snap back into place before he'd put the replacement wiper on. When the bare metal hit the glass, the entire windshield fractured into a glimmering blue-green jigsaw puzzle. When Duke told his old man what had happened and offered to pay for a new windshield, his old man nodded fiercely, hell yes, he most certainly would pay for it.

But now his subcompact hummed as he hurtled around the curving asphalt. The car had always been small for him, his knees rubbed the bottom of the steering wheel, and it wasn't exactly overpowered, but it took a corner with surprising poise. He could feel the tires flexing and straining under him but still holding to the asphalt, and he stayed precisely in the center of his lane. He was thirty-two, finishing his engineering degree this summer after five and a half years of class work. Last week, after interviews and a drug test, he'd gotten an offer to come back to work for US Axle. He knew precisely where he would clip his electronic ID badge—right-hand side, first belt loop.

About thirty feet ahead a car was laid across the road like a barge.

Duke tried to get his foot from the gas pedal to the brake, and he recognized the car, even as the rear passenger side door of his old man's Buick came quickly and improbably close—it seemed he could have reached ahead and touched it by the time he felt himself suddenly flung forward and heard a short and horrible chaos of steel buckling and ripping. His seat belt caught him and his head snapped forward then down and the rest of him strained against the belt. There was a sickening, immeasurable black moment cut from time, lost entirely.

He blinked and raised his head off his chest. The steering wheel was much closer to him than it should have been, like he'd gotten into the car after a short person had been driving it with the seat forward. The floor underfoot felt bulged and odd. The windshield was gone—it lay in a crystalline scatter over the dashboard and in his lap. The hood was doubled up, blocking his view. He managed to swing the door open and tried to get out but could not, could not move, and it took him a long, desperate moment to figure out that this was because he had not yet released his seat belt.

He pressed the seat belt button and it retracted just like it always did, like nothing in particular had happened. With both hands gripping the top of the door he stood for a moment, waiting for the road to stop seesawing. His little car had T-boned his old man's Buick like it desperately wanted to get inside, and the subcompact had taken the worst of it. Duke sneezed once and things steadied. He felt remarkably OK—not entirely clearheaded, but his limbs and organs seemed to be in working order. He could see his old man sitting in the driver's seat, looking angrily through one window then the other. With a hand on the Buick for support, Duke started around it, shouting, "Dad! Dad!"

His old man rolled down his window and said, "Duke?"

"Are you OK?"

"Duke." His old man squinted at him. "Duke, I can't believe—damn it, son. Why the hell did you run into my car?"

"Why were you parked across the road?"

"I wasn't parked. I was turning around."

Duke tugged at his old man's door. "Come on, we should get away. The car might explode."

His old man frowned. "That only happens in the movies. You've just put a bit of a dent in my car, that's all."

"It does not only happen in the movies."

"Do you smell gas?"

Duke sniffed. "No."

"Then it won't explode. Settle down, OK?"

This, Duke thought, was the kind of thing they should teach him in engineering school—how to tell if a car was about to explode. But they had taught him nothing so practical. Adrenaline buzzed in him like a low voltage AC current, and he felt too disoriented and too near collapse to argue with his old man. He breathed deep, put his hands on the roof, looked down at his old man's face—craggy and contemptuous—and felt, as he always did around this man, like he was about knee high, looking up, hoping for a pat on the head. He tried to recover the relaxed confidence he had felt earlier, the calm self-possession, the certainty of his progress. He breathed. He blurted, "Dad, I've got a job lined up."

"What're you talking about?"

"A job. Never mind. It's not important right now."

"A job? Where? California? Did I send you that article about how all the engineers are going to California now?"

"No, back at US Axle." He thought this would actually, finally, merit some congratulations, and he allowed himself to speak with the unhesitant force of authority and pride: "I'm going to be a process engineer."

His old man's lips tightened around his teeth and his eyebrows drew down. He slapped a hand on the car door. He sputtered. "You have to be kidding." He glared at Duke. Duke shook his head. "So you're going to be one of those bastards installing robots so they don't have to deal with humans and the union? Or did they hire you to pack the whole damn plant off to Mexico?"

Duke looked at the ground. "You know it's not like that."

"Shit." His old man rubbed the palms of his hands into his eyes. "Shit. Son. You embarrass me." He held his hands a few inches from his face and glared at them.

Duke was quiet. Then he said, "Look."

But his old man wagged his head, and Duke didn't really want to continue. He stood embarrassed and silent, looking across the roof of the Buick while a breeze ruffled the leaves of the cornstalks along the road, raising smells of dust, of stale fertilizer and chemical herbicides. He wished he were not here, closed his eyes and wished it hard.

But nothing changed.

When he looked down his old man was leaning forward to turn the key in the ignition. From the front of the car came a series of clicks, but the engine did not start. He turned the key again—more clicks. He sat back and said to the windshield, "Well, go ahead and fix it."

"What?"

"You're the engineer," his old man said. "It'll be good practice, fixing a broken-down car."

"We should get out of the road."

His old man glanced around. "You knocked me half off the road anyway. Just take a look."

"This isn't really what they teach us."

"What do they teach you? Different ways to push paper?"

Duke stepped away. "Dad," he said. His old man peered out the window, frowning, his forehead furrowed like a washboard. "OK," Duke said. "Open the hood."

The hood clunked and popped up an inch. Duke went to the front and fumbled to find the release latch. He had to bend to look for it while his old man scowled at him through the window. When he had the hood up, it blocked the view from the front seat, and Duke sagged in relief. He told himself that it was no small measure of success that his old man seemed to think he might actually be able to do something useful. But he looked down and knew it was hopeless. He had even taken an internal combustion engines class last semester, but it was all about efficiency curves, Otto cycles, and the relative merits of spark retardation versus increased air swirl to reduce NOx emissions. The class never looked at an actual engine. Here were chunks of metal and plastic all interconnected by tangles of hoses and wires. Nothing was obviously amiss. None of the hoses were broken. Nothing was smoking. He poked at a couple of random wires.

Engineering school was an exercise in frustration and sleeplessness for him. He studied endlessly and barely maintained Cs. The classes were packed with skinny, pimpled kids who occasionally approached to ask if he would mind buying liquor for them. They did in fifteen minutes home-work problems that took Duke an hour and a half, and they crowded the back rows of the lecture halls and whispered while he perched in the front row and took scrupulous notes he hardly understood. Worst of all, he knew from experience that none of what he was studying had anything to do with what an engineer did in the plant—resolving production problems, diagnosing and fixing machines. Instead he was learning about differential equations and the combinational forces of complex kinematic situations and how to calculate convection coefficients for spheres in flows of air or water. Once, after a particularly bewildering lecture in thermo-dynamics about the Gibbs function, an entirely theoretical construct related to various other theoretical quantities in some mathematical manner, Duke, in an agony of frustra-tion, went to talk to the professor in his office. This professor had an uneven gray mustache and thick, dusty-looking eye-glasses, and the other students snickered because he still car-ried a slide rule. But Duke liked the man because his fingers were thick and scarred with years of building experimental equipment and because he often came into class wearing lab coats that smelled of solvents and pants perforated by tiny burn holes from stray welding sparks. In the professor's of-fice, surrounded by shelves and boxes piled with a hundred miscellaneous pieces of equipment, Duke felt like this was a man who built things—not a math or computer-headed geek, but a man he could talk to. He started complaining about the Gibbs function. He wound himself up and claimed he could never, ever figure out the Gibbs function and asked, "But who cares? Gibbs won't help me fix a fried logic box. How will it help me weld one piece of steel to another, or design a machine to torque to specification? How is it going to help me install a new air gun into an assembly line?"

The professor snorted through his bristling mustache. "Look, son," he said. "This is a research institution. We teach first principles, not applications. If you want nuts and bolts and welding, you should think about one of the technical colleges."

"Oh—" Duke said, realizing, suddenly, sickeningly, that there would never be any sympathy for him in this place. He coughed and nodded and tried to look like the kind of student who might be forgiven for his transgressions. Contritely, he asked if the professor might explain Gibbs one more time. He passed the class, with a C minus.

"Got it yet?"

Duke called, "Why don't you try the key again."

His old man grunted. Clicks came from somewhere in the engine, but nothing visible happened. The clicks stopped, and Duke peered into a muddle of dusty, greasy steel and rubber, hating it all.

His old man called, "Got it?" Duke prodded one of the hoses, frowning. His old man added, "Five years of college now, isn't it? And you haven't learned a single useful thing, have you? J. H. Christ in a duffel bag."

Duke wished that they had taught him how to *make* a car blow up. But he said, "I guess you're right." He came around to his old man's side of the car. "I can't figure it out."

"Get the girl to help us," his old man said. "Where did the girl go?"

Confused, Duke turned and scanned the road. "What girl?" The road was empty, except for a go-cart a short distance away. Its steering wheel had been cleverly fashioned out of a plastic dinner plate.

"There was a girl. She could help us."

This stalled Duke. Around them the fields of corn were now dead still. Overhead, a distant plane marked the sky with white contrails. A house stood about a half mile down the road, and beyond that stood a single enormous maple tree amid the corn. This far into the back roads there might not be anyone coming along for quite a while. He supposed that they needed police, tow trucks, insurance claims agents, maybe an ambulance.

Dust hovered in the air. Behind him, Duke's old man said, "Hey. Quit standing there. Let's go."

Duke went over and leaned in the window. "You're OK?"

"Yeah, yeah. Help me out. I'll walk with you."

"Maybe you should stay and rest."

"Help me with this door," his old man said, plucking at the inside door handle.

Duke seized the outer handle and pulled. The door would not open. His old man said, "Heave. Use your weight. You've built up some padding at college."

Duke let go of the handle and stepped back. He and his old man stared at each other. It was always this way. After Mom's death, two years ago, he had taken a full week out of school to help with the arrangements while Kevin, on the other hand, flew in from his law practice in Phoenix for just a half day—it was the first time he had been back in three years. Duke picked him up at the airport in Detroit. As they drove north, toward home, Kevin made fun of Duke's little car and talked about a bachelor's party he had been to the day before. There had been strippers and something about an eggplant that Kevin found very funny. Duke did not recall Kevin being so chummy in the past. Growing up they had never really understood each other; their concerns seemed utterly separate. Kevin, for example, had never seemed to care about getting smiles and nods of encouragement from his old man, and in turn he received them constantly. He accepted them with an attitude of stifled boredom and went on with the business of making himself a success in the world. Duke suspected that Kevin's entire purpose in adolescence had been to arrange a dignified escape from this awkward, huddling, blue-collar little family and the semirural suburbs he had been born into. Despite all Duke's personal frustration, he could not help being awed and impressed by Kevin. And happy for him. He had done it, gotten away, and wasn't it a bit much to expect him to spend a lot of time looking back now? When they got to the house Kevin assumed a serious expression, and his old man, on seeing Kevin, shambled over and fell against him, weeping. Their hug went on for a minute, then two, while Duke fretted around the room, straightening the armrest covers on the sofa. It was the first time that Duke had seen his old man cry since Mom had died. Returning Kevin to the airport that evening, he heard all about Kevin's girlfriend's remarkable breasts. Several days later, when he felt he had done everything he could, Duke announced he would be going back to Ann Arbor. His old man said gruffly, without looking up, "Thanks for your help." For a moment Duke was ridiculously, glowingly elated. Then, turning angry, he had left.

Duke licked away the sweat on his upper lip. In the heat of the sun, held by his old man's glare, he felt simultaneously big and awkward in his body and small and inconsequential beneath the vaulting sky and upon the long ribbon of the road. He said, finally, softly, toward his feet, "Dad, I'm trying to make something of myself."

"I'd say you're doing a good job of making something of yourself—fat."

Duke looked at his old man again. "What if I just leave you here?"

His old man angled his head a few degrees. "Say what?"

"I might as well leave you here. You heard me." Duke set his gaze and held it until his old man's eyes dropped. Duke shivered. He could not remember backing his old man down before. The day was sunny but not hot, and yet gleaming lines of sweat marked his old man's temples. He looked pale, and his nostrils and jaw were trembling.

Duke came forward, all sense of victory abruptly gone. "Just like you," his old man said, "first make a mess of things, then leave me to clean up." But the invective lacked spirit. Duke wrenched at the door with both hands and it came open, metal screeching, and saw then that his old man's trousers below the left hip were scarlet and moist. Long, red drips scored the side of the car seat. Duke jumped back, pointing, shouting, "Dad! You're bleeding! Dad! Dad!"

His old man scowled at him. "Cut that out! What is it? Will you stop that?"

"Look!"

"What?" His old man peered down. "Oh, damn it."

"I'm sorry!" Duke said. "I'm so sorry. I'm sorry."

"Calm down." His old man felt gently along his thigh. "It's hardly more than a scratch." He pulled some broken glass out of his pocket.

"What is that?"

"This thing I won in poker. The Glass Lady."

Duke leaned closer and peered at his old man. "Dad. The what?"

"Don't look at me like that. It's this glass thing I won in poker." He dropped the shards on the ground.

"You had it in your pocket," Duke said tensely.

"Yes. Listen," his old man turned aside and coughed into the sleeve of his shirt, "you shouldn't have come around that bend so fast."

"Oh, Dad," Duke exclaimed, pointing again.

"Cut that out!"

"Look at your arm."

There was blood now on his old man's right sleeve, a scatter of red droplets. He was seized by another cough, a violent hacking that ejected a wide spray of blood onto his shirtsleeve and past it. He stared at the blood on the steering wheel and the dashboard and muttered, "Now, how did that happen?" A delicate red bubble extended from his nose and burst.

Duke whirled. "I'll take the cart!"

"Where are you going?" his old man called after him.

"For a phone!"

"Why don't you use my car phone?"

"You have—" Duke ran back to the car. "Where is it?"

His old man indicated the glove compartment, and Duke found the phone beneath a mess of receipts and gum wrappers. He punched at the buttons, but nothing happened. He calmed himself and looked carefully for a power button. There was no power button. "How's this work?"

"I don't know. I've never used it."

"Come on! What did you get it for?"

"For emergencies."

Duke poked one by one at all the buttons on the face of the phone and nothing happened. He said, "It's broken."

"It's not broken. Look at it. It's fine."

One button said *talk.* Duke hit this, *talk talk talk.* The phone did nothing. "When's the last time you charged the batteries?"

"Batteries?"

Duke dropped the phone. His old man looked shrunken and hunched. His skin had paled to a spectral blue. Duke sprinted to the go-cart. He perched on the tiny seat and fiddled with the controls. "I'll be back!" he cried and set off for the house down the road. He'd break in the front door if he had to.

The old man watched him buzz away: a big man on a small go-cart, his knees splayed in the air, his arms reaching to grasp the steering wheel. He tilted this way and that with each bump in the road. But the cart had impressive go; it dwindled quickly into the distance even with Duke's weight on it. The old man remembered him as an infant, big and red and always curling on himself. And silent; Duke was an eerily silent baby. Even then he'd been baffling. Kevin had been normal, a real screamer.

He wished Kevin were here. Kevin knew how to handle things. But this thought made the old man feel bad. Duke was a good boy. He tried hard. And if he occasionally did things like start grease fires while trying to cook the family a surprise breakfast, well, these were mistakes, not malice.

It was such a difficult thing to spread love with an even hand. Especially when one son practically raised himself while the other somehow managed never to grow up at all. These were the two things about Duke: one, he was a good boy, and, two, he was infuriating. Not the sharpest tack in the box, not the brightest bulb in the chandelier, not the quickest chimp in the monkey house. For instance, the time he accidentally killed the neighbor's dog feeding it chocolate bars. Christ, Russell still sometimes called to give him a hard time about that. And now this business about going back to the plant as an engineer. The old man still had friends working there. How much shit were they going to give him? And how long before Duke installed some machine that eliminated one of his friends' jobs?

Well, perhaps he expected too much. He was sometimes unkind to the boy, he knew, but his nature was such that exasperation always leaped in front of everything else. He lacked the patience to sort intentions from incompetence. It was a shortfall in his own character; he was not proud. But patience was not a thing he could go out to the store and buy. Mom, bless her, had always been able to forgive him for this. And Duke had had *her* approval. Why couldn't that be enough? He was just some stupid old man.

A figure emerged from the corn and approached the front of the car. The old man needed a moment to focus. It was the go-cart girl. He said, "It's the corn fairy. Where'd you go?"

"I hid."

"He's scary-looking, but he means well."

She said, "I saw him hit you."

"That's right!" The old man nodded vigorously. "You saw everything. You're my star witness."

She came around to his side of the car, stopped, stared, mouth hanging. Then she put her hands into her overalls. "Are you going to die?"

"No, kid," the old man said. "No way." She was entranced by the blood. "Kid!" She looked at his face. "Why don't you hand me that phone?"

She picked up the cell phone and held it out by a corner, as if she were afraid of touching him. He took it and fumbled a moment, dropped it in his lap, then picked it up again. He looked it over and found an on/off switch on the side. What were they teaching that boy in engineering school anyway? He slid the switch to "on" and the buttons lit up pale green.

He stared at the glow of the buttons. They seemed to dim, then light up green again. But he doubted that they had actually done any such thing. A sudden, terrible pain pierced him. His stomach clenched; he winced. The girl said, "You sure you're not going to die?"

He would have made his scary monster face at her, but he didn't have the energy. He paused a moment, trying to think, then, digit by digit, pressed out Duke's phone number. Holding the phone to his ear, he tilted his head to one side. The phone seemed very heavy. Duke's answering machine came up. "Howdy, pilgrim! This is Duke. Kindly leave a message." Same message he'd had for five years now.

It beeped. When he tried to speak, his tongue felt dry and brittle, like old newspaper, and he could not form a word. He worked his throat to raise some spittle, smacked his lips. "Duke," he croaked, "numbskull, the phone works. There's this little switch on the side." He paused a minute, listening to himself wheeze. "Look do me a favor. Get a job somewhere else. Work on bombs, better mousetraps, whatever, but by God—" The answering machine beeped and cut him off. "Fuck," he said, then glanced at the girl. "Sorry, miss." He laid the phone down and punched at the buttons with a finger.

"Howdy, pilgrim! This is Duke. Kindly leave a message."

"These machines are worse than useless. Here, before I forget again, what I want to tell you is this." He gulped. "OK, I guess we both know, God didn't give you a lot to work with. But son, you're trying. I see you trying." He clicked his teeth, nodding. Then a cough wracked him. He gasped, said, "I guess the point is, Duke, I'm proud of you. Proud."

He thought a moment, the phone resting against his head, then, just to be clear, he added, "This is your old man." He dropped the phone into his lap again.

The go-cart was nowhere to be seen. A hovering trail of dust led all the way to the house. The old man let his eyes rest a moment, then fluttered them open. He pressed 911 and gestured for the girl to take the phone. "Talk to this person, will you?"

He relaxed against his seat and looked at the ceiling of the car. Darkness swarmed and evaporated, swarmed and evaporated.

There was a voice. Duke's? "—be here soon."

"I know. We called them," the old man whispered.

"They told me to keep you talking. Gotta talk, Dad."

"Mm."

"It's a nice day isn't it?"

"Mm. No."

There were hands on him, slick, as if greasy. The old man did not know whose hands these were, his own or some other's.

"OK, Dad, listen, here's one thing I learned in my fluid mechanics class, about blood. It's a non-Newtonian fluid."

"Yeah?"

"That means it's kind of strange, that it flows differently than water and most other fluids." A pause. Hands again. "Ketchup is also non-Newtonian, and that's why you have to hit the ketchup bottle to make it go."

"Who cares?"

"Well, I don't know."

The old man groaned. "Goddamn it, Duke. I'm dying, and you're talking about ketchup."

There was a little girl talking into his phone. It was all very confusing, and everything was distant. The world darkened. The hands on him were too strong and deft to be his own. He felt like a child. Then he didn't know what he was doing, closing his eyes or opening them, but all he could see was his son, Duke.

Commemorating

I grew up on a lake in Minnesota where the winters were paper-white with trees like stick figures drawn in charcoal. One midwinter day when I was just four years old and the lake stood frozen, covered with a vast surface of snow, I was in the kitchen, finger painting. I had all the basic colors—green, blue, violet, orange, red, black—except for yellow. And I thought of a girl, a couple of years older than me, who lived in the house next door. She had yellow hair, so distinctly and startlingly yellow that people would comment on it. Thinking of her and the missing yellow paint, I knew, somehow, to worry.

Later that day, she fell through the ice on the lake. I did not actually see this happen, but the image was very clear to me: the girl running, dressed in a blue coat, green mittens, and a red woolen hat, with yellow hair just peeking out beneath. Then, suddenly and silently, she dropped through the snow, leaving only a small, dark hole.

I blamed the missing yellow paint. Sometimes life rings with that much subtlety. And then sometimes it thunders like an invasion of fully armed marines.

For the past two decades, when people have asked, What do you do? I've smirked with self-effacement, to warn them not to expect much, and I've told them that I sell insurance.

Eighteen years ago, on an early spring day in the park, I spotted a woman dressed in white standing amid a crowd of people wearing blue and brown. Lita was her name, and soon enough I married her. We rented a tiny house in the woods and filled it with secondhand furniture. We were isolated and happy, I believed, although as I think back now, I recall certain small things—the uneven keening of the winter wind, closed doors that came oddly ajar, birds that hit the windows and died.

I loved Lita for her predictabilities. On summer evenings we sat in lawn chairs behind the house and listened as the frogs and cicadas struck up their lyrics, and on these evenings, if she stretched her neck and bent her face to the darkened sky for a long moment, she would always, always, five minutes later announce her intention to go to sleep early that night. In winter months when the isolation became unbearable, we went to the movie theater in town. If the film was sad, and definitely if good people died, I knew Lita would suggest a stiff drink, usually gin.

But then, not long after our second wedding anniversary, Lita told me she had signed up for a drawing class. I was surprised and said as much—she had never expressed an interest in drawing before, never mentioned that she would like to go to a museum or buy a sketch pad. I'd never even seen her doodle. She shrugged. She said it had been in a corner of her mind for some time to do this, and suddenly she'd decided. Only in retrospect could I see the clues that might have given me notice: a little drawing of a flower that a waitress had put onto my lunch bill a day earlier, and the pattern of cracks I had noticed the week before in the ceiling of the post office—they had appeared to outline a lady in a veiled hat writing in a book, but she might have been drawing, not writing. Lita enjoyed the class, and her style was fairly distinct. She liked to work with ink to create objects and characters without shading or crosshatching, like cartoons.

One day that same winter I came home from work and began to tell her about an old woman I had seen slip on the ice outside my office. The woman tried to catch herself against my office window, only to slide down it. She had broken her hip; an ambulance had come. I said maybe we ought to call Lita's mother, just to tell her to take a little extra care.

"Sure," Lita said. She nodded emphatically, as she did when she was being falsely earnest. "Sure. That's completely logical. And while I'm at it I'll mention maybe she should keep an eye out for black cats and broken mirrors, that sort of thing."

I began to explain the difference between this and a black cat. I may have raised my voice. We'd had similar arguments in the past, but this one ended with me in the car in a sleeping bag for the night. We simmered around each other for days afterward, until Lita finally pointed out that nothing had happened to her mother, that clearly I'd been wrong. I didn't admit she might be correct, but as a peace offering I suggested a trip. This was March, and why not go to someplace warm? We didn't have a lot of money, but we had enough to fly down and take a reasonably nice hotel room for a week in Fort Pierce, one of the less glamorous stretches of Florida's Atlantic coast.

Stepping out of the 737 in Orlando, I immediately felt the humidity and smelled the salty sea. I thought of sand, of palm trees, of fruity drinks, of the simple pleasures of being alive. A man held a cardboard sign which read, "Limo for Mr. Goode." I leaned into Lita and pointed to it. "It's a good sign."

"Yes," she said with a small smile.

In the hotel lobby we could hear, in an undertone, the rumble and crash of waves. Their steadiness seemed reassuring to me, and I did not think at that moment to ask myself what I wanted to be reassured of. The sky was clear and blue and perfect. We pulled on swimsuits and ran barefoot to the beach. We swam, though the winter Atlantic water was chilly, and we laughed at the golden sun as if we had not seen such a thing in years.

We ate dinner that night in the hotel restaurant, blue crab for me and whitefish for Lita. I noticed a man, fat and balding, perhaps in his late fifties, eating with his wife at a nearby table. He had a distinct smile, displaying slightly yellowed teeth, that never disappeared. The smile nagged at my attention the way a too-loud conversation does. He held it through his entire meal.

"Maybe he has a medical condition," Lita said. But I preferred to think of him as the ambassador of a smiling land where emotions were measured only in degrees of happiness.

Over the next several days we broiled in the sun, went through novels like chocolate candies, and ate as much seafood as we could. On the fourth day, I saw a boy fishing, and I decided I wanted to do some surf fishing. Surf fishing is simply fishing with a pole from the beach, and I remembered doing it with my grandpa during a couple of trips to Florida when I was a teenager. I got a pole, some tackle and bait, and set an alarm clock for before dawn.

The next morning I left Lita asleep in bed and shuffled out with my equipment. I emerged into a dark fog. It made every gesture small and illusory, concentrating reality to the sand under me and the noise of the sea. I followed the roar down to the beach, then I walked northward along the scalloped edge of sand wetted by the push and pull of the waves.

Eventually I noticed a gray light suffusing the fog above the sea, and I saw, vaguely, the moving lines of foam rushing in. I stopped and cast my bait. Although I've felt it magnified tenfold since, at that time I thought I had never experienced such a sense of solitude. The entire universe might have shrunk to the small gray place surrounding me. I felt the fishing pole tug and snap feebly as the bait was tossed by the waves. Coded signals, I realized, sent directly to me, as clear as Morse code, if only I knew how to interpret them. I wondered a moment whether indecipherability might be a signal in itself, but I set that aside to concentrate on the feel of the telegraphs from the sea. I ought to be satisfied, I felt then, that the ocean had words to whisper in my ear, even if the words meant nothing to me.

The fog filled with light and paled. Somewhere before me the sun was rising and burning. Suddenly a phantom figure appeared, striding rapidly down the beach. It moved so fast,

I didn't have time to call out a warning before it stopped and brought both hands up to grope at the fishing line it had just walked into.

"I'm sorry!" I called.

"No, no, I'm sorry!" came the reply, a male voice. In a moment he disentangled himself and came up the sand to meet me. The smile was the first feature to appear out of the fog, and before I saw the rest of him I knew him—the smiling man from the restaurant.

We introduced ourselves; his name was Beetle Johnson. He recognized me, too, he said smiling; he had seen me around the hotel. I mean, he said this *while* smiling, through his teeth, the way a ventriloquist does. We marveled together at the density of the fog. He asked if I'd caught anything. I said, only him. He laughed. He told me he had come out to look for seashells, but he wouldn't find any today unless he tripped over them. Then, having exhausted the easy conversation, we both turned to look at the fog-shrouded ocean. He was still smiling. I wondered at the peculiarity of catching this man on my line. His smile had entered into my life as no mere passing image, but as a repeating reminder.

Then I noticed something on the water. The fog had continued to thin subtly, and I could see a heavy dark shape, low, coming in amid the waves. Then I saw another, and then a third—three of these things—like some antediluvian species coming from the mists to reclaim a place on earth. I still gripped my fishing pole, which trembled and jerked with the movements of the waves: I held on to that pole with desperate fervor. The low shapes glided silently in the water, one to the left of my fishing line and two to the right. Then they collided with the sand in a loud, violent grinding, and through the fog I heard yet more of them hitting up and down the beach.

Beetle turned. "Jack, do you see that?" he asked.

I began to reel in my fishing line.

Then the beasts opened their mouths and men ran out. Through the fog we could see that these were big men, with rifles and backpacks and helmets that made their shadowy heads look deformed. They splashed through the water and threw themselves onto the sand. Pointing their guns ahead of them, they scanned the fog and crawled forward.

"What do you think this means?" I asked Beetle.

"Means?" He giggled.

One of the marines stood and shouted orders to the others. Then, at a signal, they all rose up. Beetle giggled again. We could see a couple dozen of them, strung out along the beach. They ran ahead a few paces, dropped to one knee and aimed, then jumped up to run again. They pounded past us, one of them so close I could have put a foot out and tripped him. They scrambled up the short cliff of sand behind the beach and were gone.

A handful of marines remained on the beach. They drew little shovels from their packs and started to dig.

"Do you think that they're American?" Beetle whispered.

"Good Lord, I hope so. You heard the one issuing orders, he sounded American. What else could they be?"

"I don't know," he said through his smile. "The French."

"French?"

He laughed, and I laughed. We laughed like relieved idiots on a foggy beach while the marines climbed into their foxholes, still scanning with their weapons. Here were symbols upon symbols. Boats that emerged out of the fog as mysteriously as alien spacecraft, opening and vomiting forth their young. Dream figures that crashed through the water, swarmed around us, and passed onward. No one shouted to clear the way. The marines looked through me as if I were part of the fog.

A tap on my shoulder startled me. Here was the Cheshire cat grin again, like a toothy gap in the fabric of the universe. The grin said, "Let's go, Jack. Let's get the hell out of here." I gathered my things, and with the surf thundering portentously on our left we walked back to the hotel together.

A short time later Beetle and I brought our wives down to see the marines and their amphibious landers. The sun had burned away most of the fog, and we could now see a good distance across the water. Still feeling deeply unsettled, I walked somewhat ahead of the others, looking for marines with automatic rifles and large steel boats. But Beetle called me back.

"This is it," he said, pointing to a row of holes in the sand. The marines were gone. They had left behind nothing but a mess of heavy boot-prints and their foxholes, which now looked small, like they might have been dug by ambitious children. Lita said, "This is it?" as if she thought Beetle and I had run up and down here wearing boots, scooping out holes with our hands.

As we walked back, Beetle asked me what I did for a living. I told him, without even a smirk, that I was an insurance salesman.

Beetle was a salesman, too. He sold advertising merchandise. If someone wanted matchbooks or magnets or retractable pens printed with the name of their business, their mascot or slogan, Beetle was the man to set it up. He told me this smiling as though he were describing the greatest job in the world.

Beetle and his wife were scheduled to leave that afternoon. When we met them on the hotel patio for lunch, Beetle's wife quickly excused herself, saying she needed to pack. Across Caesar salads and iced tea, Beetle and I traded stories about our jobs. Lita worked intently with a pen on the back of her menu. When Beetle asked what she was drawing, she clutched the menu for a moment as if she were going to hide it. But then she held the page toward Beetle.

"Did they look like this?" She giggled.

My face went hot. In the center of the page, large and unmistakable, she had drawn a helmeted marine charging up a beach, holding a rifle in massive, rocklike fists, with little ringlets of fog at his knees. I was about to say something, but Beetle burst out with a great, unqualified belly laugh that shook the table and had all of us grabbing our glasses to prevent them from spilling. Beetle laughed harder, and slapped his knee. Of course soon Lita and I were laughing with him. Lita gave him the drawing. "A memento," she said, "of the invasion."

After we paid the bill, Beetle shook my hand and asked whether I had a business card. I found one in my wallet, and he stood a moment grinning at it. Then he gave me a mechanical pencil. On the barrel was printed,

Beetle Johnson
Southeast Regional Sales Manager
Advertising Stuff America, Inc.
"Your Name Here!"

and a phone number. I said good-bye and Beetle said, "Semper Fi."

After the Johnsons' departure, I resolved to say nothing; we were on vacation and I hoped for peace. But we had hardly gotten back to our room before Lita began it. Turning on me, she said, "Maybe it didn't mean anything."

"Marines!" I cried, throwing my hands up, instantly exasperated. "Armed combatants storming ashore all around us! You should have seen it, Lita."

"They went astray in the fog. You happened to be there. That's all. Why can't that be all?"

"Because we *happened* to be there. Don't you see? We happened to be there. This thing happened to *us*. It was extraordinary."

We stared at each other a second. I wanted very much for her to understand, but I could explain no better. "Whatever," she said. She turned on the TV.

I gathered my swim trunks and a towel and sunscreen, thinking that I could sit in the sun on the beach and I wouldn't have to talk to anyone if I didn't want to. Lita looked over. "Where are you going?"

"The beach."

"What about the cruise?"

I had forgotten about the cruise. We were scheduled for a half-day sunset trip. Remembering it now, a sour feeling came into my gut. I said, "I don't think we should go."

Lita lay back on the bed as if suddenly exhausted. She gazed at the ceiling. Her lips were tight and in her neck the tendons rose under the skin. "Why not?" she said. "Tell me why not."

"If we go out on that boat, I guarantee, we will disappear over the horizon and never be heard from again."

"Because of the marines."

"I think so. Yes. I feel it, Lita."

She closed her eyes. Perhaps a minute passed, then she said, softly, "All right."

"We'll skip the cruise."

"Yes," she said. "Let's skip the cruise."

I was surprised—I knew she had been looking forward to the cruise. I said, "Thank you, dear."

She just lay there, very still, as if asleep. But I could see her eyes moving under the lids, casting about rapidly.

We sat on the beach a while that afternoon, and later we watched TV in the room. A local television station carried a short news item on a marine unit participating in war games that had gotten lost in the fog. Lita and I made slow, tired love that night, as if obliged because we were on vacation, and when we were done she rolled off to sleep without a word. I tossed for hours before I slept.

When I woke, I was alone in the bed. A note in Lita's handwriting said, "Gone for a swim. Back soon." Dressed only in a robe, I ran to the beach. The fog of the day before had blown away completely, the rising sun cast the beach in strong light, and not a soul moved on it or in the water. I called for her and the gulls replied.

Even before I had walked far up and down the beach, before I had questioned everyone in the vicinity, before the police had taken over, before the exhausting search of the hotel and the surrounding landscape, before the divers had gone down, before the water had been dredged—I understood she would not be back. Like the marines, she had disappeared, and I would not find her again. I stood on that beach and I bitterly cursed myself and my pathetic, mortal idiocy, for not deciphering that moment when I had stood surrounded by the footprints of a missing invasion.

In the following months I did not see a coin dropped, did not pass a house with darkened windows, did not watch the fading of a sunset, did not experience any of the minutia of life without wondering if it might be a sign—of what happened to Lita, where she had gone, whether she was alive or dead. Sometimes the clear waters of a lake held exactly the color of her eyes, and I was happy for a moment. But later a hunched taxi driver laughed bitterly and rolled his shoulders the way she used to, and my hope shriveled. One day I was looking through her old drawings, and near at hand happened to be some road maps. Soon I found a nearly perfect match between her drawing of a child's puppy-laden wagon and a network of roads through Iowa, Indiana, and Missouri. I spent most of a month following the route before I finally gave up.

Exactly one year after the marines stormed the beach and Lita disappeared, a large overnight package arrived. I thought it must have been expensive to send, and I wondered if it might have been delivered to the wrong address. I pushed it inside and looked at the sender's name: Beetle Johnson. I had almost forgotten him, but now my heart twisted and wrung the memory out.

Inside the package, wrapped in tissue paper, were eight tall glasses, eight coffee mugs, and eight shot glasses. Emblazoned on every one was Beetle's name, my name, the words, "Commemorating the First Anniversary of the Invasion of the Beaches at Fort Pierce, Florida," and Lita's drawing of a marine charging out of surf and fog. My first thought was to smash it all to pieces. But I remembered that Beetle had left before Lita disappeared: he thought he was sending me a few trinkets in innocent fun. Recalling his unearthly smile, I left the box on the floor.

The next day the phone rang, and a voice said without introduction, "What do you think?"

"Of what?"

"Pretty funny, huh? 'Commemorating the Invasion'? I thought you'd like that."

Now I recognized him. Even on the phone he seemed to exude his smile like an electronic grin in the buzz of the phone lines.

I felt immediately I should tell him of the sickness I experienced at seeing Lita's disappearance memorialized on coffee mugs and shot glasses, but the emotions were difficult to name, and finally I simply told Beetle, yes, they were pretty funny.

Beetle laughed and zapped smiles at me. He asked, "How is your wife?"

"My wife?"

"Yeah! You know, that woman you find sleeping beside you in bed every morning."

"Lita is—well, you know. What I mean."

"Sure I do, Jack! I remember when my wife and I were your age. The world was like an oyster full of pearls. Remind me, how long have you two been married?"

"Our fourth anniversary, that was just a couple of months back."

"Wonderful! If you can make it four years you can make the long haul. There are days though—some days in a marriage are like that morning on the beach. Like, whoa! what's this, where's this coming from? You've probably seen some of that, huh?"

"Yes."

"Well, buddy, I'm here to say it gets better." He chuckled, then fell silent, and I listened to the buzzing grin. He said, "I still think about that day. The waves, the fog. Boats, shadows, soldiers jumping out. Some days, I can't believe we saw it."

"It was a strange thing."

"I'll admit, it scared the hell out of me. I'm glad you were there."

I was moved by this frank emotion. "Me too, Beetle," I said, honestly. "I'm glad we were there together."

I let the box of commemorative drink-ware sit on the floor for several days. Then I slid it into the kitchen, where it sat a while longer. Eventually I grew tired of bumping into it every time I opened the refrigerator, and I arrayed the mugs and glasses in a back corner of the cupboard. They cowered there until one day when all my regular glasses were dirty. After a second's hesitation, I drank a commemorative glass of orange juice.

The next year Beetle sent more stuff—second anniversary T-shirts, bumper stickers, and plastic shoehorns. He called and asked, "When are you two going to produce some rugrats to keep around the house?"

"Oh, well," I said. A silence ensued and extended until I seemed to hear Beetle's smile dimming. Suddenly I blurted, "We already have one."

"Oh!"

"Yes, little Jenny arrived nearly two months back. Sweetest baby girl ever."

"I don't doubt it! That's wonderful! It's amazing what can happen in just a year, a new little person can be made and named. Shoot. If I have one regret it's that we never had kids."

"It's something else being a father. But it can be a pain in the ass too."

"Yes sir, my one regret would be no little Beetles or Beetlettes to feed and toss around and teach a thing or two. I'm glad for you, I really am."

"Thanks, Beetle." Elation washed back and forth inside me, as though I were being congratulated for something that I had actually done.

On the third anniversary came ties, lapel pins, stationery, calendars, and retractable pens; on the fourth anniversary:

matchbooks, miniflashlights, bottle openers, and cheap digital watches. He called every year. I told him about little Jenny growing teeth and hair, going ga-ga and goo-goo, and getting big fast. When I felt I had been talking too long, I would ask, "How are things for you, Beetle? How's business?"

"Business is *booming!*" This is what he said every time, and he said it enthusiastically, but some subtle lonely note in his voice caused me to connect the word *boom* with the desolate tumbleweed ghost towns that follow boomtowns. He would say, "The market for 'individualized trinkets,' as I call them, is taking off. It makes all the sense in the world, if you think about it. Everyone has all kinds of stuff lying around the house. Imagine the advertising power invoked when your brand is proudly displayed on every one of those small but necessary household items. That's why I encourage my larger customers to try to achieve 'full home saturation.' That is, ideally, the advertiser has an item in every room in the prospective customer's house—a comb in the bathroom, a cup in the kitchen, a clock in the living room, a shoehorn in the bedroom, and, in the study, a mouse pad beside the computer—you see?"

I did see. For the fifth anniversary he sent baseball caps, penknives, Frisbees, pencils, and erasers. On the sixth anniversary came magnets, outdoor thermometers, a clock, more calendars, lighters, and mouse pads.

I stunned myself when we spoke that year, and I told him that little Jenny had fallen into a frozen lake and died. I experienced a sudden, horrible stabbing of loss and yearning, as though my little girl really had died. "It's hard," I told him. "An agony." I looked at the walls of my empty house. "We've decided to try for another one, another little girl or boy."

"I'm sorry, so sorry about your loss," Beetle said. "But I think you have the right spirit. Give your love a new object."

Seven, eight, nine, ten, eleven, twelve, thirteen years passed in this way. In real life I took out ads in the personals but hung up if anyone actually called. I spent my nights alone with the ticking of a commemorative clock. Still, some mornings I forgot and felt sleepily across the bed, expecting to find Lita beside me, and every time the discovery of her absence opened a fresh, exquisite pain. But all that faded in my conversations with Beetle. When I was speaking to Beetle, Lita had never left. She gave birth to twins, a boy and a girl, and I told Beetle about the children and trips to the dentist where they screamed and clung to the doorways and spilled dental implements everywhere. I told him about visits to the in-laws', the dreadful food, the pieces of the crystal the twins broke, and the uncles who shook the kids upside down by the ankles until they puked. There had been confrontations with the neighbor's three-legged pit bull and harrowing battles with a penknife-wielding kindergarten bully. I spoke about the nights of romantic relief that Lita and I enjoyed when the children were staying at Grandma's house. Beetle contributed chuckles of appreciation and bits of generic advice, things like: "You've got to give the kids room to breathe, to find their own space. But only a little, remember, only a little," or, "Teach those children to fish! Teach them to fish!"

I anticipated Beetle's call for weeks beforehand, but the stories I told him were spontaneous, as if I were the speaker for phrases telegraphed directly into my brain from an alien source. Reflecting on the lies and their complex relationship to reality, I began to see that, to find any truth in the world, I had to grasp *all* the subtle signs that floated around me like confetti.

When Beetle spoke of himself, he told me about vacations in Florida or on the Texas coast. "Exotic enough by far for me," he'd say. He made references to an old house that he seemed to be rebuilding perpetually, plank by plank. He'd also under-taken a project to trace his family roots through various librar-ies and city courthouses. "And so far all I've found are deserters in various wars and pioneers in the bootlegging trade."

I wondered why he called every year. Did he take some-thing away from this that I did not understand? Perhaps, childless himself, he gained some vicarious pleasure in the stories I told about my children growing up. But maybe he had more secret reasons. Possibly his stories held no more truth than my own. Sometimes Beetle seemed to be entirely a figment of my imagination, like an escaped dream. Or, rather, a dream captured and chained to me. Yet this was ridiculous, because if Beetle was a dream, where did all those packages full of cartoon marines come from?

I didn't realize how much I looked forward to our ritual until the fourteenth delivery failed to arrive. I fretted for several days, then I dug out the mechanical pencil Beetle had given me when we first met. I dialed the phone number on it, and a woman answered. "I'm sorry, Mr. Johnson passed on after a heart attack almost eight months ago. Mr. Calhoun has taken on Mr. Johnson's accounts. Would you like to speak with him?"

I hung up. I moved dully to a chair and sat gazing out a window. It had been gray all day and an intermittent rain was now regathering force. I had lost my only witness to history and his smile as well. Gusts whipped the rainfall against the window with a crackling noise, and the water then moved in slow trickles down the glass and around, in the lower right corner, a suction cup–mounted commemorative outdoor thermometer. It stood unmoved by rain or wind and its steady presence helped calm me.

After a minute I called back and asked to speak to Mr. Calhoun. I ordered a set of commemorative wine goblets, several pairs of sunglasses, and, after Calhoun reassured me that they would be of the highest quality, a case of sweatbands. Each to be marked with the distinctive charging marine cartoon and the customary phrase.

This is the fifteenth anniversary of the invasion, and today I told an imaginary Beetle a few things—one of the twins excels as a student but the other struggles; Lita grew gravely ill with a mysterious fever in the autumn, but now it has passed; and we've gotten a little puppy with ears longer than her legs and named her Snow. These facts are somehow connected to the reality of paint peeling in the bathroom, the fist-shaped stain on the carpet in the kitchen, the cold air. I look around, and Lita's cartoon marine is charging from the walls, from inside the cupboards, from the floor mat in the hallway. They've overrun me and surrounded me, these square-jawed fighting men. I study the lines of each, noting slight differences between the soldier on the eighth anniversary duffel bag and the one on the eleventh anniversary handkerchief, a thicker neck on this one, a meatier fist on that one, both charging toward sands they will never reach.

Electric Fence

When Elizabeth sat far away afterward, in her office or in a meeting, and her attention slid from the ceaseless managerial tasks before her to her memories of childhood and of the woods, this was the view that first came to mind: from the driveway, beside the car, luggage at her feet, looking back across the open lawn toward the line of treetops serrated by branches reaching to all directions of the sky and horizon. The view of the woods at that moment beside the car was a view separated by years from the woods of her youth, yet no different really. The relative heights, breadths, and positions of the trees created a distinct pattern that she would always know, the way some know a particular ridge of mountaintops or a city skyline.

A wind pressed a wave of disturbance through the branches, causing them to lash. The leaves lifted, displaying their silvery undersides. A bird provoked from its perch flew up, darted down. Then the wind was gone and the branches returned to where they had begun. Elizabeth lifted her suitcase and together she and Allison carried the bags into the house. The sisters had returned home.

Allison tried to appear certain, although she was not. She never felt as certain about things as Elizabeth seemed to, and at the moment—sitting at the kitchen table, bearing her best expression of firm resolution, looking at the squat, silvered urn that held their father's ashes—she envied her sister's confidence.

She watched the urn on the table and tried to make her own gaze as tough and cold as Elizabeth's, but she began to doubt herself and to feel she should apologize—though she knew she had done nothing wrong—because surely just now it was important that they not be at odds. When she glanced up, however, she realized Elizabeth was gazing abstractedly out the window and paying her no attention. The window was open and a breeze caused the curtains to draw against the screen, then relax. Both sisters were in chairs which in the past would have been considered their parents', and this heightened Allison's feeling that she was involved in something like a tense game of pretend.

Suddenly Elizabeth rose. "I'm going out," she said, moving toward the backdoor.

"Elizabeth?" But Elizabeth was already outside. Curious, concerned, Allison got up and followed. A queer rhythm entered her pulse.

The sun shone hot and bees nosed at the dandelions scattered over the lawn. Allison liked the flowers, even if they were weeds, but she wished the bees didn't like them so much. Wearing only light sandals, she placed her feet carefully. She wrapped her arms around herself despite the heat. Elizabeth had already disappeared into the sumac bushes that marked the edge of the woods. Songbirds twittered among the trees. The sky was clear, the sun high, and it seemed to Allison that the day's breeze did not cool but only blew the heat against her.

She remembered how as a child she had sometimes been sent to retrieve Elizabeth from the woods, how she had always moved slowly, hesitating in the lawn, as now. How she hated to go into the woods, that dismal place. She was an adult now, not so small and slight a creature as she had been then, and she felt a little less intimidated, but only a little. She pressed gingerly through the sumac. Poisonous stuff. It turned that bloody red color in autumn.

Elizabeth stood at the fence, birch and poplar trees on either side of her, hands on hips, still as a photograph of herself.

"Elizabeth?" Allison said. Elizabeth did not acknowledge her. Allison wondered where Elizabeth was at times like this. What corner of the mind did she crowd herself into? Allison took a step forward, thinking to touch her on the arm, awaken her, but she stopped. Elizabeth's hands were in fists, as if she were struggling with something: perhaps it would be best to leave her a minute.

Now, in the gloom under the trees, Allison felt cold.

Wood and foliage suddenly crashed and slapped behind her and Allison spun toward the noise expecting to meet some leaping predator, but there was only a single upper tree branch wagging wildly. It could not have been anything very large, so high in the trees, but something was there. "What was that?" she said. "Was that a squirrel?"

"Sounded like it," Elizabeth said.

Allison continued to watch suspiciously. She couldn't see any squirrel. The thrashing of the branch dampened quickly and soon she was no longer certain which one it had been. Everywhere the uppermost leaves twitched and flickered, agitated by a light wind.

Then there was a peculiar noise that didn't at first alarm Allison so much as it mystified her. It was a sound of metal shifting, as if someone were thrusting their hand into a bucket of pennies, combined with a low buzz, a loud variation on the droning of the bees in the lawn. She turned toward her sister for an explanation, then could not understand what she saw. "Elizabeth!" she cried. Elizabeth was recoiling from the fence with her face to one side, her eyes opened wide, her hands lifted slightly as if she were preparing for flight. She collapsed to the ground like a long coat slipping off its hanger. Allison gasped and tasted, faintly, an acrid smoke. She screamed and scrambled through the brush toward Elizabeth and, though it was unlikely anyone could hear, screamed again, and again. When she paused to breathe the woods still made all the usual sounds and this angered her. "Damn it!" she yelled. She knelt and cradled her sister's head in her lap. Elizabeth lay gasping, her legs bent under her, her eyes closed. Allison took her sister's hand and massaged it with her own—it felt warm and limp, at once dead and warm. "You're okay," she said. "You're okay. You're okay." Then she screamed, again, "Help!"

Suddenly Elizabeth's eyes were open. "Hey, hi," Allison said. "You're okay. Lie still. Are you all right?" Elizabeth squinted. She raised her head and strained awkwardly to peer down at the limbs. She nodded.

She stood a moment later, and Allison walked her back to the house with a hand on her shoulder. Red welts cross-hatched her arms and her cheek was marked by a faint upside-down L, but her clothing seemed to have protected most of her. Allison wanted to take her to a hospital, but Elizabeth said no. Please, Allison pleaded, gesturing at the marks on her arms, but Elizabeth shook her head. She spent a couple of hours resting, then, coughing lightly, came downstairs again. Allison watched her closely as she wandered into the kitchen. "I caught my foot and fell against the fence," she said. "That's all. I feel fine now."

Allison stared. "Elizabeth. How can you be fine? You were electrocuted."

Elizabeth shrugged. "All right, yes. But I'm okay. I swear."

Allison sensed that Elizabeth was lying: she hadn't tripped on anything. But at the moment it seemed best not to argue. Allison aimed a disapproving glance at her sister and let the matter go.

However, a silence then fell between them that lasted the rest of the evening, broken only when Elizabeth said, "Good night," and Allison said, "Night, Elizabeth." It seemed to Allison that her sister accepted the quiet with greater ease than she herself ever could. She lay awake a long time, curled on her side in a state of melancholy, mulling how Elizabeth's impenetrable, self-collected reserve—which Allison often admired—could be bitterly frustrating at a time like this.

Poached eggs, oranges, and coffee just as Elizabeth liked it—Allison had everything arranged by the time Elizabeth emerged from her room. The slanted morning sunlight landed directly on the table, making the colors of the food vivid. Elizabeth thanked Allison. Still, they ate in silence. Elizabeth peeled her orange carefully and ate the wedges one by one, while Allison, stricken with worry, glanced from time to time over the table at her. Elizabeth smiled when she caught her. "Really, I wish you would stop it now with the funny looks, Allison."

"What did it feel like, Liz?" Allison asked, softly. "When you touched the fence? Do you remember?"

"Like nothing," Elizabeth said. "It didn't feel like anything." Allison frowned. Elizabeth added, "I mean like nothing, it felt like an emptiness, a hollowness of feeling."

"You were unconscious."

"I guess I was."

Allison thought about this for a moment. "But you're all right now?"

Elizabeth's eyes widened with impatience. "Yes, of course." She made a short, curt gesture with her hand, as if closing a door. "Please, quit worrying."

"All right," Allison said. Sometimes she felt the possibility of understanding spanning between them, but then, quick as that, it would be gone.

Ten years later, a hand shook Elizabeth by the shoulder. "Elizabeth, get up!" Allison was saying while another voice, deeper and male, was speaking at a distance in the background. When Elizabeth opened her eyes, Allison took her by the arm and dragged her out of bed. They stumbled down the hall and into the living room, where Elizabeth, still moving under Allison's guidance, sat on the couch.

The male voice, Elizabeth realized, came from the television. The volume was up quite high. Unimpressed by Allison's panic, she stared at the rectangle of colored light. She was here visiting the old house, Allison's house now, and she had been deeply asleep in her old room—now the study. Allison's husband was away, which had been a relief to Elizabeth. Allison had been married for eight years now, or mostly married—there was an intermission when she caught her husband sleeping around and divorced him, only to marry him again several months later. Elizabeth had been angry with Allison then, had argued with her, told her that this was a mistake, that one could go too far with forgiveness. Allison replied that it wasn't a matter of forgiveness but a matter of love. Elizabeth thought this utterly unconvincing. She couldn't budge Allison, however, and she couldn't argue forever about it, so she had to give up, disappointed but not surprised. Whenever she had doubts about being unmarried herself, at thirty-eight, an examination of her sister's situation reassured her, and made her a little angry as well. Allison's husband was currently missing on a week-long fishing trip, the ulterior motives of which Elizabeth had little doubt. Sometimes it was hard for Elizabeth to say to what extent the differences between herself and Allison, who was the older sibling, simply revealed themselves as a matter of course or came about because she actively pursued such differences and defined herself by them. Elizabeth dated men but ended things if they got too serious. She had friends who thought this the symptom of a strange pathology. Allison, of all people, did sometimes seem to understand.

The man on TV, she now understood, was talking about tornadoes. Allison leaned forward, eyes wide. Elizabeth ran her hand over her face and through her hair. She wore her hair short now that it was turning a steely gray.

She had spent the last few days reading books, pacing through the rooms she had grown up in, talking with Allison and watching her fuss about. The days had passed quietly. A couple of times, in the afternoon, she had driven alone to a grassy, open park several miles away and she walked there with other people who ran wearing headphones or strolled with their children or trailed after their leashed dogs—Elizabeth wished the place were more solitary, wished the people gone. Even more, she wished she could go back to the woods she knew, the woods behind the house she grew up in. But of course there was the fence. The marks that the fence had left on her face and arms were now long gone, and she tried not to let herself feel too upset when she thought of it.

The TV weatherman gestured at the maps shifting behind him and spoke with emphatic calm. The air outside was ominously still. From the direction of town could be heard the faraway howl of warning sirens.

Then, finally, the winds began to rise, and Allison insisted that they go down into the basement. An unfinished cellar with a cool, damp concrete floor and exposed beams overhead, it smelled of mildew, dust, and sweet, decaying wood. Neither of them had spent much time here as children, and to Elizabeth it seemed foreign and stifling. Various large, unknown objects under tarps loomed in the shadows. Paperback books, yellowed and warped with moisture, spilled from large, slowly collapsing cardboard boxes. Long rolls of carpeting leaned against one wall, and nearby lay a rough pile of wood, perhaps taken out of the walls in some renovation, saved for an unknown purpose and now rotting.

Gusts slammed into the walls upstairs and curled shrieking around the corners. Elizabeth had brought down a couple of kitchen chairs. They were sitting in these, gazing at the stairway they had just descended, when, silently, the lightbulb overhead went dark.

"Do you have candles?" Elizabeth asked.

"I forgot to bring them down."

"I'll go get a flashlight."

Elizabeth stood, but Allison grabbed her arm. Her fingers felt moist and sticky against Elizabeth's skin. "Stay here," Allison said. "It's dangerous upstairs."

Elizabeth sat and relaxed. Still, Allison gripped her arm. The floor beams began to creak loudly in the black air, and beyond rose the sounds of a ripping, crashing destruction. Elizabeth wished that Allison had not forgotten the candles.

Allison's other hand felt in the dark for Elizabeth's and Elizabeth repeated a few meaningless, reassuring syllables to her.

Then the house's shuddering stopped and gradually the wind's howling settled to a mewling, then was gone. They ventured upstairs and lit candles and everything appeared to be as they had left it, until Allison went to the window and gasped. The funnel of a tornado had touched down behind the house and cut into the woods, destroying trees in a wide, brutal swath like a lawn mower through grass.

They carried their candles outside, where they burned without wavering. Sunrise was flaring over the eastern horizon and the full sky was so fathomless and clear that one might not guess there had ever been a cloud in it. Allison began inspecting the damage to her lawn and some recently planted apple and pear saplings. Elizabeth blew out her candle and walked to the woods. Entire trees lay tumbled across each other. She began moving forward between the trunks and snapped limbs. Allison called, and Elizabeth turned and waved in a gesture of reassurance, then pressed ahead.

The fence had been torn in several places by falling trees. Fence posts were pulled from the earth or bent to the ground. The path of the tornado continued on the other side, and even the largest trees were down—their thick trunks broken off in splinters the size of swords or ripped entirely from the ground to expose tumorous masses of earth and twisting roots. Elizabeth looked about for several minutes, wondering if the man who lived here might be watching. But at such a moment, she decided, her presence would be of little concern to him. The fence could not possibly be carrying a current; nonetheless, she paused a second and spit on one of the posts before she started over the flattened metal.

She felt sick seeing all these trees dead, many still bearing their leaves, still green and vibrant. She walked without plan, moving as she could. The old paths were just visible, here and there, under the carnage, and certain trees she recognized, although now they lay horizontal. The sun lifted up and she began to think about going back. But then, reorienting, she realized the old climbing tree was nearby.

She found it uprooted and on its side, its spiral ladder to the sky now a ladder to the west. It looked much like the others, its foliage still thick and green, but in the branches near the crown was a dead boy, his spine folded backward.

When she remembered to breathe again, she gulped rapidly, swallowing air. She could not know from his position whether the boy had been up in the tree or had been caught underneath as it fell. Yet, she felt certain he had climbed to that place in the tree.

A man's voice called in the distance.

Elizabeth turned so she could not see the boy, and she felt more calm. But when she looked up she felt a dizzy buzzing, and the sky itself appeared to ripple and flow like a river.

The man's voice called again. "Wilson!"

She began running toward home, stumbling in the wrecked landscape, backtracking the tornado's route. She came into the house sobbing, and Allison found her and gripped her in a hug. Then Allison was crying, and Elizabeth started to tell her everything, about the fence, the woods, the man, the boy—but Allison shushed her. "It doesn't matter," she said. "It doesn't matter."

Growing up, Elizabeth never felt as comfortable in the house as she felt in the woods. The house seemed to her to have a sepulchral quality, and she could not understand why it didn't drive Allison outside as well. Their parents were stoics, impassive and unplayful people. Their father, a salesman of solvents and other industrial chemicals, was often away on a selling circuit that took weeks to complete. Their mother was always waiting for him—either to return or to leave again. She spoke only in whispers, washed her hands compulsively, and gave her daughters somewhat less attention than she gave her own interminable despair.

The suburbs eventually oozed out around them—lots across the road were sold, houses were built, families arrived—but the process took many years and in the meantime, with few neighbors and town miles away, Elizabeth and Allison faced broad expanses of lonely, empty time. Elizabeth watched Allison move toward internal, two-dimensional preoccupations—paper, ink, pencils, books—while Elizabeth herself spent more and more time in the woods behind the house—a collection of oaks, beeches, and maples that formed a canopy across more than a hundred acres. Allison was obviously never comfortable in the woods, and it pleased Elizabeth to imagine that her own sensibilities were as alien to her sister as an Apache's.

The land the trees stood on was not owned by her family, and later she wondered if the thrill of trespass might have formed some of her pleasure in the place. But she also simply loved to be outside with her feet on the mulch and muscle of the earth, surrounded by wind, green life, and the crawl of the sun. She climbed into the tallest of the trees and clambered precariously among the high thin boughs to find a view out, or perched herself in the uppermost possible crook where, within a dappled tent of leaves, she felt so isolated and exalted that she could have passed days at a time without touching the ground if not for the necessity of meals and sleep.

As for the man who owned the woods, Elizabeth watched him from a distance, her curiosity alloyed with apprehension. It was said his family had once been significant in the paper-making industry, that he had inherited an enormous fortune, that he was a widower, that he had a daughter he wouldn't speak to. Whatever the circumstances of his family and his past, he now seemed content to live in isolation. His house was set deep amid the thickest timber, an old frame house with a newer, aluminum-sided pole barn beside it where he garaged a heavy-duty pickup truck. He was known to be utterly antisocial—anyone who approached to proselytize or peddle goods or even to trick-or-treat was greeted with a shotgun. However, outside every one of his windows he had hung bird feeders. Apparently the finches, sparrows, robins, and jays were companionship enough for him. On a daily schedule he came out and placed pieces of suet into certain feeders, loose seed into others. Into a red plastic hummingbird feeder he put sugar-water, which seemed an act of perpetual faith, or stubbornness, because the hummingbirds never came.

He never sold any of his acreage, developed it, or harvested the trees. He didn't have any barbed wire or fencing, but he posted many No Hunting signs. Elizabeth stayed quiet and hidden when she was in sight of his house and listened constantly for a footstep that might be his. But she never saw him venture more than a few feet beyond the bird feeders. She thought perhaps he saw his woods as a playground for his birds and, like most adults, had no interest in using the playground himself. She sometimes imagined that she might have an unusual rapport with him; he might be kind but tragically shy; he might secretly know about her use of his woods and be glad she was there.

They were pulling the bags out of Elizabeth's car when Allison paused to explain about the electrified fence that had been erected in the woods. Gripping a suitcase halfway out of the trunk, Elizabeth stiffened. She set the suitcase down. "These woods?" she asked, pointing. She stood gazing toward the trees.

Later Allison tried to recall, what had been on Elizabeth's face at that moment? But either memory failed her or, perhaps, Elizabeth's expression could not be read. She was always so reserved.

Allison had touched her gently on the arm and said, "You can't see it from here." Elizabeth shook her head and lifted her bag. They went inside in silence.

Allison had arrived a day before Elizabeth. When she learned of their father's death she also learned that he had previously arranged for his body to be cremated. Only the silvered urn needed to be picked up, the inheritance dealt with. Their mother had passed on some years earlier, and both parents seemed to have drifted into the next life as quietly as they had lived in this one. Allison was saddened by her father's death, but not deeply so, and this seemed both tragic and fair to her. The main loss she felt was for the opportunities her parents had ignored, for the tightly bound family they might have created but did not. She had consulted with a lawyer, met some of the new neighbors. They seemed to be kind people, and she wondered how her life might have been different if other families had lived along this road when she was young.

From them she heard about the electric fence that had been erected in the woods. Her parents held the property right along the road while the land behind, bracketed by narrow dirt roads, had always been owned by the old man with the birds. The fence had been an enormous project and it must have been incredibly expensive—expensive enough to prompt several neighbors to offer competing theories about the sources of the old man's money (family wealth, commodities trading, real estate fraud). The chain links stood nearly ten feet high and wove through the trees around all his land, surely more than two miles of fence.

It was crazy. Why, Allison wondered, had no one protested? Perhaps because he had erected it far enough back in the trees on his own property that it wasn't an eyesore. Even the signs posted regularly along the fence—large, yellow and black warnings: *Danger! High Voltage!*—were invisible until you came through the woods right up to the fence. If anyone should have gotten upset it should have been Allison's father, with his strip of land bordering the fenced area, but apparently he had done nothing.

Allison didn't know anything about the fence when she first arrived. She had gone straight into the house, which she found mired in a dark, stale, unloved atmosphere. The first thing she did was throw open all the windows. Then she sat a while in the empty house, now bright with sun, and soon began thinking she might enjoy living here again. It had always been to her a place of protection, and she liked that the suburbs had come out around here, that other houses had been built up and down the road. She was glad of the new chances to socialize, happy to see children playing in yards, bicycling in the street. She did not wish to be withdrawn from the world, not in the way she had been when living here as a girl.

She was surprised by how quickly Elizabeth settled her things into her old room, then appeared in her jeans and an old shapeless smock, ready to begin. Allison trailed after her as she took an inventory of the appliances and utensils in the kitchen, the furniture and books in the living room, the power tools in the garage. In the bedroom closet they found their mother's clothes on hangers and her shoes stacked in boxes. Allison said she wasn't sure if it was spooky or romantic that their father had never thrown them out. Probably just laziness, Elizabeth said. A couple of decades-old porn magazines were hidden under the mattress. A wedding ring lay at the bottom of a drawer. Elizabeth said, "He wasn't much of a father."

Their father always seemed to Allison a sad man, defeated by she knew not what. "He did his best," she said.

"He never invested himself in us," Elizabeth said. "I see no reason why I should expend sympathy on him."

"Elizabeth!" Allison exclaimed. "How can you say that?"

"Well, what reason is there?"

Allison's thoughts seemed to have lost their order, like sheets of paper subjected to a wind. After a moment she sighed. She said, "He was our father."

"Happenstance." Elizabeth was taking dresses from the closet and throwing them, arms and hems aflutter, toward the bed.

"Oh," Allison said, "Elizabeth, please don't. Don't be cruel."

Elizabeth bent and in a two-armed embrace lifted the loose clothes off the bed and crammed them into a cardboard box. She hefted the box and took it downstairs.

Allison stared after her, then followed.

She found Elizabeth in the kitchen, seated in the chair that had always been their father's. Allison took Mom's chair. Beside her sat the box of clothes, exuding odors of mothballs and dust. Elizabeth stared at the window, the green space of the back lawn. Allison watched the urn on the table and tried to make her own gaze as tough and cold as Elizabeth's, given courage by her anger at Elizabeth's lack of reaction. But soon she began to doubt herself. Then Elizabeth rose and went outside.

When Allison cast back over all of it—from the moment Elizabeth arrived in the driveway until they stood at the fence with the squirrels overhead playing pranks—seeking some indication as to what had led Elizabeth to walk into the fence, it remained impenetrable, and she could only fret vaguely, worrying in all directions at once. She sometimes thought Elizabeth seemed not so complicated, a simple person hidden inside a careful arrangement of shields. But now, in a moment like this, Elizabeth seemed to be moved inside by currents of a depth and complexity beyond anything she could grasp.

She would have liked very much to have had the kind of sister she could talk to every day on the phone, with whom she could exchange every possible secret, a sister she could know and sympathize with profoundly and intimately—a *sister*.

Allison carried the silvered urn out to the back lawn while Elizabeth followed slowly behind. She was still marked with crisscrossing red welts like war paint. She had discovered herself reaching unconsciously, again and again, to touch the lines on her face, and now she kept her hands in her pockets. Allison opened the urn and offered it. Elizabeth glanced inside, but shook her head. "You do it," she said. Allison brought the ashes out in tiny pinches that she tossed overhead, and a gentle wind carried them toward the sumac and the woods.

For the last couple of days Elizabeth had been trying to analyze and understand what she had done. She had awoken flat on the ground, just inches from the fence, and when she regained sense enough to understand what had occurred, it had been a surprise to her. She recalled that she had walked straight into the fence, but she could not remember, or even imagine, why. Despite the welts on her flesh she still couldn't quite accept the reality of it, as if its presence in her memory might have been due to a particularly cogent, evil dream. Watching the dust thrown by her sister wisp aloft and vanish into the trees, Elizabeth decided she needed to go see the fence again, to try and fathom it—both her actions, which were hazy and improbable, and the physical thing itself.

She got up at the first light of day, well before Allison, and stepped quietly across the dewy lawn, through the brush and into the woods, to the fence. The old path still ran under it and onward, but weeds had begun filling it in. To Elizabeth it was as if her own fingerprints were disappearing. A squirrel several feet away on the opposite side zigzagged across the ground, sniffing and testing things with its teeth. The fence itself was silent, just a thing in her path, and whatever had caused her to step forward before was gone now. She was relieved, but also annoyed; she could not summon any sensible conception of what she had been thinking. The squirrel came to the fence and reached up with a paw. In the past Elizabeth had seen squirrels make some spectacular long-distance leaps from tree to tree; as a girl she had envied their ability to do that. But she had never seen a squirrel jump like this—backward and probably four feet in the air. It hit the ground tumbling tail over head, found its feet, and frantically skittered away.

Then the woods stood quiet again. She had keen memories of the light here, coming down in long shafts filtered by leaves moved by fingers of wind into green-stained, kaleidoscoping patterns. But the foliage seemed thicker now than when she was young, allowing less light to earth, and the birdsongs were not as dense as she recalled.

At the sound of a foot on a dry leaf or a small branch, as if she were a girl again, fearing the bird-man had found her out, she took a step away.

She recognized the approaching figure—his height, thin chest, and broad shoulders: the man she had watched fill bird feeders years before. She was surprised by how he had aged— heavy creases marked his face and he looked about seventy. A boy was at his side, thin and maybe six or seven years old. Holding the boy by the shoulder, the man halted a short distance from the fence. "Hello," he said.

"Good morning."

"You're on my property."

"I'm sorry."

The man grunted and switched his grip from the boy's shoulder to his neck.

"Hello," Elizabeth said to the boy.

The boy stared. The man tapped the boy's neck with a finger. "What do you say?"

The boy said, hurriedly, as if the longer he stretched the syllable the more dangerous it would become, "Hi."

"Hi," Elizabeth said. She smiled at the boy.

"What are you doing?" the man asked.

"You put up this fence?"

"Yes."

"Why?"

"It's my goddamn land."

"I'm not going to argue about it. I'm just curious."

"Everything's an argument."

Elizabeth stood watching this man watch her through his electrified fence and wondered if her silence constituted an argument, if this fence did. Certainly the fence did.

He said, "You're the one that shocked yourself the other day, aren't you?"

"You saw that?"

Now he was silent.

"Did you see that?"

"I know what happened."

Elizabeth shifted her feet, setting them more firmly on the path. "You must be glad, then, that I'm okay?"

He nodded. "Sure."

"What about him?" She looked at the boy. "Aren't you afraid he'll run into the fence someday?"

The man chuckled. "My grandson's not that dumb."

The boy's eyes were big and dark as a deer's. Elizabeth leaned forward, putting her hands on her knees. "You like this fence?"

The man interrupted. "You be careful. Leave the boy alone. I've got video cameras up in these trees, recording all this."

"You do not." Elizabeth scanned the foliage. She didn't see a camera, but there were a couple of squirrel nests high in the trees that might have concealed something that size.

"What I want to know," the man said, "is why you're messing with my fence. You going to do it again? You shouldn't even be where you are now; that's my land too. I got to push the fence all the way out to the property line?"

"I'm not going to do it again."

"Well. I'm glad to hear that."

"I don't know why I did it."

"One might guess either stupidity or craziness."

The boy crouched, picked up a stick, and scratched in the dirt. Elizabeth said, "I'd be worried about your grandson."

The man snorted, hocked, spit. The saliva crackled on the fence like water on a frying pan. "He's exactly what I'm worried about. There are crazy people everywhere out there."

"That's absurd. It's cruel to shut a child in." She said to the boy, "You get to play with other boys and girls?"

The boy dropped his stick. "I'm home schooling. It's better."

The man added, "You've seen what's going on out there. I'm supposed to send him into a war zone? I'll teach him everything he needs to know."

"There's a great tree to climb, just over there," Elizabeth said. She pointed. "A huge tree, perfect for climbing. You can see everything from there. Miles and miles."

"You know these woods?" the man demanded.

She had not been to the climbing tree in a long time, and she wondered if it was still there, still climbable. She didn't know these woods anymore. The trails were vanishing; the fence created an irreconcilable disjunction. She thought she understood what had impelled her to press herself against the fence: it hadn't been an impulse to suicide or a strange masochism but the fence itself, its existence, how it cut her off from the woods, from her own past, which left her clawing inside with anger, and she felt that anger starting to scratch in her again. She said, "No, I've never seen this place before in my life." Turning away, she saw the boy watch her with an expression of utter concentration.

"She's a liar," Wilson's grandfather said. Wilson looked up at him. His grandfather strode along, scanning the shadows and the branches to either side and over the path. "I remember her, when she was a little girl, slinking around here like she had something to hide."

Wilson contemplated what she might have hidden and where it could possibly be as they returned to the house. It had a new coat of paint his grandfather had put on earlier in the summer, a white that shone so hard in the sun it hurt Wilson's eyes. To the west of the house stood the pole barn where his grandfather stored the truck and his woodworking and metalworking tools. East of the house, in the shade of a large elm, was a small, covered entryway and a set of concrete stairs that led down into a bunker. They went into the house, and his grandfather told him to finish his breakfast—orange drink from concentrate and instant oatmeal. They didn't have any video cameras, but an alarm went off every time there was a power draw off the fence. Usually it was just a squirrel or a bird that managed to touch the electrified wires while also touching ground, but this time it had been more interesting. The oatmeal was cold, but Wilson ate it, thinking about the lady at the fence.

She represented a singular event in a fog of otherwise similar days. His grandfather gave Wilson lessons in mathematics, science, spelling, and reading (books of history, the natural sciences, the encyclopedia) for six hours a day, seven days a week, fifty-two weeks a year. During the remaining hours of the day Wilson was free to go about as he pleased, within the fence's limits. Gradually the details of what had happened that day at the fence became tangled with fragments of his own imagination. He recalled a beautiful, sad woman who stared at him while she talked with his grandfather. Wilson stood mute. His grandfather spoke angrily for some reason. The woman pointed into the woods behind Wilson, then walked away into shafts of light driven down like spears through the trees. His grandfather said she had been hiding something, and Wilson wondered what she had hid, and where it was.

The woods constituted a world for Wilson. His sense of them grew from an intuition for their stillness and rhythms, for growth and decomposition. He observed: the order in which a spider spun the strands of its web, the building of robins' nests and the fattening of their chicks, the unfolding and the wilting of trilliums scattered under the trees. He stood at the foot of a single, unremarkable tree until he believed he could actually see it growing. On a windless day following the first hard frost of autumn, when the sumac beyond the fence had already turned to flame, he sat under a maple while its yellow leaves came down in a steady, random, falling drift, and it seemed to him, tracing the entire motion of a single leaf from branch to ground, that he understood everything.

However, he knew nothing really of what lay beyond the fence. His grandfather told him that this was simply how people had to live now, and occasionally he showed Wilson enough television to make the point. Wilson knew he had once lived outside the fence, but he remembered nothing of that, nor of his parents—they were a pair of wisps, less substantial than sunset's long shadows. A man had murdered them, his grandfather said. Wilson did understand as he grew older that his life had a certain emptiness, but it was an unconscious understanding, pervasive and colorless as air, and it only caused him to try to fill the emptiness with ever more minute details: the tiny, intricate branchings of leaf veins, the patterns of scent that rose as the sun set, the hundred individual sounds created by a wind—the heavy flap of oak leaves and the patter of poplar, the rattling of locust pods and the shushing of maple boughs. To dig under the fence or to find a tree that extended over it and escape would have been easy. But, while he considered the possibility and even noted the places to dig under or climb across, he was like a person who stands at the edge of a cliff and looks down, idly picking out the particularly jagged rocks.

He was not a tree climber. He was slightly built and, sensing his own frailty, the difficulty of scaling a trunk intimidated him, as did the idea of putting weight on the branches. Trees swayed in a wind, and he had no desire to be up there when that happened. The thought of an earth far enough below to hurt frightened him. So he preferred to stay on the ground. There were many things to do without going up into the trees, many things to notice. He wandered around, observing, often wondering what the lady at the fence had hidden in the woods.

He was nine and finding something amazing seemed possible, even probable. A buried treasure, perhaps. He started by going back to the place where they had met the woman, and he tried to find the precise spot where he had stood. He visualized his grandfather beside him, then the woman on the other side of the fence, her arm raised. He turned and memorized the tree trunks there, the hang of the branches and the leaves, setting the direction in his mind. He dug dozens of small and large holes along that line for the better part a summer before he finally gave up. But he did not forget, and a couple of years later he asked his grandfather to let him build a metal detector as a science project. He spent another summer working the detector back and forth between the trees.

His grandfather seemed to pay little attention to what Wilson did with his free time as long as he did not leave the woods. His grandfather kept the bird feeders full and watched them through the windows, and once a month he took his truck—painted flat olive green, with tinted windows and a winch mounted on the front bumper—out for supplies. They stocked fresh goods in the bunker and carried older supplies into the house, exactly enough cans, dried goods, and bottled water to last the month.

His grandfather was a mystery, a summation, encompassing like the sky, and if his grandfather changed at all during these years Wilson could not perceive it. But there were no photographs in the house, and in the woods Wilson had come to understand that time was fluid, like water: it leaked through his hands if he tried to grip it. His grandfather had the habit of disposing of things that seemed to him not immediately useful. The walls of their house were blank. The bookshelves were stocked with heavy reference books and how-to books. If Wilson brought a flower, a leaf, or a feather into the house, it was gone the next day. His grandfather believed only in self-reliance. On birthdays, Wilson received a pocketknife or a magnifying glass, a compass, a calculator, binoculars, or a book of knots, a field guide to birds. He liked these things and arranged them on shelves that his grandfather built for him in his room.

Time continued to trickle by more or less unnoticed until Wilson's sixteenth birthday, when he woke and came into the kitchen and, as usual on this day of the year, a brown paper package lay on the table. This time it was very small, the size of a matchbox. Breakfast had not been laid out. Dawn light colored the room gray. His grandfather sat tight-lipped and stern. "Good morning," he said. "Happy birthday."

"Thank you." Wilson opened the package. Inside was a single key, with a black plastic grip and *Subaru* printed there in small raised letters.

His grandfather said, "We're going to eat breakfast out."

"We are?" They sometimes went to eat dinner with some of Wilson's cousins in the area—second cousins, third cousins, twice-removed cousins. Wilson could not keep them straight.

He didn't like them, and he passed these dinners in silence, remaining always at his grandfather's side in order to avoid their questions and teasing. But he had never before gone out for breakfast. He had never even considered the possibility of eating out for breakfast.

His grandfather led him to the pole barn. A button activated a motor that winched up the door. His grandfather stood looking at Wilson while it rose. Inside was a green station wagon.

Wilson frowned. "What is that?"

"It's yours. Got it used, but it's in good condition." His grandfather walked around to the passenger side. "Let's go. You have the key."

Wilson looked at the key in his hand. He unlocked the passenger-side door for his grandfather, then his own. His grandfather directed him out of the pole barn and up the driveway. They stopped at the gate and his grandfather opened it with a garage door clicker, which he then clipped onto the sun-visor above Wilson and told him to swing left onto the road. Wilson sat with his foot on the brake, and his grandfather repeated, "Left." The road was empty of traffic. Wilson turned left.

He had driven his grandfather's truck before, up and down the driveway and around the house, but this was the first time he had ever driven on the open road. His fingers hurt around the wheel and he tried to relax them. "Go faster," his grandfather said. They went faster.

It began to seem easier after a few stops and turns. The world moved around the car at Wilson's command. "I like this car."

"Don't forget to check your rearview mirrors," his grandfather said sternly, but he smiled a little, and Wilson knew he was relieved. His grandfather had given him a bicycle a couple of years before and told him that he should get out, meet some friends, explore the neighborhood. Wilson felt too exposed on the bicycle. He'd gone out cautiously a few times until a large dog charged out of a ditch and nearly got a piece of his calf. He rolled the bicycle into a corner of the pole barn and left it. Sometimes his grandfather brought it out and washed it, checked the tires, greased the chain, and left it leaning against the barn door. Wilson dutifully rode it down the street a half mile, returned, and put it back inside the barn. He had not seen it now in months.

His grandfather pointed Wilson into a McDonald's parking lot. They ate Egg McMuffins and hash browns and drank from little cartons of milk, and his grandfather explained that Wilson needed to get out more. "Wilson," he said, "I'm beginning to worry about you." He spoke in a way that seemed rehearsed. He said Wilson needed to make friends, meet girls, needed to see more of the outside world to understand it. Wilson was a man now, old enough to stand his own ground, old enough to recognize when others were trying to take advantage of him, old enough to assess risks and make his own decisions. His grandfather had kept him alive this long, and now Wilson needed to learn to protect his own hide.

"I see the world on TV," Wilson said. Some years before his grandfather had begun allowing Wilson to watch an hour of TV each day, and Wilson liked TV, it was amusing, but this place made him uncomfortable. It had smells that he didn't like, and he didn't like how the people behind the counter looked at him—he always felt uncomfortable when people looked at him. He did not feel ashamed of anything in particular but he was unused to bearing scrutiny and it made him clutch inside with self-consciousness. He asked, "Can we eat in the car?"

"TV has very little to do with the real world, and no we can't eat in the car. You can do what you want later, but don't stink it up yet. For the next couple of weeks I'm going to be in there with you, teaching you how to drive. Those'll be your lessons each day. Then you're going to go take the driver's license tests. Then you're going to get out, maybe join a bowling league."

Wilson set down his McMuffin. On his milk carton a missing boy was depicted. A few booths down sat a fat man who stared. "Bowling."

"Yes, it's a great way to meet people, see the world. I used to bowl. I used to be pretty good."

After a moment Wilson picked up his McMuffin. "Okay," he said.

A month later he dutifully passed his driving tests. He went to a bowling alley where he was assigned to a team with three other men, all much older than himself. He was terrible. He had no idea what to do when the other men slapped him on the back or shouted advice or made catcalls at passing women. He felt battered and confused. How he understood the world seemed to have no application here. What interested him was the way the pins flew about, the complex arcs of spinning, bouncing, simultaneous motion, and the way a ball felt dangling from his hand, dead and heavy on three fingers like a kind of terrible growth. He listened carefully to the cacophony of the balls crashing into pins and the machines resetting the pins and the balls skidding down the lanes and the many people talking and calling and slapping and stomping, all merging into a smooth, nearly musical flow of noise that was completely unlike and somehow independent of any of its individual parts. But obviously no one else noticed or cared about such things. Wilson sat to one side, they ignored him, and he was relieved. The following week he drove past the bowling alley, circled around for a couple of hours, then went home and lied. The lie simply came out—it was the only thing he could think to do.

He got into the habit of taking the car out every day after morning lessons. He drove for hours, often into the night, traveling as much as two hundred miles away and back again, sometimes staying near home, but always remaining secure in the isolation of the car. If he could have kept something like the protection of a small electric fence around him, he would have; the car was a compromise solution. He visited the parking lots of strip malls and supermarkets, cruising through or sometimes just sitting. He found an appliance store with several TVs in the display window, and he could park a short distance away to watch the multiple glowing images. He also watched people. Girls and boys his own age entered and left the stores, slouching, bickering, laughing, driving cars that emitted discordant music. Old people hobbled around with walkers. Couples clutched one another as if nothing else in the world were solid.

One day he saw a woman leaving the supermarket who seemed familiar. He followed her sedan out of the parking lot and down a series of roads. Dreamlike, it was as though she were leading him back to his own house, until she suddenly turned off into a driveway, where, as he rolled by, she unloaded her bags. In the following weeks he often returned to cruise by.

Later that summer he saw two women on the front lawn, bent over a new rosebush near the house. He slowed nearly to a stop, and one of them glanced at him. She said something, and both women turned to look. One was the woman from the supermarket. The other was similar in appearance, but thinner, and she held herself with a particular, proud posture.

His tires squeaked. He drove a half mile, turned down a dirt road, and parked at the edge of the woods.

As soon as she pulled into the drive Elizabeth noticed the neat row of newly planted pines in the backyard along with a number of sapling silver maples, apple trees, and pear trees. They looked very odd to her. As long as she had known this yard it had been absolutely flat and empty. The saplings Allison and her husband had put in were small, like branches shoved end-first into the earth, but Elizabeth could imagine them growing, and she could see they would change the character of the place utterly, creating shade and a sense of the vertical as well as the horizontal. She could not blame her sister; Allison needed to make the place her own. Later, when Allison toured her through the most recent changes— new paint in the entryway, new bookshelves in the study, new trees in the backyard—Elizabeth noted that the pears were particularly surprising because Allison had always hated pears. But Allison said she had come to a sort of reconciliation with pears. It was a small thing, but it caused Elizabeth to recall that Allison had really, always, been as much a stranger to her as she was to Allison.

As a result of relentless work Elizabeth's career was accelerating, and during this visit she often caught herself feeling guilty about taking time from the office. But she was glad to see her sister, and it was of course good for one to spend a few days in idle conversations and aimless walks. She was also glad, however, that she did not live here now, that she was merely a visitor in this dull place, this fragment of her own history.

That evening Allison made gin and tonics, and they sat on lawn chairs in the backyard and watched the sunset fold to a dull glow while the night expanded behind. Allison talked about the past; Elizabeth talked about her work. Peepers and cicadas called. The air chilled. Elizabeth saw him first, a shadow shifting among silhouetted trees. She watched him a minute before Allison started, leaned forward, and called, "Who is that?" He was drawing quite close, a gray shape materializing. Allison began to rise, but Elizabeth put a hand out to stop her.

It was just a boy, a teenager. He halted before them with his face more hidden in the shadows than revealed in the house lights. "Do you need help?" Elizabeth asked. "Is something wrong?"

"Excuse me," he said. "I remember you." He gestured vaguely behind himself. "I could let you in."

"What?" she said.

"I could let you inside the fence."

"The fence? What for?"

He turned his head a little and looked at her sidelong. He said, slowly, "To get what you hid there."

"Hid?"

"From where it's buried."

"I don't understand." Elizabeth looked at Allison.

"Who are you?" Allison said to the boy.

"I don't understand," Elizabeth repeated to him.

The boy shifted his feet, like he was preparing to run. "That day. You talked about it."

Another second passed, then it came to Elizabeth. "When I saw you," Elizabeth said, "I think I said something about a climbing tree. Is that what you're thinking of?"

"No—" said the boy, but a confused expression came over his features. He frowned. "Maybe." He looked at the ground, squinting as if to see something far away. "Yeah, maybe." He shrugged and turned.

"Wait," Allison called. "Let me get you something to drink." He stopped to look at them, then shook his head and walked on into the dark. "God," Allison said. "Maybe *we* should put up a fence. Who was that?" She turned to Elizabeth. "How did he know you?"

Elizabeth didn't know what to say. She tried to think of a lie. She had never told Allison about any of it—about going back to the fence or about the old man and the boy she had met there—and she absolutely didn't want to explain it now. It was her own memory and her own place and to share it all now would have felt like taking a hammer to an exquisite piece of glass.

She said, "He was selling magazine subscriptions door-to-door."

"He was? I've never seen him."

"He came by the other day when you were out. I told him I didn't think you wanted any magazines. We talked a little."

Twilight had become nighttime. Allison peered at the motionless, night-blue trees, as if thinking he might come back for that drink after all. "He seemed very odd. Wasn't he weird?"

Elizabeth shrugged.

Allison giggled. "Kids are pretty strange these days, aren't they?"

"He was weird." Elizabeth laughed and looked at the sky. "He was offering buy two, get one free on the magazine subscriptions." The lie felt fine. She was comfortable with it. She saw Allison smiling toward the trees.

Allison was in the attic. Dust lay over everything and the air had a dry, stagnant feel and it seemed to sit heavy in her lungs. The exposed lightbulb hanging from the rafters lit the center of the attic with an unflattering harshness and left the corners enclosed in darkness. Elizabeth was downstairs. Her arrival had made Allison recall the tornado, and somehow she could still hardly believe that the house had not been touched. She had come up here half-seriously expecting to find a hole or something, something somehow unnoticed for months now. But she saw nothing wrong. "Looks okay," she said aloud, to stir the air. "Looks just fine." There were stacks of cardboard boxes that had not been opened in many years. She began pulling apart their interfolded flaps. She found the tarnished urn that had once contained her father, then a pipe rack with two pipes in it—though as far she could recall her father had never smoked—and a wooden box in which her mother had abandoned a series of heavy eyeglasses with scratched lenses and badly unfashionable frames. She found clothes she and Elizabeth had worn as children—little dresses and overalls and jeans stained at the knees and tiny, matching pink jumpers. She found a button-eyed rag doll. She gazed at it, confused, because it was not one of her own. Then she recalled: Elizabeth had played with this as a child. Perhaps, she thought, the two of them had not really been so absolutely different then as it now seems to her. There had been many days when it rained or the winter weather was too cold for Elizabeth to go outside and the two of them had played, and fought, together in the house. But somehow those days were never the ones that came readily to mind.

She opened the urn and peered inside as though something might be there, but of course it was empty. She closed it and put it into its box. She sat crouched on her knees, gazing at the wooden rafters. During the tornado, in the basement, it had seemed the wind would pick up the house and throw it aside as one might lift and toss a ball cap. She had imagined she saw things moving in the darkness, had imagined she could see the basement ceiling bowing out and in like the ribs of a breathing man. She had been so glad to simply be alive when it was done.

She wondered now if she should say something to her sister about the things she had been ready to pour out when she came back from the woods, just after the tornado. She wondered if she should tell Elizabeth that she had already known Elizabeth was lying, for example, about the boy and the magazines. If she should tell Elizabeth that she wasn't a very good liar. That she understood Elizabeth needed to have her secrets, her hidden things. That it did not matter to her what Elizabeth had hidden in the woods.

But no, Elizabeth had recovered her self-possession now. She would not want to talk about it, would try to deflect the conversation. She might become angry if pressed.

What had shocked her was that Elizabeth had broken down—had *cried*. She had never seen her do that before, and at that moment she would have said anything to Elizabeth to calm her.

Why could Elizabeth weep over this boy, but not her own father? She had read in the papers about the boy that had been killed—a tragedy, he had been buried beside his parents, already dead many years. Allison had concluded that was the same boy who had stopped in their yard one evening. Beyond this, she couldn't make anything of it.

She opened a small box of unpaired socks and gloves.

These secrets indicated only a fraction of the chasm between her and her sister. Allison could see it yawning before her in the darkness of the shadows across the attic floor. The trust of children seemed to her to be the only human variety that was truly infinite, and maybe trust that had not been completely formed in childhood would always find its limits.

Old toothbrushes. Why had anyone kept these?

She heard Elizabeth, downstairs, calling to her, but could not make out the words. "I'll be down in a minute," she yelled back. She sat still and the house was quiet. The exposed pink of insulation had a disturbing, fleshy appearance. There was a faint, earthy odor that might have been the smell of stale mouse droppings.

Elizabeth's head appeared through the trapdoor. "What's going on?" she asked. "Are you okay?"

The question filled Allison with a peculiar, mellow happiness. "Everything is fine," she said. She held up the rag doll for Elizabeth to see. "Remember?" she said. "When we were kids?"

Elizabeth shrugged. "Sure," she said. She shrugged again, ducked, and vanished. Allison stared at the square hole of the trapdoor in the floor. She had known Elizabeth would react that way, had forgiven her in advance. She wondered if that was love.

Wilson stood beneath a thick elm, looking up into the branches above, the sprawling sun-spangled canopy. How did one go about this? He circled around the elm until he decided it was simply too intimidating, then pressed deeper into the woods. He found a maple, smaller and thinner than the elm, with a strong low limb. On his toes, he could reach up and grasp it firmly. He held it a minute, then let go and sat on the moldering leaves below. He found it strange to think that once he had been so small he could not possibly have grabbed that branch. He remembered what his grandfather had told him, about the need to become independent, a man. He remembered his embarrassment, his *fear* in the bowling alley. He stood and rubbed his hands together, then placed them again on the big, low branch. For several seconds he remained there, toes on the ground, hands gripping the rough bark, his body stretched between tree and ground. Then he scrambled with his feet against the trunk, pulled with his arms, and began moving upward.

Quickly his old fear of climbing seemed absurd, a childish notion he had somehow forgotten to dispose of while he grew up. He climbed dozens of trees before he started up a vast oak he knew immediately was the one, knew exactly what she had meant. Its branches went around the trunk with startling convenience, like a staircase spiraling to the topmost boughs. From there he had views across all the land that his grandfather owned, the houses around the periphery, and beyond, to fields, houses, woods, the town in the distance. The branches did sway with the wind, but the movement was exhilarating.

He climbed the tree repeatedly, and he began to prefer the windy times when he could perch near the sky and feel the rush of the air and watch the horizon fall and rise. He went into the woods whenever a big wind started. The first time he was out in a storm, he was thrilled by the thrashing of the branches and the leaves, the crash of the rain, the danger. Soon he knew the big oak so well he could climb it by moonlight. The rush was even greater in a nighttime storm, a chaos of motion and wet blindness. And when the storm passed and uncovered the stars, it was a kind of miracle to cling so close to them and wait and watch while a blush of color grew on the horizon, then unrolled and unrolled until all the air was lit with blue and bright as day.

In her office, still packing her briefcase, Elizabeth phoned Allison and warned her she would be late. Allison said okay, she would keep dinner warm. Elizabeth told her not to bother, just go ahead and eat. It would take her hours to get there. And Allison said all right. Yet both of them knew that when Elizabeth got there the dinner would be waiting, warm. Allison kept waiting for her. And she kept returning.

Then she was on the interstate, pointed toward home— the house, the woods—but traffic lay at a standstill for as far as Elizabeth could see. She sat unmoving in a car in the midst of an endless ribbon of unmoving cars, the sun setting and coruscating in a thousand reflections off all the glass and chrome. She hated this feeling of being trapped in her own car. Certain moments—at the fence, beside the boy's body—would return relentlessly, unbidden, into moments like this. And all these other things were dragged up behind.

Sometimes, still, the unexpected broken appearance of that body came back so vividly it made her gasp for breath. Was she guilty of something? Surely not. Yet, she could not think of the boy without a terrible sensation forming inside her. And if not her, then who? The grandfather? Surely he had done everything he could, went to excessive lengths trying to protect the boy. No one's fault then. These things happened. Nothing could be changed now. She tried to think about the tasks before her. But, in the interstices of the day, these things welled up.

At certain rare moments—ignited perhaps by a smell of acrid smoke or, as now, by the way reflected sunlight rippled along a stream of cars edging into motion—a memory exploded vividly in her: standing before the fence, her anger gathering and concentrating into a twisted, searing fiber within her. Suddenly it expanded immeasurably and she was light, airy—invincible—and she stepped forward, without hurry, toward all the familiar oaks and maples, the hollows and glades and groves, the places and paths she had known.

Radio Ads

This was the summer of Uncle Lewis, also the summer of the new Three Trees Shopping Mall. The radio ad ran every hour, blandly worded but emphatically read by Uncle Lewis: *"Shop where shopping is the thing and bargains are king. Shop at Three Trees Shopping Mall, one place where you can do it all!"*

Whenever Uncle Lewis's voice came on the radio, Billy stopped what he was doing—model building, exploding aliens on his Atari, knocking golf balls across the piece of artificial turf that his father had given him—and he listened. If he was standing he sat down, as if to stand would divert too much concentration. Uncle Lewis never did TV ads, just radio, so whenever Billy watched television he kept a radio going in the background.

Uncle Lewis had other commercials on the air as well, this summer of 1985: *"You think you know beer. But you don't know anything until you've had Stray Tooth Beer."* And, *"Pizza Joe's exclusive eight-cheese, nine-meat, ten-vegetable pizza. There's never been so much pizza in a pizza. It's the pizza with every-thing. Get it at Joe's."* And, *"Diamonds. Diamonds. Diamonds. King Brothers Jewelers, the place to buy diamonds. Diamonds. Diamonds . . ."*

That voice, its projection of salesmanship and confidence, awed Billy. Uncle Lewis lived not far away, and, before Billy's parents divorced, he had come over now and again for a drink. He arrived in his Mercedes convertible, top down. The adults joked in the kitchen, gathered their drinks, then roosted in the living room where Billy sat to one side and listened to Uncle Lewis's voice. It was huge and slow as a cruise ship, and it did not quite fit the physical facts of him. He was short and narrow, easygoing but capable of bursts of energy. Dad was the bigger, taller man, with the weight of an imposing belly suspended before him. Dad's voice shared Uncle Lewis's deep timbre, but Dad tended to hurry his words, as if he couldn't wait to be through his sentences, as if he felt contempt for the clumsy customs of spoken language. It sometimes made Billy a little nervous when his father spoke.

After Billy's parents divorced, his dad moved into a new house that was closer to his work and closer to Uncle Lewis. Billy stayed with Mom, but Dad got Billy for the weekends. Mom and Dad didn't like to see each other anymore, so Uncle Lewis was nominated by Dad, and accepted by Mom, as a chauffeur between the two houses.

Every Friday Uncle Lewis arrived in his open-top convertible. He swooped with Billy along roads and interstates at seventy miles per hour, the rushing wind all around, delivering Billy from Mom's doorstep to Dad's. Every Sunday evening they followed the route in reverse.

The wind made conversation difficult. Sometimes they just listened to the spinning noise of it, or sometimes Uncle Lewis twisted the radio knob to blast Top 40 songs. When one of Uncle Lewis's commercials came on, Billy listened to the voice and watched Uncle Lewis. His lips did not move. *"Pride laundry detergent makes your clothes Pride-fully clean. Don't forget your Pride!"*

Occasionally, Uncle Lewis shouted a comment through the wind. On the very first trip, while barreling down the interstate, Uncle Lewis looked suddenly at Billy and boomed, "Do you want to drive?" Billy, throat throbbing with terror, refused. He began to regret it immediately.

Billy's mom said, "Uncle Lewis is a gentleman." So Billy learned what a gentleman was by watching Uncle Lewis. A gentleman arrived in an expensive car and gave a distinctive three-two knock on the door, then stood with hands clasped behind the back and a broad smile. A gentleman wore a tie. He wore a heavy gold watch. A gentleman said—his voice deep and full and somehow containing its own echo, as if he always stood at the center of an empty room of enormous size—"Hello!" A gentleman took Mom's hand and kissed it, which made Mom laugh.

And laughing, she backed away. "Do you have everything you need, Billy?"

Billy lifted his duffel bag and set it one inch closer to the door.

Uncle Lewis followed her inside. "How are things, Carol?"

"Oh fine, you know, the usual. Billy, you have your toothbrush? Clean underwear? You forgot your toothbrush last time."

Billy nodded.

Uncle Lewis said, smiling, "My offer still stands, of course, Carol. Anytime you'd like to come down to the studio to see how things are done— You never know who you might meet."

"Eventually, maybe, I'll have some free time. I think Billy's all set, aren't you Billy?"

Billy nodded.

"Of course," said Uncle Lewis. He tipped an imaginary hat toward Billy's mother. "Hop along, Billy." He held the door and shooed Billy outside. "Can't keep my ladies waiting."

A gentleman spoke often of his ladies.

Billy's mother laughed again, and Uncle Lewis gave her a little wave.

In conjunction with its grand opening, the new mall was having a promotion: *"Hey kids! Every store in Three Trees Mall has four, that is four, unique, lifelike figures of your favorite Movie Heroes for sale. Just collect all 112 and you'll win a Galactic*

Starfighter with realistic action sounds, movements, and wea-
pons, plus amazing liquid propellant engines. Check out the dis-
play in the mall courtyard!"

Mom and Billy visited early in the summer, shortly after the mall opened. Mom bought kitchen towels and a romance novel. For lunch they got huge soft pretzels like Billy had never seen before. In a glass display in the central courtyard hung the Galactic Starfighter, suspended from wires as if in flight. It was the size of a large suitcase, and it had flashing lights and made electronic sounds. Its motorized, retractable wheels could propel it over any alien surface. A placard said it could fling its missiles twenty yards (in earth gravity) and it boasted twin pressurized water rockets for launches to the interstellar regions. Arrayed beneath it were the 112 Movie Heroes action figures in action poses. Each was molded in one piece of plastic, the face dabbed with pink paint. Billy bought three at the nearest department store, $1.49 each.

Dad owned a large and busy golf shop with a driving range and a putt-putt course. It was located in a cluster of gas stations and strip malls beside a tangle of looped interstate ramps. The parking lot was nearly always full of vehicles and dotted with people standing over their car trunks, getting out golf clubs for the range or putting away the new clubs they had just bought.

Dad loved his shop. Even on weekends, or especially on weekends since weekends were the busiest, he did not have much time for Billy. When he did find time, he wanted to stay close to the action, so he would take Billy out on the shop's thirty-six hole putt-putt course, where they played round after round. Dad knew how to sink every hole in one putt, and he often did. It never took him more than two.

Billy spent most of his weekends alone at Dad's house, eating pizza from the fridge and watching TV, or poking at the balls on Dad's billards table. Dad's new house was a man-ufactured home in a subdivision of manufactured homes that all looked alike, except that some had concrete driveways and some had asphalt. Dad's was asphalt. Sometimes Ralph, an older boy who lived at the end of a concrete driveway next door, came over to see Billy. He was tall and lean with a long neck and a crewcut. He always pretended he had forgotten Billy's name during the time Billy was gone. "Bobby?" he would ask, squinting. "Or is it Buddy? Or Betty? Or Willy?"

When Billy and Uncle Lewis returned in the Mercedes on Sundays, Mom would open the front door and call, "You boys stay out of trouble this weekend?"

"Well, we had to go three rounds for the steering wheel," Uncle Lewis raised his hands and air-punched toward Billy. Then he laughed. "Everything went fine."

"How's your brother?" Mom asked, looking at Uncle Lewis.

"The usual. You know him." Uncle Lewis swung an imaginary golf club. "Working."

"Working." Mom's face puckered. "He won't give anyone time unless they hit him in the head with a fifty-percent-off nine iron or kick him in the shin with a pair of red-tagged cleats."

She said to Billy, "Remember that your father loves you. He's just not a very good dad. Not like Uncle Lewis. Uncle Lewis is a good uncle."

Uncle Lewis beamed.

At Dad's house, Billy noticed a pattern. Every Saturday morning, a red pickup truck pulled onto the concrete driveway next door. Five to ten minutes later, Ralph came over to see if Billy wanted to come out and do something. When Billy asked Ralph about the truck, Ralph rolled his eyes and then he made a circle with his left hand and poked his right index finger into it a few times. This, Billy knew, meant *sex*. "My mom kicks me out of the house so that she and her boyfriend can do it."

Ralph suggested that they sneak around to the bedroom window to watch. They ran and ducked behind the red pickup and crawled on hands and knees to the house then, using their elbows and dragging their legs behind, they hauled themselves around until they lay directly under the bedroom window. Billy's breath sounded to him like tearing rags, and he was afraid someone might hear. But, alongside Ralph, he pushed himself gradually up to the window.

The shades, however, were closed, and they could see nothing. They collapsed to the ground and crawled away. Ralph shrugged. He said he had seen it before. Sometimes they forgot the curtains.

On Sunday afternoon Billy was alone in the house, lying on his back in front of the television. He was throwing a golf ball in the air, trying to get as close to the ceiling as possible without hitting. Hearing Uncle Lewis's muffled voice, Billy dropped the golf ball and charged toward the front door, only to realize it came from the stereo. *"Three Trees Mall . . ."*

Later, during a stretch of silence in the drive home, Uncle Lewis said, "Billy, never turn your back on a woman." He tapped the steering wheel significantly.

For days afterward Billy tried to always be facing toward his mother, until one afternoon when she was moving between the bedrooms, taking out dirty laundry and putting away clean, and Billy was tracking her movements with the precision of a robot. She stopped suddenly and yelled, "Will you stop that!" He did.

One day at Dad's shop a man dressed as a giant golf ball was doing jumping jacks beside the road. Black holes for eyes were cut in the huge, white, dimpled sphere of him. He jumped and waved underneath a banner that said, *A Free Bucket of Range Balls with Every Purchase!* The parking lot was almost full, and they left the Mercedes in a far corner.

In the shop people hefted clubs, peered inside golf bags, fingered knickers. Dad saw Billy and Uncle Lewis and started toward them. Someone shouted from across the store, and Dad yelled back, "Wait a minute!" He said hello, rubbed Billy's head, and punched Uncle Lewis on the arm. "Was my ex-wife hitting on you again today?"

"Me?" Uncle Lewis shrugged, shook his head slightly.

Dad looked at Billy. Billy picked up a divot repair tool. Dad said, "She was, wasn't she?"

Uncle Lewis said, "I'm just the driver." He lifted a driver from a nearby rack of clubs and waggled it.

"Krazy Lefty's burgers: the licking-est good burgers around. And, they're always cheaper than Mickey D's, guaranteed."

Every Tuesday, Billy received an allowance of six dollars and fifty cents. Every Tuesday evening Mom took him to the mall, and Billy bought three or four Movie Heroes action figures. Then they went to Krazy Lefty's and ate burgers. When he had finished his burger, Billy licked the wrapper.

Billy ate Pizza Joe's anytime he could, he encouraged Mom to use Pride laundry detergent, and he wished he could buy diamonds and Stray Tooth Beer.

One weekend he took all the Movie Heroes he had collected to Dad's, forty-seven figures altogether. He arranged them into a panorama of gunfights and close quarters fisticuffs that sprawled across the living room from sofa to television.

When Ralph showed up, Billy brought him inside to see. Ralph picked up one of the figures and laughed. "These suck!" He kicked over several. They fought, but only briefly—Billy was quickly pinned and sobbing under Ralph. Movie Heroes lay scattered around like the corpses of a slaughter, and Ralph stalked away, stiff with disgust.

Billy rebuilt the panorama. Just wait, he thought. *Wait until Ralph sees the Galactic Star Fighter in my hands.*

The following weekend Uncle Lewis arrived late to pick up Billy. He apologized and asked Mom, with the familiarity now of an old joke, "To make it up to you, how about we do that studio tour this weekend?"

Mom said, "Sure, why not?"

Everyone looked surprised. Mom touched her hair.

It made Billy nervous too, and excited. He felt all his cells winding and compressing, like millions and millions of tiny watch springs tightening, preparing for something.

In the Mercedes, Uncle Lewis said, "Your mother is a pretty woman, isn't she?"

Billy pressed back in his seat and tried to consider this. Prettiness and his mother were difficult concepts to hold in relation to one another.

Uncle Lewis glanced over and said, "But then, you already know that, don't you?"

Billy, relieved that the answer had been provided for him, shrugged, said, "Sure."

They rode without speaking for a time. A commercial came on in Uncle Lewis's voice. *"Three Trees . . ."* Uncle Lewis muttered something as he came up behind another car. Billy reclined his seat and gripped the armrests and tried to feel again like he had entered into another world.

"Billy, does your mother ever have any other men visit?"

"Um," said Billy. "No."

The next weekend, and for several weeks after, Uncle Lewis was silent in their rides together. They arrived at the golf shop and Dad slapped Uncle Lewis across the back, and Uncle Lewis shrugged and smiled and left.

When Uncle Lewis brought Billy back to Mom's, he left Billy in the drive and he waved as he backed out. Mom smiled. She brought Billy inside with the usual questions: How was it? Did you get dinner? Did you get to see Dad at all?

Billy stood on the putt-putt course with Dad, considering his shot into the mouth of the huge, sad-eyed dog that lay panting over the twenty-second hole. Its tongue lolled up and down, and the idea was to putt the ball through while the tongue was up. Dad said, "Do you ever see Uncle Lewis over at Mom's place? Aside from when he's there to pick you up?"

"No."

"Does he ever call on the phone during the week?"

"No."

Billy bounced his ball three times off the dog's tongue before getting it to go through, and once he did get it through, he had to tap it again into the cup. Dad's first putt went under the tongue, spiraled around the dog's curled tail, and dropped cleanly into the hole.

The next Friday when they arrived at the golf shop, Dad asked Uncle Lewis if he would keep Billy for the rest of the day. Uncle Lewis frowned. He said, "The ladies will be calling."

Dad laughed.

Uncle Lewis glanced at Billy. "Really," he said, "the ladies—"

"Lewis, I've had one employee quit today and a girl who called sick. We've got this huge sale going on, and I can't leave. Billy would just be in the way here, and he'd love to hang out with you."

Uncle Lewis looked again at Billy. Dad put in, "To top it all off, the ball-gathering machine for the driving range has broken down. Come on, Lewie."

When Uncle Lewis shrugged his resignation, Dad was already moving away, calling thanks as he went. Uncle Lewis took Billy by the shoulder and led him outside. "Your father," he said, "is a very successful businessman."

In the median by the road, the giant golf ball energetically flapped his arms.

As he drove, Uncle Lewis wondered aloud, "What does one do with children?"

Billy slouched.

Uncle Lewis answered himself, "One wears them out so that they will sleep."

They tacked down a series of streets until they came to a park with a scattering of picnic tables, a swing set with rusty chains, a crooked merry-go-round, and two small, dented iron elephants mounted on coil springs. It overlooked a dark pond ruffled with a crisscross of waves. Uncle Lewis got out and ambled to the nearest picnic table. Billy followed.

Uncle Lewis gestured toward the swings. "Don't you want to play?"

"Not really," Billy said, disappointed that Uncle Lewis had even asked.

Uncle Lewis watched him for a moment, then turned toward the lake. "I guess, really, I'm not very good with children."

"That's OK," said Billy.

"Are you hungry?"

"Yeah."

Back in the car, rolling into town, Billy felt it again, the sense that he was not in the ordinary world but in some rarified realm, traversing the earth in the chariot, tickled by the fingers of the wind. Uncle Lewis sat godlike behind the wheel. The road hummed, the radio sprinkled notes around, the mundane world outside the car was blurry, and he had a feeling of moving at tremendous velocity.

At a stoplight a commercial come on: *"Pizza Joe's exclusive eight-cheese, nine-meat, ten-vegetable pizza . . ."*

The voice was electrifying, deep, full of gravel. Uncle Lewis seemed to not hear it. He sat with his hand on the gear shift, watching the light. Ahead was a Pizza Joe's storefront, a small, glass-fronted building with customers visible inside. A sign on the roof said Pizza Joe's, with the *o* in the shape of a pepperoni pizza. Billy pointed. "We could eat there."

"No."

They came to Uncle Lewis's house, a small structure located on a narrow lot surrounded on three sides by towering white pines. They were like the biggest Christmas trees ever. Across the road were cornfields.

"This is the love nest," Uncle Lewis said, flipping on lights. Billy had never seen such an empty house. The walls were blank. The living room had two chairs facing a TV that rested on the seat of a third chair. The kitchen had a small table and two plastic chairs. They watched the television, and Uncle Lewis ordered Chinese food.

Billy had mentioned a few things about Mom and Uncle Lewis to Ralph. Ralph grinned. "I'll bet they're doing it together."

"No," said Billy. But he had already thought of this himself.

They were out in the street, picking pieces of asphalt out of the crumbling edge of the road and hurling them into the air. When the asphalt came down it exploded impressively, skittering fragments everywhere. Ralph threw one more, said, "That's what you do when you're an adult." He made the finger gesture.

Billy began explaining to Ralph who exactly Uncle Lewis was—an awesome voice, the voice of Three Trees Mall, of Joe's Pizza, of Krazy Lefty's.

"Oh yeah?" Ralph picked up a big, two-handed piece of asphalt. "So the hell what?" He considered the asphalt's heft, then dropped it so it broke into three smaller pieces.

"He's cool." Billy took a breath. He looked at the broken asphalt. "He's famous."

Ralph took the three pieces and one by one threw them up high, higher than Billy could throw. They jumped back and hid their eyes as shrapnel exploded around them.

Ralph turned to Billy. "That doesn't mean anything. He's just some guy."

"He's on the radio! He drives a Mercedes!"

Ralph shrugged. "Calm down, Willy." He started off down the street, and after a minute Billy followed. They began poking sticks at the Cullers' Dalmatian.

Dad dumped Billy on Uncle Lewis for another Friday night. This time they skipped the park and went straight to Uncle Lewis's house.

Uncle Lewis rummaged in the refrigerator. "Tap water here tastes terrible," he said. "Do you drink beer?"

Billy remembered the missed opportunity to drive a car. "Yes."

Uncle Lewis swiveled. "You do?"

Billy nodded.

Uncle Lewis shrugged. "Guess one can't hurt." He bent again into the light of the refrigerator. "Are you a Heineken or a Miller man?"

No Stray Tooth. Billy peered over, hoping for some clue. "Miller?"

"Very good. Miller." Uncle Lewis tossed a can over and directed Billy to the chairs in the other room. "Hang out while I find us some food."

The previous winter Billy had touched a shed door latch with his tongue, and beer reminded him of that latch— metallic and cold and bitter and painful—but he forced it down his throat and followed it with another sip and then another before he could think too much and gag. After he had gotten a few swallows down, it didn't seem quite so bad. In the kitchen he heard Uncle Lewis rattling in the drawers and cupboards. Billy stared around the living room, but there was nothing to look at. A car went by. Beyond were rows of corn and, in the distance, some high-voltage power lines strung between large, multiarmed steel frameworks.

A blue van came up from the left, slowed, and turned into the drive. Billy sipped his beer. The van parked behind Uncle Lewis's convertible, and a woman got out. She was short and thin with long, brown hair and eyes that bulged as if they were about to burst out. She strode toward the house in a pair of shorts and a T-shirt that stuck to her. Billy said, raising his voice, "One of your ladies is here."

"What?"

"Someone is here. One of your ladies." She was a very pale person.

"One of my ladies. Of course." Uncle Lewis came out of the kitchen with a beer and a saucepan. The woman was at the door, ringing the bell. Uncle Lewis looked at the van in the drive. "Oh, God!" The bell stopped and a fist hit the door.

Uncle Lewis pulled the door open. The woman stood with arms akimbo and an expression like a bulldog's. "Lewis!" She held up a cassette tape. "You gave me the wrong tape!"

"You drove all the way back?" He stepped away, and she barreled inside.

"After driving two hundred miles out there, I had to apologize to everyone, reschedule the studio for tomorrow, and then drive two hundred miles back here." She gestured at her arm. "My A/C gave out on the way and I've been roasting my arm in the sun for four hundred miles. Look at it!" Her arm was lobster red. Her voice was interesting to Billy. It was husky, full, rhythmic and powerful, and it seemed familiar. It was, Billy realized, after a moment, a radio voice.

Uncle Lewis put his hand out as if to touch her arm, but then stopped. "Josie, that looks bad."

"Listen, you. We're going to the basement, we're going to find the right tape, and we're going to know it's the right tape because you're going to play it for me, and then I'm going to drive straight back out of here." She looked at the tape in her hand, then threw it down at Uncle Lewis's feet. "You can do what you want with that." Uncle Lewis knelt to retrieve the tape. She glanced at the sofa. "Who are you?"

"Billy."

"What are you drinking?"

Billy held up the can of beer. "Hey!" She walked over and seized it from Billy. "Lewis, did you give this to him?"

"What?"

"Man's an idiot." She stomped into the kitchen, taking the can with her. "I'll get you something decent to drink."

Uncle Lewis and Billy followed her. Assessing the cans of

soup on the counter, she asked Uncle Lewis if he planned to eat these for supper, then she scoffed. After a glance in the re-frigerator, she grabbed the phone and ordered sodas and two with everything from Pizza Joe's. Then she went down into the basement with Uncle Lewis. After a moment she called for Billy to follow.

Whereas the living room and kitchen were nearly empty, the basement was filled with open boxes, strewn books and papers, several chairs, and an entire wall of recording equip-ment—speakers, microphones, amplifiers, cabinets and con-soles, knobs and switches of mysterious purposes, and also tapes—racks and racks of cassette tapes.

Uncle Lewis played one tape after another, dozens of them, and he could not find the one Josie needed. She sat beside him and tsked and sometimes delivered a slap to the back of his head. The tapes contained practice takes and retakes of com-mercials that Uncle Lewis had done—the same commercials were repeated over and over with slight variations of voice. Billy was taken aback, then fascinated. This was a library of gods' voices. When Uncle Lewis finally found the one Josie needed, all that was on the tape was Uncle Lewis saying, cu-riously, "Oh, yeah?"

Then Uncle Lewis began pulling cassettes from a different rack, and the sounds were of passing cars or jackhammers or ringing doorbells or bird songs or someone with the sniffles. Josie explained that Uncle Lewis kept these tapes of random sounds that he found. It was his only charming feature, she said. Uncle Lewis blushed.

When the pizza came, they ate it on the patio behind the house where towering pines surrounded them on three sides. Uncle Lewis and Josie sat in lawn chairs and leaned to whisper to each other. Billy lay on a reclining deck chair with his hands behind his head. Josie mentioned the missing tape again, but teasingly. Suddenly Uncle Lewis called for silence. "Listen," he said, "listen." Josie giggled, then fell quiet. From his deck chair, Billy looked straight up the long trunks of the trees. As the wind pushed and released, they swayed slightly and creaked, popped, groaned, in an eddying rhythm, a rain of crisp, wooden sounds.

Uncle Lewis ran inside, and a moment later he came out with a reel-to-reel recording machine. He set this down, pressed a button, and the reels began to turn. He carried a microphone into the trees, as far as its cord would allow. Tape vanished slowly off one reel and materialized on the other. Billy closed his eyes and felt the noises of the trees drift down and land on him like a fine dust. Uncle Lewis and Josie began whispering again, and their voices ran underneath the other sounds in a steady current. Perfect, it all seemed just then, these sounds of nature at dusk and the mythic voices and, somewhere in it, Billy's own breathing, all of it immortalized on a tape machine in the trees.

The next day, Ralph introduced Billy to the phone book. They looked up the numbers of neighbors, then they called and breathed heavily, or waited in silence to see how many curse words a person would use before hanging up. They called bowling alleys to ask if they had eight-pound balls. But Ralph became bored, so they went outside and threw gravel at the sparrows.

A couple of weeks later, while at home with his mom, Billy looked up Uncle Lewis's number and called, hoping to hear his voice. But Josie answered. Billy breathed heavily, hung up, and laughed.

The red pickup was in the driveway next door. Ralph came over and frowned at Billy. "We're moving," he said. "We're moving into the boyfriend's place."

They watched TV. Billy said, "Well, maybe it will be OK."

"I hate him," Ralph said. "I hate him. Let's go slash his tires."

But Billy did not move and neither did Ralph. They sat in front of the TV through the afternoon, then Ralph stood and said he had to go. They did not say good-bye. Through the window, Billy watched Ralph walk away, watched how Ralph's crewcut glowed in a fuzzy, sunlit blur.

Billy and Uncle Lewis were waiting for Dad amid long ranks of golf bags that smelled like lawn chemicals. Uncle Lewis was unzipping the pockets of the bags, feeling inside with one hand, closing the zippers. Billy maneuvered a pair of Movie Heroes figures against each other on a shelf. "What are those?" Uncle Lewis asked.

"Movie Heroes from Three Trees," Billy said. "Like your ad. I have seventy-eight out of one hundred twelve."

Uncle Lewis shut a zipper and looked at Billy for a moment. He knelt down and stared, and Billy felt forced to examine Uncle Lewis's eyes in a way that he had never before examined another person's eyes. Eyes were complicated, moist things with blood vessels in the whites, striations of color in the iris, an unreadable darkness at the center. Uncle Lewis said, "Billy, will you do a favor for me?"

"Yes."

"Do you promise? This might not be easy."

"I promise."

"A good salesman never, ever buys his own pitch. OK? And I don't want you to buy it either. Never buy anything I tell you to in my radio ads." Uncle Lewis nodded slowly. "In fact, whenever possible, I want you to do the exact opposite."

Billy smiled, until he realized that Uncle Lewis was serious. He said quietly, "OK," and then he held very still, steeling himself as vertigo hit.

"Thanks." Uncle Lewis stood.

Billy excused himself and went to the bathroom. He felt horrible and thought he might vomit. He bent over the toilet, but nothing happened. When he came out, to his relief, Uncle Lewis was gone.

"Dad," Billy said. They were on the eighth hole, the windmill hole. Billy's putt slipped through the windmill, ricocheted around two right-angle turns, and trickled into the cup.

"Yeah?" said Dad. "Good shot."

"Have you ever been to the studio where Uncle Lewis works?"

"He told me it's not very interesting."

"I guess he took Mom."

Dad's first shot deflected off a windmill blade. "Really?"

"I guess."

Dad grimly bounced another putt off the windmill, and the next as well. In all, he mistimed five shots before he got through. He needed two more strokes to drop the ball into the cup. Winning a hole over Dad was so unlikely that Billy felt slightly sick in his glee.

"Why," Mom wanted to know the following Tuesday, "do you suddenly not want to go to the mall? What about the Starry Galactic thing?"

Billy looked down. "It's…"

"You've put a lot of money into it already."

Billy, sullen, nodded.

She tapped him on the head. "You need to learn follow-through."

They drove to the mall. Billy bought four more Movie Heroes, and Mom donated funds for a fifth. He threw all his figures into a box and put them on a shelf in his closet.

That afternoon he played Atari Pac-Man, game after game after game. His fingers grew sore and cramped. Mom was reading a romance novel. A carpet store commercial came on the radio. It was Josie's voice. She said, *"Carpet Land's triannual clearance-athon begins tomorrow and goes until everything is gone!"*

"Her left arm was sunburned."

Mom let her book tip down. "Who?"

"On the radio. She had long brown hair. She drove a big blue van."

"Billy, who?"

"Josie. I met her at Uncle Lewis's. She's there all the time, pretty much."

Mom set her book aside. Billy cleared fourteen consecutive Pac-Man screens. Mom got up and went into her room.

The next time Uncle Lewis drove Billy to the golf shop he hunched close to the steering wheel and darted glances at the rearview mirror. He left Billy at the door and did not come inside.

Sunday night, Dad came home from work and said that Uncle Lewis would not be taking Billy home. Dad would drive Billy home.

In the car Billy asked, "Why?"

Evening shadows flickered on Dad's face. "You won't be seeing Uncle Lewis as much anymore."

"Why not?"

Dad concentrated on passing the car ahead. Then another. Finally he said, "Uncle Lewis is moving far away."

He left Billy in the driveway. Mom opened the front door to let Billy in, and Billy saw a look exchanged between the two adults. She asked Billy if he had had dinner.

From then on, Dad picked Billy up on Fridays with a honk of the horn from the driveway. Sunday nights, he drove Billy back.

Once he actually had the Galactic Starfighter in his hands, Billy was impressed by it all over again. It launched missiles at speeds that appeared seriously dangerous. It came with a hand pump to pressurize twin water tanks that blasted it sixty feet into the air. It was really big. Even Ralph might have admitted it didn't suck.

He loaded the Starfighter and took it outside for launch. Unfortunately, it landed in the Cullers' yard. The Cullers had a new puppy, a big, rambunctious beagle with neck muscles like a hyena. It got hold of the Starfighter and Billy watched while the toy was reduced to several pieces of shredded, indistinguishable plastic.

One day he was looking through the phone book for Ralph's address. He could not find it. Idly, he looked up his own name, and discovered Uncle Lewis's. He was not very surprised to see that Uncle Lewis had never moved.

The radio continued to emit Uncle Lewis's voice in a steady stream of commercials. At first to hear that voice was troubling, like a phantom haunting him, but in time it became merely irritating, and eventually the voice was just background noise, another guy peddling tennis shoes, tax services, gasoline, supermarket discounts, car batteries, rock concerts, tuxedo rentals, milk, bread—just more salesmanship in a world saturated with salesmen.

Telescope

She found the box, a long, narrow box of dark-stained wood with a small metal clasp in front and tiny hinges in back, found it in the far corner of the closet where she hung her winter coats, dumped the ice skates she had used only once, propped the skis that her husband might still use except her husband was dead, and she actually didn't remember what was in the box until she carried it to the kitchen table, wiped off the dust, opened it, and there was the telescope, beautiful, after so many years she had forgotten how beautiful it was (she had forgotten last time too, the last time she had "found" it again, found it that time lying in the grass of the yard, re-discovered the grain and varnished sheen of the wooden segments, the bands of shining brass, the glossy smooth glass lenses, the precise slide of its expansion and collapse, but her husband had glanced at it and said, "I don't want to see that thing ever again" (they both associated the telescope with their son, Michael, who had twice torched their house with gasoline when they refused to give him money for heroin, associated it with their anguish over him and particularly their anguish following the second fire when her husband had told the police he did indeed wish to press charges, after which, so far as they knew, no one ever saw their son again, and her husband said forget him, said, "We are childless," upon which announcement he actually did seem to forget him and she played along because otherwise he became angry, though sometimes she wanted desperately to be able to talk about her son and sometimes her husband wept and still would say nothing although she knew it was the loss of his son that leveled him this way (these emotions triggered by, among other things, the process of filling new closets, which the second time felt like an act of pitiable déjà vu, and the hollow strangeness of a house in which almost nothing was old, except the telescope, both times the lone surviving object, easy to hate (Michael claimed he had used the telescope to focus the sun— the way a child burns ants with a magnifying glass—to ignite the gasoline he had spread around the house, which seemed unlikely when a Zippo would have been so much easier and was also exactly the sort of elaborately pointless lie he liked to tell at the time, but it was a fact that while everything else in the house was destroyed, both times, the telescope alone was found safe, placed on the lawn well away from the fire, so after the second fire she hid the telescope deep in a closet, perhaps hoping at the same time, uselessly of course, to hide the ways in which she could not understand her son (one day they had received a notice that their son had missed a day of school, then another of these, and another, until these notices began to seem almost routine, although she tried not to treat them that way, then the first call from the police came when Michael shoplifted five pounds of hamburger and a dozen D-cell batteries, for what reason he refused to explain, but the store manager had let the matter drop and then Michael seemed to be behaving better, going to school, listening to his father's lectures, eating her good meals, accepting her cautious smiles, her love, until six months later when he was arrested for breaking and entering, stealing power tools from an old man's garage, and he spent several weeks in a home for juvenile delinquents, and his disappearances began, a night now and again, then several nights, then weeks (no, she could not say how or when exactly things began to go wrong, but, in hindsight, perhaps the first misstep went back to the telescope, when the neighbors' daughter accused Michael of spying on her bedroom window with it, and he denied it, said he was only watching birds, and he was so young then that she, his mother, believed him and told the neighbors there had been a mistake, and a year later, when the neighbor girl's room was broken into and ransacked, she, his mother, still did not quite begin to make the connections—but she could only fitfully imagine the steps and reasons of his descent, for she had no experience herself in that world, and when she realized that he had entered it she felt helpless and terrified, remembering well it had been a nightmare of hers, when she was younger, that she might have a child who turned out like this (he never was an adept student and he always had a temper but he could at times be so fiercely loving—she remembered how he clung to her skirts, how he brought her pretty stones he found, really such a sweet child, a boy who said excuse me before leaving the dinner table, a small boy who tidied his own room without being asked, and the telescope was intended to be a reward (but he had opened the box and looked at the telescope with dismay, absolutely crestfallen: he had wanted something else and she never knew what, couldn't guess, and what use had she thought a boy would have for a telescope? birds! had that been the beginning of the problems? but she shouldn't blame herself, or so her husband had told her many times (she found it in an antiques store, in the window, displayed on a red velvet pad, and she thought, oh, Michael would love it! (but really: really it had been she, hadn't it? she who loved it, all those years ago, she who wanted it (the telescope), and she collapsed the telescope, put it into its wooden box, and the next day she pawned it for thirty dollars and spent the money on a large bouquet for the mantel—asters, irises, lilies, heather—beautiful things that would fade and then could be thrown away.

The Prototype

The vehicle looked as if someone had attempted to armor plate it with cushions from a black vinyl sofa. Only the overall dimensions allowed Martin to recognize it as a truck—a sport-utility vehicle. Black plastic panels hid the painted surfaces and crowded the side and rear windows, narrowing them to portals the size of arrow slits. The headlamps peered out of a masklike construction over the grille. The wheels were painted flat black.

It pulled in with something dragging in the rear, lifting dust from the gravel parking lot. Martin had just closed the shop and stood watching in stained coveralls with a rag in his hands, trying to work the grime from under his fingernails. The truck stopped and two men got out wearing khaki trousers and electronic gadgets—pagers and cell phones—on their belts. They said they were engineers from Detroit, conducting tests on this vehicle. But a rear suspension link had busted. One of the engineers was quite young while the other had gray hair and lines in his face. Martin said, "Kind of a long way from Detroit, aren't you?"

The older one peered at the name embroidered on Martin's breast pocket. "Things are pretty flat around Detroit, Martin. We come out here to feel how the truck performs on the more aggressive mountain roads."

The younger one said, "The vehicle is a prototype."

"Uh-huh," Martin said. "Of what?"

The older one said, "If we told you that, we'd have to kill you." He grinned. "Ha-ha," he said.

Martin drove the truck into the service bay and raised it on the lift. The suspension link—a curved steel bar with joints on the ends—had sheared in half; the two pieces hung down awkwardly and the wheel camber was badly off as a result. Martin came out and said, "That isn't a standard part."

"Yeah, it's a prototype design," said the older one. "Won't be able to order one from your nearest dealer. But it's a pretty simple piece. We were hoping you'd know someplace where we can have some bar stock formed. Then we just need to cut off those end pieces and weld them onto the new link."

"Well," Martin said, "that's possible. The thing is, technically, we're closed. There is a guy in town who can form a new link for you, but he'll be closed now too. Pretty much the entire town is shut up at this point. Best I can offer is to get it done first thing in the morning. Have you out of here by 10 a.m."

The two men looked around, as if there might be another mechanic across the street.

Martin added, "Next town's some thirty miles along, but I can lock your truck in our garage overnight. We've got a good alarm system."

He led them into the office and made a couple of calls to verify that everything was closed. The older engineer said, "Pretty goddamn stupid, getting ourselves stranded in a backwater like this." He looked at Martin. "No offense."

Martin shrugged. "You'll be gone early tomorrow." He filled out a work order. While the engineers looked it over he asked, "How much does it cost to build a prototype like that?"

"A half million, isn't it?" said the younger engineer.

The older one shrugged. "More, I think. Depends on how you divide the costs. We make only a couple dozen of these prototypes. Mid- to upper six figures per truck." He clapped Martin on the arm. "You insured for that much?" He laughed.

Martin locked the truck into the service bay and drove the engineers to the motel in town. The engineers had no bags or overnight supplies with them, and as they trudged into the motel they appeared bowed and forlorn. Martin tapped the

horn at them and waved. Then he drove back to the shop, unlocked the office, and went to the phone.

Martin did not often have plans. Generally, he did not
think much of the future; he mostly took things as they came.
But now he had a plan and it gave him a giddy, erratic feeling,
as if his heart were a four-cylinder engine and one of the cylinders was misfiring.

One thing Martin knew for sure about Eileen was that she
liked trucks. The sight of a truck often sparked thoughts of her.

It was Eileen who answered the phone, and, after hello
and how are you, he asked if she wanted to do something tonight. She said, "OK. What do you have in mind? I don't think
I want to go to a bar or anything like that."

"That's all right. I sort of have this thing I'd like to show
you. It's a surprise."

"Oh," she said, "really? Actually, I guess I kind of have a
surprise too."

Martin agreed to meet her at her parents' house later and
hung up. He went into the garage, unbolted the broken suspension link, and hurried with the pieces to the metal shop—
Mike's Metalworks. Martin had known Mike since grade
school. He fetched the key from its nail among the rafters in
the rear and let himself inside.

He kept the lights low while he worked. Around him the
shapes of saws and lathes and milling machines formed omi-
nous shadows. He heated and bent a piece of bar stock until it
matched the shape of the two broken pieces fitted together, then
with a band saw he cut the end joints off the broken link. The
welder cast the shop into white relief and threw sparks of bright
metal that fell and bounced on the concrete floor. In a little
more than an hour he had finished the new part. He returned
to the garage and with some hammering made it fit. He put the
bolts in, torqued them, lowered the truck to the ground, and
went home to wash and change. A clean button-down shirt,
jeans. He scrubbed his nails until his fingertips felt painfully
raw, even though he knew he could not get the black out.

He had not seen Eileen for several months. She had left a message on his answering machine a week earlier, letting him know that she was in town visiting her parents, but until now he had been delaying, day by day, not quite able to find the courage to call her back.

Thin and delicate, Eileen didn't seem particularly like a woman who would love trucks. But she surprised you like that sometimes. She was a generally quiet, sensible girl, but sometimes a headstrong notion or a peculiar talent popped up amid her day-to-day common sense. Origami, pottery, and horseshoe throwing had all been pursued intensely. She played poker with relentless aggression. Once for Martin's birthday she had prepared an entire sushi dinner; he'd never had sushi before, and found it not really to his taste, but he had been impressed nonetheless. She had quite a nose, a surprising nose in the face of a small woman; it had taken Martin a while to figure out how to kiss around a nose like that. She was the first woman Martin had ever made love to in an actual bed, which had been a transforming experience for him. They had dated through their senior year of high school, almost ten years ago. After graduation Martin stayed in town and worked for his father. Eileen's going away to college wasn't her choice so much as her parents'—at least that's what she said—and Martin figured she would come back soon, since it wasn't really her choice to go. But she surprised him; she liked college, liked being away. "Martin," she said on the phone a few months later. "Martin—" She hesitated between words. "I just don't know how to make this easier. But you're still there and I'm not. You see?"

"See what?" Martin said.

"I hope we can still be close, Martin," she said. "I care for you a lot, but we're going in different directions. I hope we can still be friends."

Martin recognized the cliché, but when the conversation was over he clutched at that idea—still being friends—and in the weeks, seasons, and years that followed, he never let it go. He sent letters, about once a month, maintaining a careful distance in them. Just friends. Friendly, she wrote back. Once or twice a year, when she came home to visit her parents, she called her friend Martin and they met for breakfast or lunch and he was carefully polite, affectionate, but not too much so. They hugged briefly on meeting and parting and, otherwise, did not touch. He was afraid that if he went any further or said what was in his mind, she would never speak to him again. Afterward, Martin went home and drank whatever form of booze he found in the cupboard, and the next morning, hungover and miserable, he'd resolve to put her out of his mind for good. But this could not be done. He had relationships with other women, but none of them ever made his brain and body buzz the way a two-sentence postcard from Eileen did.

He turned into her parents' driveway and parked behind their old pickup truck. Her father had used the truck to haul a stock car around to the racetracks for several years, until the hobby nearly bankrupted him and he had to give it up. He used to let Eileen drive practice laps in the race car, taught her some maneuvers, but she always preferred the truck. It had been old then and looked like a battered antique now. The tailgate was missing; the body panels were mottled with faded paint, patchy rust, and naked-pink Bondo. Martin gazed at it, hesitating. He wondered why the confidence he felt dealing with metal never extended further into his life—to women, to his future, to his grasp of his own desires.

Finally he got out and rang the doorbell. Faintly, he heard Eileen call, "Come in!"

The living room was empty. Eileen's voice came from behind the closed door of her old bedroom. "My parents are gone, Martin. I'll be out in a second."

"OK," Martin said, to the door. He sat on the sofa. From here he could see nearly all of the house—the shower curtain slumping into the tub, the dishes stacked beside the kitchen sink, a cluster of racing trophies on the dresser in her parents' bedroom. It was a small house.

Martin briefly entertained a fantasy in which Eileen came out nude and seduced him.

She called, "Ready?"

"Sure."

She was smiling and fully clothed. Her nose seemed different. "Hi," she said.

Martin squinted slightly. Something had happened to her nose. This was definitely not the nose he recalled; this nose was smaller. Martin wondered for a moment if he was looking at the wrong woman, if this could even be completely the wrong house. But it was Eileen—same gray eyes, same long brown hair, same thin lips. Then he remembered that this was possible, people nowadays could have their noses changed, although he had never personally seen such a case before. But here it was, a new nose.

Martin realized he was staring. "Hi," he said. He looked away. "Um," he said. He glanced at her and she was looking at him. He said, "The nose?"

She raised her hands toward her face but stopped the gesture halfway and instead put her hands in her pockets. "That's the surprise," she said. "You think it looks better?"

"Yeah," he said.

"Yeah?"

"Oh," he said, "oh, yeah." He nodded slowly. He couldn't think what to say. Then he thought of something. "It looks like a movie star's."

"Like Sigourney Weaver. That's what I told them I wanted."

He peered. "Oh," he said. "Yup. That's exactly it." Eileen had Sigourney Weaver's nose.

"Her nose is distinctive yet graceful. At least that's what the doctor said."

"I see what you're saying. I mean, I see it right there."

"I'm still a little self-conscious about it, especially here. I haven't really been into town. I know how people will talk."

"Well," he said. "I'm sure they'll get over it."

"Yes," she said. "I guess so." She smiled a little. "I'm glad you like it."

Martin smiled—he hoped it looked like a real smile. He looked around.

She said, "It feels awfully small now. The house, I mean. After having been away and come back."

Martin said, "It's not really that small."

"The trees seem bigger, though," she said. "I guess that's because they are."

They talked for a while about the people they had known in school, what they were doing. Martin watched her nose, how it moved up and down, just slightly, as she spoke, her nose that wasn't her nose. Most of their classmates were still in town. Most, like Martin, now did the same things their parents did. Martin asked, "Are you planning to leave again soon?"

"In about a week," she said. "You know, you should get out of this town too, Martin."

Martin looked at her. Did she mean he should come with her? No, surely not. But that he should visit her? He said, "I like it pretty well here."

"I know, but I think it would be good for you to get out. You might be surprised. You might like it."

"Uh-huh," he said. As a girl, Martin knew, Eileen had traveled often and far with her father, pursuing small-purse races at all the little tracks within a five- or six-hundred-mile radius of town. She had stayed in cheap motels, had eaten in greasy diners, truck stops, and race-themed saloons, had watched thousands and thousands of miles of countryside blur by. Ever since she had left for college she had continued to travel and move on; her address changed almost every year. Martin, on the other hand, had never been more than a hundred miles from the town limits, on short excursions to the city to visit the junkyards or to buy the things his mother couldn't get in town. Otherwise he didn't leave the mountains. His parents were not travelers. His father worked nearly every day of the year, taking on small engine repair jobs, or even vacuum cleaners, VCRs, and washing machines, if he couldn't find a car around that needed fixing. The additional income wasn't necessary; he just liked to take a thing that was useless and make it useful again. Now, as Martin picked up the work at the garage, his father was doing even more of these small jobs, often for no pay.

Eileen gestured with a long sweep of her hand. "There's a whole world out there, Martin, a very big world."

"Maybe. But I usually feel like there's enough of a world right here."

But once he'd said this, Martin was uncertain how much he believed it. On a number of occasions over the years Martin's father had assured him that, really, there was no need to go anywhere when everything he needed was right here. It made sense to Martin when his father said it. There were good people here. He had steady work that he mostly enjoyed and the opportunity to one day take a business and make it his own. But when he thought of Eileen he wasn't so sure, wasn't at all sure that everything he needed was right here.

Eileen looked at the floor. "You're probably right," she said. "There's stuff here I don't appreciate as much as I should."

Martin felt embarrassed. He watched a silent pair of headlamps slide by in the night-black window.

Suddenly Eileen stood. "So, what's your surprise?"

"Oh." He cleared his throat. "I had something unusual come into the shop at the end of the day. A truck."

She smiled. "I like trucks."

"This one is a prototype, from the labs or whatever in Detroit. These engineers had it wrapped in black plastic to disguise it. They broke a rear suspension link."

"A *rear* suspension link? So, it's got an independent rear suspension? Not a solid axle?"

Martin nodded.

"That's interesting. They must have done that to improve handling."

"That's what they were out here testing. Handling."

"Does it look good?"

"I couldn't tell with the disguise on."

"And now they're gone."

"No. Actually, I lied. I told them I would have to keep it overnight. Want to see it?"

"Martin, you lied?"

Martin felt his cheeks heating a little in embarrassment. It was pretty unusual—Martin tended toward honesty and caution in most things. He felt again the surging, fluttering feeling he had when he picked up the phone to call Eileen, an exhilarated feeling, the feeling perhaps of taking hold of the wheel of something significant and turning it to an unfamiliar direction. He said, "I was curious what it looks like under the disguise. But I haven't taken it off yet."

"You were waiting for me?"

Martin's throat closed up. He nodded.

"Thanks," she said and smiled. "Let's go see it."

Outside, Martin held the car door open for her. While they drove back through town, she said, "Really, what do you think of the nose?"

He glanced at her. Nose, he thought. He steered through a turn, rubbed his cheek. "I think it's pretty amazing what they can do these days."

She was staring at him. She said, "I guess you don't like it then."

"I like it. It's very nice. But I liked it before. It's just different."

She was silent.

He said, "The nose doesn't matter much, one way or the other. It's you I like."

"Well, that's sweet," she said.

He ground into the gravel of the parking lot and stopped. Actually, he couldn't decide what to make of the nose. It was too strange. That first impression, that he'd gone to the wrong house and picked up the wrong woman, hadn't completely gone away. She talked more and with more confidence now than she had when they were in high school. He had seen this change before, had seen it arrive gradually in her previous, occasional visits home. But his memory of her always reverted to when he had known her best, and the surprise of who she had become felt new every time he saw her. It made him wonder, had he changed too? He had, of course, though he rarely thought of it. He essentially ran his father's shop now, and that would have been inconceivable a few years ago. And—this deception of the engineers. He never would have done this when he was younger, and it struck him as a little worrisome that with age he was perhaps growing not wiser but more foolish.

He led her through the side door and into the service bay. The darkness was nearly complete; only a bluish glint of light here and there suggested objects. He flipped a switch. The fluorescent lights flickered, then held and brightened.

They stood looking at the prototype truck. The lights buzzed.

Eileen said, "It's not really a truck. It's an SUV."

"An SUV is a kind of a truck."

"I suppose."

Martin frowned. While Eileen circled around the truck, scrutinizing, he picked a washer off the floor and set it on the table beside him. After a minute he tapped the plastic panel covering the hood and said, "Guess we might as well take these off and see how it looks."

The panels attached with Velcro peeled away easily. Others were strapped on, or attached directly to the sheet metal with screws or cotter pins. Tacky patches of adhesive, small holes, and furry strips of Velcro marred the paint beneath. Bundles of wires ran from the gap around the hood down into the front grille and back to the passenger-side door. But once the disguise was off the intended appearance was obvious— the sheet metal swooped into sharp creases at the corners and narrowed toward a snarling chrome grille bracketed by wide headlamps with mirrored reflectors shaped with dozens of intersecting flat surfaces, like intricately cut gemstones.

"It's very modern," said Martin.

"I like it," Eileen said. "And, think, the only people who have seen this are some engineers and designers, and you and me."

"True."

"Plus, I like the color," she said. It was a bright red.

The black plastic panels lay on the floor. Martin kicked one to the side. "Well," he said, "go for a spin?"

"You said it's broken."

"I already fixed it." Martin pulled the keys from his pocket and pressed a button on the key fob. The truck bleeped. The locks whirred. He held out the keys, and Eileen snatched them. She grinned and he grinned and she ran, literally ran, around to the driver's door, as if afraid he might try to get there first. And Martin felt good then, great even, like maybe this wasn't the dumbest thing he'd ever done. Maybe—he allowed the hope to surface and float happily in the back of his mind—maybe this would turn out to be worth it.

A mess of wires erupted from the dash. Many of them fed into a portable computer on the floor that Martin kicked up into the footwell. Eileen flipped open the armrest between the front seats. "Six-CD changer," she reported. "It also says 'DVD.'" Martin reached up and pushed a button to roll open the sunroof. Another button dropped a small screen from the ceiling; it displayed a detailed map of Southern California with a large you-are-here arrow. Martin pressed another button and static swarmed the screen. He pressed it again and got more static. He said, "I guess we don't get cable." But he hit the button once more and an Internet website popped up. Eileen turned the key and the speedometer and the tach appeared in glowing digits on the foot of the windshield. "This is so cool," she said. "I wish we had some CDs."

Martin pushed the video screen closed and looked at the steering wheel, the center of which was open, black, and empty. He said, "Looks like they took out the airbags."

"Well, I'll drive carefully," Eileen said. She then revved the engine and sprayed gravel as she backed out of the service bay, spun in the parking lot, and swerved onto the road.

She drove fast. They were out of town in a minute, and the twists in the road rushed on them from the dark. Eileen hit the brakes, lurching them into their seat belts, and squealing around the turns. Martin was pressed into the door, then pulled away. She hit the accelerator as a curve began to straighten, and they were set back into their seats while the engine grew noisy. The truck generated speed quickly, even when pointed uphill. Martin said, "Must be some engine they've dropped in here."

Air rippled through the sunroof with a noise like a flapping flag and the stars there swayed and twisted. Martin's stomach clutched a little when Eileen crossed lanes to hit the inside of a curve, but he actually didn't feel too nervous. There didn't seem to be anyone else out; they tore through an unremitting darkness like the only moving vehicle on earth. And he knew that she knew what she was doing with a truck. She had always been a better driver than he was.

"What do you think?" he asked.

"The steering's on-center feel is a bit sloppy," she said, "and I'm surprised by the tendency to oversteer in the corners." She grinned. "Other than that, it's great. It handles almost like a car. This engine could tow the *Titanic* up a mountain."

"It's a nice truck," he said. "It'll be even nicer when they get all this junk out of here." He toed the computer on the floor. "I'm glad you like it."

"I'm glad you invited me out. This is fun. I haven't been getting out."

Martin nodded.

She slowed the truck. "God, Martin, I don't feel like I know anyone here anymore. I mean, you, yes. But the people in town, the people we spent all those years with in school seem practically foreign to me now. The difference in experiences is too much, I guess. I feel like a stranger."

"You're not a stranger to me."

"I know," she said, and she scuffed the top of his head.

He wasn't sure how the gesture was intended, but it made him feel like an amusing pet, rubbed between the ears for loyalty. He slapped the door. "My turn to drive."

She pulled to the side of the road, miles from anywhere now. They crossed in front of the truck, through the glare of the headlamps. Her nose again.

Martin sat in the driver's seat and adjusted the mirrors, gripped the steering wheel. It was wrapped in soft leather.

"You're not going to baby it, are you?" she asked. "My dad used to tell me that a good race driver always has either the gas or the brake pedal floored."

Martin looked at her. "Is that true?"

She smirked. "No. But it's a good place to start."

Martin drove hard, making the body roll back and forth and the tires scream and scrub sideways around the turns. The yellow markers in the center of the road shot by like bullets. After a few miles he began cutting off the corners, as Eileen had done. Occasionally the backend caught a bit of gravel on one side of the road or the other. He was squarely in the opposite lane during a long leftward curve around a brush-covered slope when he saw the glow of lights spreading across the pavement ahead. He tweaked the steering wheel to the right as twin white headlights appeared suddenly before them, very near. Eileen yelped as they swerved. If the window had been open, Martin could have reached out and tapped the roof of the other car as it passed. The shadowy figures of the driver and a passenger looked at him. Martin didn't feel the adrenaline rush—nerves burning like fuses—until the sound of the other car's horn had faded around the hill.

"Very nice!" said Eileen.

Martin kept his foot hard against the gas pedal. His breathing had slowed and his nerves were steady again about a mile later when he saw a dirt road branching off to the right. He took it. The wheels slapped into ruts, the trees on either side blurred. "Hey, four-by-four," said Eileen, pressing a glowing button on the center console. There was a clunking sound and Martin felt the front wheels begin grabbing and it seemed he could take on anything with this truck. They emerged into a meadow where the road opened out and vanished into dry grasses and low rocks. The truck jumped among the stones and undergrowth, and Martin struggled—gripping hard to keep his hands on the wheel and flailing a bit with his foot—to keep the truck under some control.

He knew this meadow and the steep downhill ahead, but he had forgotten about the single tree, in all this open space, until it came into the lights. He spun the wheel, already imagining the head-on collision. The truck, however, lurched suddenly rightward, rebounding off a luckily positioned rock, or something. The truck hit only a few low leaves that slapped the windshield and slid along the side of the truck as it scuffed to a halt.

A moth flashed whitely in the headlights. "Wow," said Eileen. Dark space opened where the hill dropped away before them, to a dry riverbed far below, invisible and silent.

Martin unclenched his fists from the steering wheel. He chuckled nervously and wiped his face. He was dripping with sweat. He said, "I guess this was pretty stupid."

"We're OK," Eileen said. "For a while there you were really driving. It was fun."

Martin sat without touching the steering wheel, looking into the space where the truck's lights projected out and were lost. He said, "It was a little much. But it was fun. That was a lot of fun."

Eileen touched her nose and gazed at the black valley before them. She said, "You ever feel like the whole world is just too much, too big?"

Martin considered this, listening to the slow, irregular tick of the cooling engine. He said, "I do sometimes. I think that's why I stay put, stick with what I know."

"Really? I think my instinct is to resist. I want to keep moving away from here, to see as much as possible."

They were quiet.

She said, "I guess that's the difference between us."

He didn't want to admit it. "It's not such a big deal. I've been thinking you might be right, maybe I should get out, see someplace new."

"Really?"

"Well, sometimes. It's confusing, you know? It's comfortable here, but I wonder what I'm missing."

"Do you miss me?"

Martin's instinct was to change the subject, but he fought it down. "Yes," he said. "Yes, of course. And I admire what you've done. I really do. I have for a long time. I think you've got a lot of balls."

"Balls?"

"So to speak."

"Thanks. That's very flattering."

"I'm serious," he said.

"Me too." She laughed.

Martin looked at her and wondered, did he like this nose? Yes, he decided. Yes he liked this nose. She had the courage to change things, to do and try new things and to make her face new and she looked beautiful. She was still smiling. Martin felt happy to see her smile.

It occurred to him that this moment was utterly unique. That this might be *the* moment.

He had been through this kind of thing before and should have known better, but, again, he was disappointed to find that, in the moment, he was moved by neither reflex nor some instinctive force of animal desire. Instead he sat frozen and hyperaware of himself—of the noise of his breath, the twitch of his toes against his shoes, the clutch of the muscles in his chest. His body refused to move unbidden. Anything he did would have to be forced by an overwhelming and very conscious command.

Eileen looked out her side window. The moment—if this was the moment—was slipping away. She would ask what he was waiting for, and this opportunity—and what better might there ever be?—would be over.

Feeling as though he were trying to move through an atmosphere congealed into some high-viscosity fluid, Martin lifted his hand off the armrest and pushed it toward her.

He put his hand on her knee. No one moved. The light of a sickle moon faintly delineated the peaks across the valley. An owl called. Martin began to feel awkward, sitting with his hand there. What now? She gave no indication. It was as if the air had solidified around them, locking them like bugs into amber. Millennia from now someone would dig them out, and what would they think? They would think these two had been in love.

He slid his hand up her thigh, three inches. He could feel the warmth of her through her jeans.

Two inches more.

"Martin," she said. "Is this what this has been all about?"

He did not move.

She said, "I thought—I don't know. I mean, we're not in high school anymore. Thank God."

Martin took his hand away. His face was hot. He said, "I didn't mean that."

She said, "How about we just go home now."

"Wait, please—"

"Actually, no, it's a nice night, and I can walk back from here, OK? It's not too far. I guess I thought maybe you'd grown up. Thought by now maybe you would have started looking for something other than sex in a backseat. Thought maybe you were a more interesting person. But, you know, thanks anyway for showing me the truck. It's pretty cool."

"Eileen, don't." She opened her door and stepped out, and he watched in the rearview mirror as she strode away, lit taillight red. He got out. "Eileen!" he called. "Eileen! Listen to me for a second!"

"What?" she said.

He could hardly see her. He said, "Just—" And he didn't know what to say. He cast about as though there must be an answer somewhere within reaching distance.

There was a scratch on the side of the truck.

"Gah!" he cried. It was a long gouge, taking off paint along both the driver's side doors and the rear fender. Had the tree done that?

"Gah?" said Eileen.

If he put the camouflage panels back on, maybe the engineers wouldn't notice. But of course they would notice eventually. He turned toward Eileen. "The truck," he said, "There's a scratch on the truck."

"Oh," she said. "There's a scratch on the truck." She turned and was gone into the dark.

Crickets jumped at Martin's feet.

He looked at the damaged truck, his hands clenched into fists. He felt as though his insides were being scoured, as though his blood was laden with grime and iron filings. Where before he'd felt frozen, he now had to strain to keep himself from doing something, anything, anything. His jaw was clenched vise-tight. He had to do something.

He looked at the darkness vaulting out beyond the truck, where the hill fell away.

He turned and shouted, "Eileen, please wait! I—"

Several seconds passed. From somewhere in the distance she called, "What?"

"Look!" He opened the driver's door and notched the gear shift into neutral. He ran to the back of the truck. He called to her, "I don't care about this truck! I don't care about anything but you! I'll go anywhere, do anything! I don't care!" He put his right foot up on the rear bumper. He shouted, "I don't care about it! I care about you!" He strained against the truck, leaned his weight into it, but it seemed immovable as a brick wall. He groaned with despair, dropped his foot, and fell forward against the truck, put his hands against it, put his body against it, and pushed. The rear window glass pressed cold against his hands, his shoulder, the side of his face.

He felt a miniscule give and tried to push harder. The truck rose slightly, up and over some rock or root, and began to creep away. He took a step after, just his two hands on the truck at arm's length. Then it was gone, only air on his fingertips, space opening between himself and the slowly accelerating prototype. The metal and glass were invisible in the dark and only the twin glowing rubies of the taillamps marked the truck's bouncing progress downhill. Suddenly an alarm system went off, screaming but fading. The bouncing grew more violent, more side-to-side and twisting. Tree branches cracked. The underbody could be heard encountering various rocks. The truck veered left, and then it flipped sideways, the lights whirligigging, metal crashing and glass crashing, until, with a last, violent clamor, it came to a halt. The alarm stopped. Somehow the truck had ended upright, and the dome light was on, making the interior glow with a light the color and size of a candle flame.

A new silence opened and it appalled Martin.

He squinted toward where Eileen had been, then down at the truck, that small distant light, and when he looked around again she was standing beside him, looking at the truck. She was a presence, a shape hinted by the light of the moon. "Martin—" she said. "Wow." She drew in and blew out a deep breath. "That was really, really dumb."

Martin looked at the truck and felt nauseous.

She said, "I don't know what to say. I'm kind of stunned."

Martin said, "Eileen—" His gaze had gotten stuck on the light below and he felt he might never look at anything else again. Its position there seemed hardly creditable. Never before had he done anything like this. He felt Eileen touch him, just below his neck, felt three individual fingers there. Then the touch was gone. He heard her moving away. Still he could not bring his gaze off that truck, could not imagine what he would tell the engineers. Down there lay his ruination. Mid-to upper six-figure ruination.

The light below seemed to grow smaller and he seemed to rise, a sensation of flying—of vertigo, really, but he tried to let it carry him, as much as it could.

But then the light winked out, and Martin, in darkness, earthbound, thought despairingly of the sleeping engineers, of the empty service bay. Of Eileen. He gazed at the absent light a moment, then turned and started back. He could not see Eileen, and he thought her gone. He stumbled over a stone and strained to see in the meager light of the moon and made his slow, slow way toward the oil-black shadows of the trees across the meadow, where he heard Eileen say, "Martin," and she took his hand in hers and pointed out that the same road that would take them back to town could also take them away.

Two Thousand Germans in Frankenmuth

The television is on. Katherine's mother sits in her easy chair, absorbed in the sorcery of shining images, while on the sofa Katherine slouches over a basket of laundry. She is matching socks. The room is growing dark, lit only by the TV and an end-of-day sky in the window. The shelves behind Katherine's mother are crowded with knickknacks—smiling porcelain figures, artificial flowers in chipped vases, framed needlework platitudes. The green carpeting shows the wear of repeated passage along routes determined by a furniture arrangement which has not altered in many years. To Katherine, even with a pile of fresh laundry before her, the air smells shabby and stale. As is usual, the only sound in the room is the noise of the TV. In the years since Dad died, Katherine has seen her mother remove herself from the world and decline into a spiritless television habit of such fixation that Katherine now sometimes feels as if she were tending to a kind of vegetable that required TV-light to survive—the last time she dusted the room and moved the TV to wipe beneath it, her mother's face followed the screen like a sunflower tracing the sun's arc.

When she glances up from the laundry, the sky in the window is wildly aflame.

"We should go to this," Katherine's mother says.

Startled, Katherine turns. "What?"

"We should go." Her mother gestures toward the television. "We might get on TV."

The local news is on. A reporter is saying, "—next month Hans Kraus will come here, to Frankenmuth." He stands on the main street in town, and behind him is a building with whitewashed walls accented by dark wooden beams and bright window box flowers. "Which just goes to show," he says, "Frankenmuth, Michigan's little Bavaria, truly is 'world famous.'"

"What?" Katherine blurts again. "Who is Hans Kraus?"

Her mother smiles and says, "We could be on TV."

The reporter explains that Hans Kraus is the star of the most popular talk show on German television. In a brief clip, a tall, balding man waves his arms and shouts something in German while the crowd at his feet laughs and applauds. "Here," the reporter says and gestures toward the park: an image of the park's amphitheater is shown. "Indeed—" the reporter lowers his voice dramatically "—Hans Kraus will bring not only his show here to Frankenmuth to tape a program, but he will also be accompanied by an entire audience of some two thousand Germans." The reporter nods soberly, as if anticipating the viewer's incredulity. "Two thousand," he says, "real Germans, from Germany."

"Mom, you want to go to this?" Katherine exclaims. "Everyone on the show will be speaking German. You don't speak German, do you?"

"So? It's television."

"It's television but we'll never see it in this country. It's German television."

"Television is television. Millions of people will see it." Her mother turns again toward the TV. She adds, her voice fading as her attention drifts, "Hans Kraus's is the most popular show in Germany."

The reporter has signed off; the news shifts to sports. Katherine looses a breath of exasperation, glares at the sunset, returns to the laundry. She has friends who complain that their mothers try to dictate their lives. Katherine envies them. Better that, she believes, than this vacancy. At least she would know her mother cared.

She makes inquiries at work the next day. She is a receptionist in one of the town's large hotels, and her manager points her toward his friend's sister-in-law, who happens to be the mayor. During her lunch hour, mentally estimating the balance in her bank account and preparing emotional appeals, Katherine drives to the town hall. A secretary tells her that the mayor is out, but listens as Katherine explains her purpose. Then she opens a drawer and hands her a pair of tickets. "First come, first served," she says. "You're first come."

When Katherine gets home she doesn't even take off her jacket before stepping between her mother and the television. Her mother looks up, blinking. "Look Mom," Katherine says, "I've got tickets for the two of us. The Hans Kraus show!" Katherine waves them, and her mother watches the tickets move back and forth. "Here, look. They're printed in German, I don't know what it says. But it means that you're going to be on TV, Mom."

"Oh, yes, the German TV." Her mother takes the tickets and turns them, one after the other, looking for something recognizable in the tangle of letters and umlauts. She hands them back. "I can't understand these."

"I told you, the whole thing is going to be in German."

"The most popular show in Germany," her mother says.

"And we'll be there." Katherine puts the tickets into her purse. She sits on the couch to take off her shoes. "It's pretty exciting, isn't it?"

Her mother says, "Yes," but when Katherine looks up she can see the filament of her mother's attention drawn to the TV screen, like a taut fishing line disappearing into placid water.

The next three weeks are exactly like all the preceding weeks, except that Katherine allows certain vague hopes to accumulate. Anticipating Hans Kraus's show provides an opportunity to imagine her mother in a new context and to suppose—a fragile optimism—something might change.

On the morning of Hans Kraus's show in Frankenmuth, Katherine wakes and throws aside her sheets. She can hear the

TV barking in the living room. She has taken the day off work and has nothing to do but go to the show. She rises and says good morning to her mother. A program about dog training is on: dogs fetch, dogs sit, dogs play dead. She makes breakfast and, with everything set on the kitchen table, calls to her mother. The TV clicks off. Her mother shambles into the kitchen and turns on the little TV perched on the microwave and sits for her meal. Somehow her mother is able to smear jam on her toast and fork her eggs without looking down. "Aren't you excited?" Katherine asks. "Today is the big day."

"Oh yes." Her mother smiles in Katherine's direction, but then she turns back to dogs jumping tall fences, dogs catching Frisbees.

"We need to be there at one," Katherine says. "I thought we could get lunch at one of the restaurants beforehand."

"Oh," her mother says vaguely. Three little dogs spin in somersaults. "Why don't we eat here?"

"Just this once. It'll be fun."

Her mother shifts her gaze slightly, uncertainly, and Katherine decides to take this as assent.

At eleven o'clock she checks that the tickets are in her purse and urges her mother to get ready. Her mother looks around the room for a minute before she switches off the television. She disappears into her bedroom, and when she emerges she has her walking cane in one hand and in the other a little purse that Katherine has not seen in years. Shiny leather shoes gleam under her mother's long skirt; a short-brimmed hat printed with a floral pattern covers her gray hair. Her mother so rarely dresses to go out these days that the sight forces Katherine to see her anew. She had been very pretty once: Katherine remembers this from the old photographs. Her mother's features were sharp, elfin, mischievous, but over the years, and particularly since Katherine's father's death, the angles have softened so that the mischievous quality seems only vestigial, at best. Where, Katherine wonders, has that person gone?

A five-minute drive brings them into streets laden with gift shops and tourists. They go to lunch at the Bavarian Inn, a huge restaurant complex with a complicated assortment of dining rooms. The hostess, dressed in puffy white sleeves and a green dirndl, leads them to a table over which hangs a wooden shield cut with Germanic heraldry. Little boys and girls polka on the tablecloth. The waiters wear suede lederhosen and jaunty hats of green felt. *Wurst* and *Kartoffelkloesse* appear on the menu, but the specialty of the house is the less foreign sounding "chicken," and this is what Katherine and her mother settle on. Bread arrives under a clear plastic dome, like a small rye-laden UFO, and Katherine's mother examines it, turning it at its base, before opening it. Katherine watches as she extracts a slice and butters it meticulously. She says, "Mom, you and I need to talk. We never talk anymore."

Her mother bites into the bread, chews thoroughly, swallows. She says, "What do you mean?"

"I mean we never talk about anything." Katherine leans forward. "For example, every day I come home from work, and you never bother to ask how my day was."

"Well," her mother says, "when you were in school, you hated when I asked that."

"That was years ago! You never ask if I've met anyone, done anything interesting. I mean, Mom, we've never even talked about how we felt after Dad died. About the fact that I still live with you. You never ask me about my plans, my hopes."

Her mother says, "I felt terrible after Dad died."

"I know you did, I could tell. But, you know, I didn't feel all that terrible myself." Katherine opens the bread dome and shuts it again. "When Dad died, I didn't care much, not much more than I would have if a favorite goldfish had died. Dad drank like a fish, and when he wasn't in the bars he was out on the water trolling for trout or muskie." She felt she hardly knew who her father was. He worked; he fished; he played cards and watched baseball games with his buddies; he drank.

He wasn't a violent drunk, but he wasn't much fun either as he sat licking his lips, tugging stupidly at his own hair.

The waiter arrives with two plates of chicken and little side dishes of mashed potatoes, coleslaw, cottage cheese, and sauerkraut. When he leaves, Katherine's mother asks, "Do you think real Germans wear those funny leather pants?"

"I doubt it. Maybe for holidays or bowling leagues or something."

"You think they wear them for bowling?"

"No. You know what I mean."

After a second, her mother nods. "Your Dad wore those awful nylon shirts to the bowling league."

"Dad wore those all the time," Katherine says. "He slept in them."

"He only slept in them when he'd been drinking."

"He was always drinking."

"Well, anyway," her mother says, "the poor man was a terrible bowler."

"Because drinking came before bowling."

Her mother studies her plate. "He could fish though."

"He could think like a fish. It became a permanent state of mind for him."

Katherine's mother looks up and shakes her head. "Don't be unkind, dear," she says, "it doesn't suit you."

"Mom, don't you understand? I viewed the man as a kind of really big fish." Her mother seems to be listening, more or less, so Katherine goes on. "When he died, and at the funeral, the only thing I felt bad about was you. I used an eyedropper to fake tears at the wake, because I thought you would feel even worse if I wasn't crying." She hesitates, but she can't help herself: she wants to make her mother react. "Then at the graveside service, it was raining so hard, and I thought, oh, how appropriate. Water."

Her mother's attention, however, is elsewhere—she stares full-faced at something over Katherine's shoulder. Katherine glances around but sees nothing unusual. She wonders, in frustration, what her father really meant to her mother. Clearly he meant something to her, because she lost her equilibrium after his death and never recovered. Facing sobs that burst out unpredictably, Katherine took on the responsibilities of the household. When the sobs became less frequent, her mother fell into her vapid television fog, losing contact with the things outside of their little house, then with her daughter, and everything, except what came in through the TV. "Mom," she says, "you're not listening to me."

"What language are those people behind you talking?"

Katherine glances around once more. "It's German. They must be here for Hans Kraus."

"German?" her mother says. "Oh, yes, German."

The waiter brings ice cream adorned with plastic red and green dancing German figures. Katherine pushes her ice cream around in the dish while her mother eats hers and licks clean the little plastic man. Leaving, they hear more German in the hallways, bursting from clusters of people who seem happy and pleased with themselves, even though they speak what sounds like guttural gibberish. Katherine's mother is leaning on her cane by the time they reach the car, and she looks tired and worried. "Think, Mom," Katherine says, wanting suddenly to cheer her, "we're going to be on TV!"

During the drive to the park, Katherine glances at her mother and starts to speak, but stops. Her mother's attention is on the scenery: half-timbered houses, a covered wooden bridge, a horse-drawn carriage, potted flowers hanging from the streetlamps. She and her mother used to go out together, when she was a child, leaving her father alone in his slobbering stupors. Standing on the banks of the river they tossed bread crumbs to the ducks; they danced to the polka bands at Oktoberfest; more than once they had driven all the way to Lake Huron and skipped stones out across the measureless expanse of water. "Don't tell your father," her mother would say as they returned to the house. "It's a secret between us." Not that her father would have asked, or cared, but still it was nice, the idea of a secret between her and her mother—secrets were bonds. Now she wonders, is this the reason she feels entrapped here, because once she and her mother fed ducks together?

Several long flatbed trailers have been pulled onto the grass near the amphitheater. TV cameras are mounted on tall structures of aluminum scaffolding. Technicians unreel wires and tape them down. The stage has been done up to resemble a living room, with a couch and armchairs gathered around a coffee table. Stacks of stereo speakers rise at either end. High above are three huge TV screens. The words *Guten Tag* hover on all three.

Katherine gives her tickets to the man who stands at the gate. He hands the stubs back to Katherine and says a few words in German. Katherine smiles. Her mother stares, and Katherine tugs her sleeve to get her walking again. Their seats turn out to be just a few rows from the stage. They sit, and Katherine realizes that the amphitheater is empty. Where are the Germans? She looks at her watch. It reads half an hour to show time.

What has to be admitted is that her father had loved her mother. In his drunkenness he sometimes fell on his knees before her and begged forgiveness for his faults. In surprising, sober moments he brought her mother clumsy, ugly things— all those knickknacks. Occasionally her mother touched her father, on the arm or the thigh, and an extraordinary current filled the air. There was something between them that excluded Katherine entirely, and it had evidently been stronger than what was between Katherine and her mother, because when her father died her mother had drawn into herself and looked from there for comfort not toward Katherine but toward the insubstantial stuff of television.

Still, it is years later now and Katherine has never left her mother's side. Why? What does she want exactly? What is she waiting for? Katherine is not certain. Sometimes she would settle merely for some acknowledgment.

"What are those, up there?" her mother asks, pointing above the stage.

"Those? TV screens."

"That's just what I thought," her mother says. "They're huge, aren't they?" She looks over at Katherine's watch. "Well then," she says, "where is everyone?"

"Germans are very punctual," Katherine says, but she twists to look around.

"I hope that they will show us, you and me, on those big TVs. That would be exciting, wouldn't it?" Their plastic seats are small and uncomfortable, and the sunshine begins to feel hot. Her mother has fixed her attention on one of the TV screens, apparently studying those words, *Guten Tag.*

"What is it between you and the TV?" Katherine asks.

"I don't know what those words mean. Do you?"

"It's German," Katherine says, to which her mother does not respond. Katherine taps the arms of her seat. She feels it isn't asking too much: a simple acknowledgment. She has given up a lot to tend to her mother, and her mother might at least turn from the television for a few seconds to say thank you.

Diesel engines rumble. A convoy of touring buses lines up outside the amphitheater, and Germans climb out. The men wear flat-front slacks and dress shoes and tiny eyeglasses. Many of the women also wear small angular eyeglasses, and their hair is cut in short, severe styles. Many of them carry backpacks in strange styles and colors. They laugh and talk a loud, throaty talk, and the entire crowd files into the amphitheater in about five minutes.

A family with two boys come down the aisle, and as they squeeze past one of the boys jabbers at Katherine. The boy moves on, but his father pauses to say a few words and gesture apologetically. Katherine fixes a helpless smile on the man until he turns away. More people slide by, talking and talking in German. Her mother is fascinated; her gaze shifts about like a bird's. Katherine knows she hasn't got a chance at her mother's attention, but she starts talking anyway. "When I think of the opportunities sacrificed in all these years," she says, and she shakes her head. "I'm thirty-seven years old now, Mom."

People in blue jackets climb to the cameras on the aluminum towers, and others prowl the aisles with cameras on their shoulders. A man makes some announcements to the crowd, and the crowd groans twice, cheers once. Whatever it is that's going on, it's going on in German. Different words flash on the huge screens over the stage. There is a montage of Frankenmuth streets and buildings, then a long glide through a Bavarian Inn dining room. Scattered applause begins, gains strength. A camera pans around the sunlit bowl of the amphitheater. A woman comes out and says something, and the crowd roars its approval. A man steps onto the stage and grins, and suddenly all the Germans are cheering crazily—whistles, screams, people standing, jumping, waving. The man raises his hands.

He has a halo remnant of frizzing hair and wears a dark suit that looks tight, as if it were a size too small. His shirt is also dark, so that his tie—red, white, and blue—stands out like fireworks. He picks up a microphone and begins talking. After that the main thing is laughter. He keeps the crowd in a continuous uproar, eliciting laugh after laugh with hardly a pause between.

Through this, Katherine is saying, "Don't you see, Mother, the sacrifices I've been making? Tying myself to this small town? Staying with that dead-end hotel receptionist job?"

Her mother leans toward her and asks, "What is that man saying?"

"God, Mother. I don't know. It's German."

"They should have someone who speaks English. A translator person."

Katherine glares at her. "I told you all this would be in German. It's a couple thousand Germans here, and you and me."

"It just seems like a translator would have been a nice gesture."

The man on stage is engaged in some sort of antics, kicking his legs out. Katherine says, "Tell me, Mom, why did you love Dad?"

Her mother is watching the three big TV screens, where the man is kicking in triplicate. She says, "You did get good seats for us, I must say. We can see the stage very well. I'd been a little worried about that, but we can really see the stage very well, and we have those big TVs up there too."

"Have you even noticed, Mom, that I haven't married yet? I'm thirty-seven and still haven't married."

Her mother blinks. "You'll do fine, dear." She looks over her shoulder. "Better than most seats by far. Look at all these people. Who'd have thought there could be so many Germans."

"Mom, all these days of watching you watch television. It's too much, the TV. Endless talk shows, nature shows, news shows. The infomercials. It's so frustrating, to watch you do that."

The man with the American flag tie moves down into the audience. He passes the microphone to people, talking and joking with them.

"What is it between you and the TV?" Katherine asks, her voice rising. "What is it?" But her mother is watching one of the huge screens.

Katherine feels as if hands are closing around her throat. She stands. Her vision is blurry. Pulling the collar of her blouse, she flees past a row of knees to the aisle, then hurries up the stairs. Seized with laughter, the Germans seem not to notice her.

Nearing the top of the stairs the choking sensation begins to diminish. She wipes her eyes dry. She can breathe again. When she reaches the back fence of the amphitheater she pauses, but then decides she will not allow herself to turn and look for her mother. Instead, she walks out the gate. She's not certain where she's going, but she's intent on the car, sure that that is the first step. No more, she resolves, no more of this futile, unappreciated sacrifice to her mother. Her mother can learn again to cook, to clean, to take care of herself. And she, Katherine, is only thirty-seven, with decades still ahead of her, not at all too late to build a life, to start getting out, meeting people, go back to school, buy new clothes, stop slouching, dance, buy a tennis racket—

An American voice booms from the amphitheater. It says resonantly: "Hello?" Midstep, Katherine stops. The voice is her mother's. "Hello? Yes?"

Kraus has greeted her in German, causing some confusion, but he now makes a joke which rocks the crowd with laughter, then he shifts into an accent-free, smarmy English.

"Where is the lady from?"

"Right here, Frankenmuth, Michigan," her mother says proudly, and the crowd applauds.

"And you are enjoying the show?"

"Oh yes, yours is so much more urbane than the talk shows on American TV, even if I don't really speak the language." Katherine cannot seem to move. Her mother sounds younger than Katherine has heard her sound in years. Also, Katherine cannot imagine where on earth her mother found the word *urbane*. Certainly Katherine never heard her utter it before. And the conversation continues: her mother talks eagerly, brightly, about America, Americans, and American TV. The crowd laughs at each little joke, as if every one of the Germans understands English perfectly. The host makes fun of American television; he waves his star-spangled tie; her mother's laughter shoots off in sparkles.

"Is there anyone you would like to say hello to in Germany?"

"Well, I think my great-grandmother was German, but I don't know anyone in Germany now. Hello to all the Germans, I guess. And, if I may, to my daughter, wherever she's gone. And my departed husband, I'm sure he's listening. I love the both of them so much." Then, as if suddenly realizing where she is, Katherine's mother adds, almost apologetically, "My husband, he could drink beer like a Bavarian."

The Germans love this.

Katherine overcomes the paralysis in her joints and turns. There, above the amphitheater, is her mother's face, smiling brilliantly, the face of a lively, engaging woman. Hans Kraus says something, and her mother's face finds room to smile even more widely. She puts a hand into the air and she waves,

waves with the enthusiasm of a nine-year-old. Three of them on three screens, three mothers in a life where one is hard enough, and these are as big as the sky, floating and glowing like moons. Katherine no longer hears what her mother says, but she cannot escape the familiarity of that thunderous, stereophonic voice. The three images move in unison, like a mirror of a massive mirror of a towering mother, waving and glittering. Her instinct still is to flee, yet she dares not turn: more mothers are likely to be there, carved into the clouds and hills, or projected onto every wall. Flight is impossible—Katherine feels small as a thing just born, knows only: here is her mother. She holds her breath and waits, hand at her chest while the show goes on. Two thousand Germans are cheering.

Take Your Child to Work

I check my watch: 7:38 a.m. I am arriving at work nearly an hour later than usual.

Accompanying me today is my daughter—Angie. At the double-wide glass doors I press my ID badge to a sensor and the bolts clunk open. Angie inquires as to how that happened and I briefly explain that the badge is magnetically encoded. The hallway ahead is large enough for two diesel tractor-trailer trucks to pass through side-by-side. Scattered along the walls are pieces of dusty experimental equipment. Only a couple of individuals are visible. Most people will already be at their desks or in meetings.

I would like to get through this entire day without encountering Angie's mother—Laura. But from a statistical perspective that is unlikely to happen.

We walk quickly and our footsteps create along the hall a rapid syncopation of tap and echo. Angie keeps up despite the shortness of her legs and I am proud of her. She has been growing. Today she wears a pair of khaki trousers and a button-down shirt that I have given her so she will be dressed like myself and the other engineers. Her hair is pulled straight back and she looks very businesslike.

We pass through another badge-accessed doorway and enter a space filled with portable five-foot-high foam-core walls demarcating hundreds of individual office cubicles. The room is nearly as large as a football field. (This calculation can be quickly made by measuring the floor area of one's own cubicle and multiplying that area by the total number of cubicles and adding an estimate for the aisles.) I am able to see across the entire cubicle grid to the wall of windows on the far side. Angie unfortunately cannot see over the short gray walls. She stands significantly less than five feet tall. She is only nine.

My own cubicle lies three-fifths of the way across the room and we set out for it. Angie does not take my hand. I suppose she has outgrown the clinging instinct. She looks around with an expression of interest. In the cubicles engineers are working at computer workstations glowing with documents and graphs and component designs in 3-D wire frame. Most of the cubicles are cluttered with poster-size reference charts and shelves of three-ring binders. Yellowing plants. Photos of spouses and children. Taped-up *Dilbert* cartoons. Whiteboards. Pieces of experimental hardware and competitors' products. Graphite-colored twelve-way adjustable rolling office chairs—these are new. I received my own twelve-way adjustable chair just last week.

While we proceed Angie remains very composed. I think it is impressive for one so young to remain so composed in a new and strange environment.

We see no other children.

Angie is here through a corporate initiative named: "Take Your Child to Work Day." It is new and not well promoted. The only advertisement was a paper flyer that arrived among all the other office mail we receive daily notifying us of such corporate trivia as minor revisions to the 401(k) plan or the cancellation of an underattended weekly yoga class. Those less scrupulous than myself about examining incoming mail might have easily overlooked the flyer.

The idea of taking Angie to work seemed to me a good one. Angie has always known that my work is important to me. Even when she was very little she would run up when I came home from work and shout: "Daddy! Look! I've been working too." She would show me crayon sketches she had done like engineering prints. They included dimensions and material specifications. Iron. Steel. Diamond. Chocolate. She drew cars. Boats. Airplanes. A cow. I explained: "People don't design and manufacture cows."

She frowned. "Who does then?"

I explained about DNA.

At that time I was still married to Laura. She complained: "Angie never does that when I get home." I reminded her that Angie could not do math yet. I pointed out that she was unlikely to produce a crayon fiscal year budget.

Laura works in finance. She is what is commonly called a "bean counter."

Due to work-site encounters I probably see Laura much more often than most ex-husbands see their ex-wives. I would like to report that this gives us the opportunity to confer and communicate about what our daughter is doing and coordinate both of our schedules to her benefit. It does not. Rather it gives us the opportunity to frequently feel awkward and/or glare at each other in passing.

Matters are further complicated because Laura appears to be sleeping with my boss.

(Note: "Sleeping with" is a misleading euphemism. *Sleep* is not a likely element in the process of fucking someone in the middle of the day on a desk blotter.)

8:22 a.m.: Today's unique challenge is to balance the work side of the equation with the daughter side of the equation—to not fall behind in my work-related duties while providing Angie with insight into the nature of those duties.

I have introduced Angie to my coworkers in neighboring cubicles. I have found an extra twelve-way adjustable chair for her to sit in. At the same time I have taken two business-related calls on my cell phone. I have told her: "Your job today is to observe." Angie has informed me that she is hungry. I have procured Pop-Tarts and an orange soda for her from a vending machines down the aisle. I have checked my voice mail. While Angie eats I am able to check my e-mail. She bounces. I tell her: "Quit bouncing. Today you need to act like a professional." She pouts but stops bouncing.

8:25 a.m.: Angie finishes eating. She gets off her chair and kneels on the floor to examine certain of the chair's levers and knobs. She tilts the chair on its side to get better access to a plastic button under the seat. She announces: "It's like a pneumatic pump powered by your butt." I tell her that is roughly correct. She pushes the button so that we can hear the air hiss out.

Laura contends that Angie is "troubled." I have not observed this. Laura says Angie is insolent and makes mischief. She makes crude capacitors to store static electricity and deliver shocks to people. A chemistry set I gave Angie was taken away after a series of combustion-related experiments climaxed in the charring of Laura's heirloom walnut table. Also taken away was a one-half-scale guillotine built from plywood and a baking pan. Apparently its functionality had been successfully demonstrated on a variety of dolls and stuffed animals.

I have no discipline problems with her myself. I have noticed that sometimes she will burst into a room without knocking. Because I sometimes work at home when she is visiting this can be disruptive. She has been known to call me on my cell phone for no particular reason which is nice except that she sometimes does it when I am in the middle of important meetings or racing to complete paperwork for some deadline. But these are minor transgressions. During her weekly visits with me I try to give direction to her creative energy. In my apartment she has several projects ongoing that she is able to pursue quietly and with minimal supervision. A miniature dollhouse with working appliances. A remote control airplane. A small mechanical horse. (I am afraid the mechanical horse project may be doomed to failure but one learns from mistakes as well. Her approaches to some of the problems of articulation and power supply are at any rate certainly ingenious if impractical.) Moreover I have always found that Angie responds willingly so long as I address her sternly and logically and without shrillness or condescension. Insolence has never been a problem. I have pointed out to Laura that there must be some root cause variation(s) in the separate environments we provide for Angie that would account for the differences in her behavior. I have proposed that we try to learn from this. Laura does not like to hear this. She says I am being "unfair" and I am "belittling" her parenting skills. I tell her this is not so and I only think we should learn from all the available data points. But she will not listen to me.

Laura also complains that Angie's behavior and interests are not "normal for a young girl." This notion seems to me so outdated it does not even merit reply.

8:53 a.m.: I have a regularly scheduled weekly review meeting at 9:00 this morning with my boss—Roberts.

I ask Angie if she will be okay alone for a little while. She says yes. I believe her. I roll her chair in front of my computer and tell her to go ahead and explore. Just don't alter any files or send any e-mails in my name.

She nods. She says: "I have things I need to check on the Web."

I gather several files and step into the aisle. Roberts does not have a cubicle. Roberts has a real office. I proceed until I reach the end of the long row of cubicles and I turn out into the main aisle and Laura is coming toward me. I consider ducking back. But this would be futile as she has already seen me. My ex-wife stands tall and thin. She assesses me with a curious look. She says: "Derek? What are you doing here?"

I say: "Hi."

"What did you do with Angie? I thought you were going to spend the day with her."

"I am. She's at my desk."

"Lord. Can't you take just one day off?"

"It's Take Your Child to Work Day."

"It's what?"

"Perhaps you didn't see the memo."

Laura repeats: "Take Your Child to Work Day." She glances around then speaks to me low and with a hiss that reminds me of the pneumatic chair: "You could have mentioned this. You could have mentioned that my daughter would be here at work with us. I might have appreciated knowing that."

"I have a nine o'clock with Roberts. I have to go."

But Laura holds my arm. "Why isn't Angie with you? Why take your kid to work if you're going to leave her alone at your desk?"

"Please. Laura. I have to go."

"You're unbelievable. I thought this would be a fun day for Angie. I was excited for her and you. But you bring her here to work and you just leave her in your cubicle."

"I have a meeting with Roberts and I didn't want to confuse her. I thought she might have met Roberts at home."

Laura scrunches her eyebrows as if puzzled. But a red color appears on her neck. She did not know I knew about her and Roberts. They believe they are discreet. But of course everyone in the building knows. She says: "Why would she have met Roberts at home?"

I am not surprised she feigns ignorance. This is what people do. I say: "Because the two of you are having sex every day in his office."

"We are not!"

"Won't he meet you outside the office? That's not normal. He may be taking advantage of you."

She stares at me with her mouth slightly open. She says: "You don't know anything about normal."

"Doing it in the office is a punishable violation of company policy. I've checked."

Laura glances around. A young man standing at a nearby copier looks quickly away. In a low urgent whisper she says: "You're absurd. Nothing is happening between Roberts and me."

"I can prove it."

She laughs. "No. You can't."

I hesitate. She is right. I say: "I have proof. I can get you both fired."

She shrugs. She says: "Stay out of my life."

She walks away. I feel angry. I think: I should quit. It would be easy. Walk into Roberts's office and tell him I am done. Hand over my company badge and my cell phone and my digital micrometer. Walk away.

I have of course fantasized about quitting before. But I have never had to regard the idea with any seriousness and now the thought makes my stomach hurt. My head.

I love this company and my work. My hope has been to work here until I retire. This company has been my solace—it has given me a structured organization within which to place myself and know myself. I have wondered if after I retire they will let me come back to visit.

But the fact is that the relationship between Laura and Roberts places me into an extremely awkward position. Roberts's dealings with me to date have remained business-like. But I doubt that Laura is whispering into his ear compliments regarding my project-management skills. As long as their relationship continues my prospects in the company are dubious. The matter is also frankly embarrassing.

I take my cell phone and my badge off my belt. I look at them. I think: I should just turn them in and be done.

But now I am struck by another idea: Proof. I clip the badge back onto my belt. At the nearest cubicle I ask if I might have some duct tape. The engineer swivels and opens a drawer. He has three different kinds. I select one and we cut off two pieces and I thank him. I walk back to my desk. Angie is on the computer. With my cell phone I dial my desk phone.

When the desk phone rings I pick it up and press the "hold" button then return the handset to its cradle. I form the pieces of duct tape into loops—sticky side out—and affix them to the backside of my cell phone.

Angie has been watching this.

I say: "Hey there. Everything going all right?"

"Is your phone broken?"

I say: "Not exactly. This is just a little improvisational engineering. Dad is late for his meeting. Back soon."

9:10 a.m.: Roberts's office has an elliptic conference table in the center of the room with six chairs around it. His desk stands beside the windows. His computer monitor shows that screen saver involving a tiny man mowing grass that grows at such a rate that when he has mowed back-and-forth from the top to the bottom of the screen it is time to mow the top again.

Roberts says nothing about my being late. He says: "Having a great day?" His standard greeting. Roberts has a binary smile. One or zero. On or off. During the standard greeting his smile is in the on position.

I say: "Fine. Yourself?"

"Fabulous! Please have a seat. Be comfortable." He and I sit on opposite sides of the conference table and now the smile turns off. Roberts talks about a company-wide reorganization of the product development process that upper management intends to implement. He wants his department to be "out in front of" this. I nod. Roberts is lanky and square-jawed. Thick curly hair. Handsome. Tall. (Studies have shown that tallness is statistically correlated to corporate promotability and managerial effectiveness.) He and I hired into the company at the same time. He has been a manager for three years now.

Roberts's promotion came about a year after my divorce. He and I had worked together and knew each other well. I considered him a friend. In a way I felt comforted by his promotion. I thought it indicated my own rise would soon follow and one manager even said as much to me. But three years have passed and Roberts has doubled the size of his department and my position has not changed. (Indeed during the recent distribution of new office chairs I was among the very last to receive the upgrade. Perhaps this is petty. Perhaps nothing should be read into it. But as I sat in a worn and technologically outdated chair while my nearby coworkers perched atop new twelve-way adjustable chairs I looked around and found it difficult not be disheartened.)

Laura is the finance person for several departments including ours. Roberts and Laura probably met years ago at one of the office social functions. Softball. The Christmas party. I probably introduced them. But I do not think anything was going on then. I do not blame Roberts for the dissolution of my marriage.

I first noticed this thing between them only three weeks ago. I cannot be certain how long it may have been going on before that. (But the frequency of their meetings has been increasing steadily—it is now daily—and using the known data to solve for a best-fit quadratic equation an extrapolation can be made backward through time to find an initiation point 5.5 weeks ago. But with the minimal hard data available the margin of error is rather large.) Their meetings and the frequency of their meetings is not in itself inexplicable. An annual departmental budget review is upcoming and Laura has lunchtime appointments in Roberts's office. Roberts is well aware of the "bottom line" in all corporate decisions and he likes to make his numbers look as good as possible. Indeed much of his success might be attributed to a keen understanding and control of the department budget. But other small factors spur suspicion: Consistently smudged lipstick. Disheveled hair. Wrinkled pants. The door is kept closed during their daily meetings and these occur during the lunch hour when most employees are in the cafeteria or out of the building entirely.

Roberts asks me about my work. We discuss material specifications. Supplier facilities. Project timelines. As we talk

I realize he and I have never been friends. We are acquaintances pressed together by circumstance. It strikes me that in the years that have passed since his promotion I have even forgotten Roberts's first name Harold? Harry? He signs documents with an initial: H. Roberts.

I sit across from him and describe how my work has proceeded in the past week and am tempted to confront him. But I do not. I hand him some graphs and spreadsheets and while his attention is fixed on these I do this: I slip my cell phone under my chair and tape it into place.

9:36 a.m.: Angie is playing something like baseball with the handset of my desk phone and the tracking ball out of my computer's mouse. Angie tosses the ball in the air and swings the phone. The crack at impact sounds as though it might indicate fracturing in the plastic phone. The ball pops a couple of feet into the air. I say: "Angie. Give those to me."

She looks guilty. Hands me the phone. The mouse ball.

I am already regretting my maneuver with the cell phone. I do not know how I am going to recover the phone from its hiding spot.

I reassemble the mouse. I check the phone line. I can hear Roberts's voice. But muffled and thin so that I cannot distinguish more than one word in ten. An ordinary cell phone is not the ideal technology for this application.

9:42 a.m.: Angie says: "Dad—can I go outside and play?"

I hit "hold" and set the phone aside. I say: "No. When we're at work we can't just go out and play anytime we want. If we did that I wouldn't get a paycheck."

Angie points to an empty cubicle across from mine. "He went outside. Twice."

"He's a smoker. He goes outside to smoke."

"Smoking is bad for you."

"That's right."

"Can't you have some other kind of break? A bubble-gum break?"

"I don't have time for bubble-gum breaks."

"Why does he have time? Does he work faster than you?"

Angie is very smart. Sometimes her questions are difficult. I say: "I don't know. Dad needs to work now. Dad needs to finish writing this memo on sourcing options for second- and third-tier suppliers. Here." I hand her a thick design manual full of graphs and flowcharts and assembly drawings. "Look through this and we'll touch base in twenty minutes to see if you have questions."

I return to my work. I put all the other things out of my mind.

10:03 a.m.: Laura's face peers over the cubicle wall. Sometimes when I see her there is a confused and vertiginous feeling I have in me that I no longer dare to call love. But it is something. She says: "Hi. Where's Angie?"

"She's here." I look around. She is not here. "Angie?"

"Yeah?"

She is on her hands and knees and half under the desk involved in further inspection of the levers on her chair. She presses a lever and the seat back pops forward about two inches. She says: "These chairs are cool."

I say: "Get up and say hello to your mother."

She stands. "Hi."

Laura says: "Hi. You look cute." Angie looks down at her clothes and Laura glances at me with a peculiar expression. She says to Angie: "What do you think? Think you want to grow up to be an engineer?"

"I think so. But it's a little boring so far."

Laura laughs. I chuckle—to be a good sport. Laura says: "You want to come see what Mom does at work?"

I put my hand in the air. "Wait. She's mine for today. You agreed to that."

"But you didn't tell me you were bringing her to work. It'll just be a little while. Until lunch."

"You can bring her to work next year."

"Derek." She circles around the cubicle wall and stands over me. "Don't be like this."

"I'm not being like anything." I stand. Laura is about an inch taller than I am. "Let's not argue now."

We both glance at Angie and Angie stares at us.

I say: "She's mine today. You agreed to that."

Laura gazes at me in a way that seems calm but she holds it on me for a long time and it somehow makes me want to run away. Finally she says: "You make me sad. Every time I talk to you it makes me sad. I wish you could hear yourself." She turns to Angie. "Honey—I'll see you tonight. Be good. I hope your father will pause in his work long enough to actually show some of it to you."

I say: "Laura? I do hear myself but I'd been looking forward to this—" However she is already moving down the aisle.

Laura and I were once happy together. I thought we were. We were both pleased when she was able to find employment at this company just a few months after my own job offer arrived. We shared the commute and talked about our work in terms of great detail and shared interest.

Laura works with numbers and when I married her I thought she was a very rational and logical person. But apparently neither of us was quite what the other thought. "Bad chemistry" Laura once called it. (But chemistry is a metaphor for human relationships that I have never understood. Chemistry has certain fundamental principles that are scientific and unchanging. Equations can be written and precise calculations can be made as to how certain compounds will interact with one another and such has not been my experience with human relationships.)

When Laura told me she wanted a divorce one of the reasons she gave was that she saw and feared that Angie was becoming just like me. That was a difficult thing to hear. That my daughter was becoming like myself and this was viewed as a problem. I consider myself an adequate model of human being. Better than most. The things I broke around the house that day were of little or no value and I regret only that Angie had to witness it. She will certainly never have to see anything like that from me again.

11:35 a.m.: People are leaving for lunch. Angie has been asking some questions about the book I gave her and I have tried to explain about measurement systems and control points and the difference between a process engineer and a product engineer. About the work of design and manufacture at a major consumer products corporation. But interruptions arise. Engineers stop at my desk to make inquires. E-mail arrives marked "urgent." I must run off to look at this or that problem in the labs. Angie accepts these interruptions with admirable patience. At one point she starts to fidget and I cannot talk to her immediately so I hand her my laser pointer and tell her she is not to point it at anyone's eyes under any circumstances. She dances the red dot around on the ceiling. Then she digs out of my desk a couple of magnifying lenses and a piece of shiny aluminum sheet metal and manipulates the laser beam with these in various optical configurations.

There comes a moment when I want to make a phone call and feel at my belt for my cell phone and then remember.

11:43 a.m.: I look at the desk phone. It is still on "hold." A small red LED glows to indicate this.

Is it possible I am wrong about what goes on in Roberts's office at lunch?

Roberts pursues department finances rigorously. I see the way my coworkers glance at that closed office door and the way they look at me but they could all be wrong. This (sex) would be just the sort of misunderstanding that would induce people around here to circulate silly rumors and give me embarrassing looks.

At any rate Laura and Roberts surely would not do such a thing on this day. Not while Angie is in the office. I was tremendously foolish to plant the phone in Roberts's office. What if it is discovered? Sometimes when I am emotional I do things that are obviously dumb. As soon as I realize I am doing such a thing it becomes inconceivable to me and I shut it down. But sometimes the thing is already done. Then I must address myself to the consequences.

I glance at Angie and she is staring at me. I realize I have wasted two or three minutes in transfixion on the "hold" light. I wink at Angie and pick up the phone. Click off "hold."

The grunting and gasping coming through the line seems incredibly loud—even as reproduced by the tiny cheap speaker in this phone. I wonder at the amount and type of sound insulation some unknown architectural engineer must have surrounded that office with in order to successfully block the noise of such caterwauling. It is a horrible sound.

With the intention of recording this for evidence I look for my answering machine. Then remember I have no answering machine. We switched from answering machines to voice mail more than a year ago. I am not thinking clearly at all today. I try to remember if there is some way to make the voice mail system record this. I look in a desk drawer for the voice mail instruction booklet. I try another drawer. Did I throw it away?

Behind me Angie says: "What's going on?"

Perhaps I appear tense. I try to relax my shoulders and re-form the expression of my face. I look at Angie. An idea arises. I say: "Mom wants you in Mr. Roberts's office. It's just down the aisle there and to the right. Number 4131. Why don't you run over there?"

Angie looks in the direction I am pointing but hesitates. I say: "Go on."

She says: "Okay." She clambers off her chair and walks away.

I press the phone hard against my ear. The huffing continues and I listen for interruption. A knock. Gasps of confusion and the stumbling about of hurried dressing.

11:47 a.m.: There has been no knock. No interruption of the ongoing copulation. I feel worried. I stand. The aisle is empty and the door to Roberts's office is closed. The cubicles are empty. Everyone has gone to lunch. I call: "Angie!"

No answer. I drop the phone and move down the aisle. I begin to jog. I go up and down the aisles between cubicles and duck into several to peer under desks. An engineer eating in his cubicle stares. I ignore him but stop to ask the next engineer I come across if he has seen a little girl. He shrugs without turning from his computer.

11:49 a.m.: I am becoming alarmed. I stand on a desk to get an overhead view of the room. The room seems incredibly large and my child is a very small person. She is not anywhere in sight.

And suddenly I know where she is. Angie would not disobey me. They forgot to lock the door and she walked right in. They did not hear her and she is standing to one side quietly observing. Angie is capable of that.

I sprint to Roberts's office. I stop. I hear: The buzz of fluorescent lights. The whir of a distant laser printer. The hiss of cooling fans spinning inside computers. A couple of people talking loudly into their phones.

I put my hand on the doorknob and apply torque. It turns. Not locked.

I throw the door open.

Naked legs. Shirts. (When you really look at sex it's nothing more than a kinetic interaction of bodies. Piston and cylinder. Tongue and groove. Tab A and Slot B. Bolt and nut. Hydraulic cylinders. Stamping presses.)

The door crashes against the wall. Laura gasps. They have their shirts on and are naked from the waist down except that Roberts has his socks on. And his tie. His tie: I actually double check this. With these new twelve-way adjustable chairs the seat back can be leaned all the way to horizontal and the arms dropped down out of the way. Laura is on top. Roberts curses. While they struggle to get up the chair rolls out from beneath them and Roberts falls to the ground. Laura is crouching to cover herself and feeling on the floor for her panties and staring as if she does not recognize me.

I advance. I say: "You people." Roberts's face appears from behind his desk and he seems confused because his smile is on.

I seize a heavy stapler off a nearby file cabinet and hurl it at him. But miss. It hits the wall near the ceiling. Roberts does not flinch and perhaps does not even realize he was its target. The stapler clatters and spews staples across the floor. Roberts's smile switches off and he says in a loud whisper: "Derek! Keep it down. Please." He appears to be having trouble with his pants. Snagged on something. I have already realized that throwing things will solve nothing and I have stopped. Roberts says: "Close the door for godsake."

I close the door. Then I wonder why I have done this. I say: "You people. Do you have any idea how many articles and subsections of company policy you are violating?" Roberts has freed his pants and is putting them on. Laura appears to be finding it difficult to get her panties on without revealing herself. I say: "Moreover there are the moral considerations. The immoral considerations. Look at what you are doing. Look at yourselves."

Roberts says: "Derek. Shut up."

I say: "I work hard and have always worked hard for this company and my dedication to this company has been unswerving. But I find my loyalty to the company compromised by your individual actions. As my superior I hope you feel upon you the full weight of what you have done."

Roberts has his pants on now. He stands and glares at me. Threatening. Rivulets of sweat on his forehead. Laura has turned to face the wall and button her pants. She has given up on the panties and they lie on the floor. I say: "Laura? Do you do this to hurt me? Then you have succeeded." None of this appears to have an impact on anyone. I say: "Laura—the man wears his tie while having sex. This cannot be what you want."

Roberts glances down at his tie and Laura looks at him and there's a quiet. What is it I want out of these two? Their embarrassment?

Yes. I want their shame. Then I want them to vanish from the face of the earth so that I can go on undisturbed with my work and with my daughter.

And Laura's thoughts have somehow arrived at an identical point—she says: "Where is Angie?" as I wonder the same.

How can I have forgotten Angie? It never fails when I am under great duress: my thoughts become scattered and stupid. How can I have forgotten my daughter? I hurriedly peer around the file cabinets. Under the conference table in the middle of the room. Laura takes a step toward me and says: "Where is she?"

Could she be under Roberts's desk? I lean across it and the situation is such that Roberts perhaps thinks I am lunging at him. He grabs me and wraps his arm around my neck and squeezes. A "headlock." I can barely breath. My vision clouds. I scratch at his arm and struggle and things I cannot see are being knocked off Roberts's desk and crashing on the floor. I flail. I kick chairs over. Laura is screaming: "Stop it!" She pries at Roberts's arm with one hand and her other hand presses against my face and her finger is in my eye. Roberts loosens his grip and she pushes us apart. I slide back. Rub at my throat. Straighten my shoulders. Once again Roberts and I stand on opposite sides of his desk. My eye is watering and I cannot see from it.

Roberts says: "Back off." This is unnecessary. I am backed off.

I say: "She's not under the desk?"

Laura says: "No!"

I say: "Why didn't you two have the door locked? How do you know someone didn't come in?"

Roberts looks at Laura. "I thought you locked the door."

Laura shrugs. "I guess I was in a hurry."

Roberts's smile switches on.

I interrupt: "I thought Angie was in here. No one should have to see this." Suddenly it strikes me that it perhaps was not the right thing to do: to try to send my child into this room when they were doing what they were doing. I feel a surge of shame.

Laura is looking at me with her eyebrows all bunched up. She says: "You lost Angie?"

I lie: "She just wandered off."

We all together start toward the door but I am the first one there. Once again I throw it wide. And there like a prize for us—though we surely do not deserve anything of the kind—is Angie. She stands just outside the doorway and beside her is an office chair that she has modified and I jump back because she has the seatback cocked like the sling of a catapult and loaded on it in the compartments of a plastic desk organizer are the small hard ammunition of several computer mouse tracking balls while projecting from the cushion are a dozen or more bristling pens and pencils. And taped to an arm of the chair is my laser pointer serving as a kind of targeting device. Its red dot glows on Roberts's stomach. Angie has a string in her hand which is tied to a lever under the seat of the chair. She looks very composed and professional in her trousers and button-down shirt. She might be about to make a presentation on low-cost manufacturing strategies or rapid prototyping technologies.

Laura says: "Honey—what do you think you are doing?"

Angie pulls her string. The chair back snaps forward. The massed array of weaponry flops ahead about two feet and drops to the floor with a clatter muted by the ubiquitous gray short-pile carpeting.

Laura sighs. Angie gazes with a puzzled expression at the items on the floor. Roberts says: "Well." He straightens his tie. He sees the red dot on his belly and steps out of its way.

Laura says: "Now you've made a mess. Why did you do that?" Angie does not answer. Laura shakes her head. "Honey—you're going to have to pick up all these things."

For several seconds Angie stands looking at the floor but not moving. I fear she might cry. Laura says: "Angie. Please." Slowly Angie crouches and begins to gather things. Behind me I hear Roberts right one of the chairs I kicked over in our struggle. I pick up a mouse ball that has rolled to my feet. An engineer passing in the aisle peers at us curiously. Laura is saying to me: "This is the kind of thing I've been telling you about." But at the same time Roberts says: "Hey. What is this?"

I remember the cell phone.

I say: "Angie. Never mind that. Let's go."

I start for the doorway. Laura says: "Where are you going? She's got to learn to clean up her messes." From behind her comes the tearing noise of duct tape ripping away.

I push the chair/catapult out of my way and take Angie's hand to pull her upright. I say: "Come along dear."

I glance back and Roberts has his smile on. He asks: "Is this yours? Derek?"

We are walking away. Laura says: "Derek."

Roberts says: "Derek!"

Angie and I move steadily away. They do not follow. I suspect they fear making a public scene. It would not help Roberts's career. Or Laura's.

12:12 p.m.: Angie says: "Dad. You're crying."

"I've got something in my eye." It is my left eye. The one that was poked. I have to close that eye in order to see my watch.

12:33 p.m.: Angie and I have been walking the halls. My vision has cleared up. We have passed: Machine shops. Audio testing labs. Fatigue testing facilities. Manufacturing simulations. The cubicle clusters of various small departments.

Teleconferencing rooms with stadium-style seating. Loading docks. Storage areas. It would not be easy to find us if we were being searched for. I do not know if we are.

Angie is trudging heavily and strands of her neatly pulled-back hair have come undone and drift airily about her head. She let go of my hand some time ago.

I will most likely be fired. I have no proof of what was going on between Roberts and Laura. Even though everyone knew of it. They however have my cell phone taped to the bottom of a chair in Roberts's office and dialed into the phone on my desk. He is my boss. I will most likely be fired.

I look at Angie and I am struck by a lurch of awful feeling: might she have slipped into Roberts's office and out again before I got there? I say: "You didn't go right to the office like I told you. Did you?"

She glances at me. I cannot read her expression. I say: "Did you?"

She does not answer.

I have a terrible feeling. I begin: "The act of sexual intercourse between a man and a woman—"

Angie interrupts: "Sometimes I hate Mom."

I stop and gather myself. I frown. "Well. You don't really hate Mom. She loves you."

"Maybe. I guess." Angie glowers at the floor. "But I hate Herb."

"Who?"

"Herb."

"Herb?" It takes me a few seconds to substitute "Herb" into the correct equation. "You mean Herb Roberts."

"He came to the house once. Mom thought I was asleep but I wasn't. They were talking and I was listening and I don't like him."

"Well. That's fine. You don't have to like everyone." I look at her. "But you have to be polite toward them. Even if you don't like them. People are not perfect. People make mistakes. People are unpredictable. Nonetheless you must respect them and you cannot fling office supplies at them because you don't like them."

Softly she says: "I'm sorry."

"You really shouldn't have done that with the chair. Someone could have been hurt."

"I know."

"One of the things we have to do when we invent something is think about how to use it responsibly."

She nods. But then she scowls. "I don't know why it didn't work. It should have worked."

I know how she feels. I hate it when things don't work. I say: "That's why we build prototypes and test them. We experiment. I can show you the process sometime."

"Okay."

I am trying to be stern but I am feeling proud of her. Not because she attempted a catapult assault on Roberts. Not only because of that. But because she's such an incredibly inventive and clever girl.

She says: "I'm tired."

"We will be there soon." But I have no idea where we are going. I feel we should do something together. But what? What is there to do besides work? What?

When I had my girl and my work and my wife I had all I needed. The great equation seemed perfectly balanced.

12:40 p.m.: Angie and I have found the storeroom where all the old office chairs are being kept until the corporate bureaucracy decides how to dispose of them. The room is about the size of the library at Angie's school with a smooth concrete floor and concrete walls painted white and lit by overhead fluorescent lights. The floor space is entirely covered by uniform ranks of worn office chairs and dozens more have been thrown in to lie across the precise rows at awkward angles or stand upside down with their casters in the air. For several minutes Angie has been quiet. Suddenly she turns and says to me: "Dad—Mom didn't really want to see me, did she?"

I hesitate. "I guess not."

"Why did you say she did?"

"I'm sorry." This is all I can think of to say.

"Was it an experiment?"

"It was a mistake. I'm sorry." My vision blurs again. It is both eyes now. I think: I am a terrible father. I am an awful failure. "Can you forgive your father for making a mistake?"

She gazes at me but says nothing. I can see she is considering. She understands this is a grave question. Quietly I meet her gaze. Blinking rapidly. At last she says: "Yes. But you must not do it again."

"I promise to try."

"Okay. So long as you really try."

"I will really try."

"Okay."

I say: "You don't hate me?"

"Not ever."

I feel relieved. I feel happy. My vision clears.

Angie is looking at the chairs. After a minute she says: "You could catapult a lot of stuff at once."

"These old ones didn't have the variable tension recline feature." I press on the nearest one to show her.

"They don't have the springy back."

"That's right. They don't have the springy back feature."

"Is that why they're being taken away?"

"Kind of."

Angie sits in one. "It feels okay."

"I suppose they're really not bad. But people want the new thing. People want the springy back feature."

"I feel bad for these."

"Don't. The chairs don't care about anything."

"I know."

"They're inanimate."

Angie says: "I know." She spins the chair she is seated in and then climbs into the next. She keeps climbing and crawling over the rows of chair backs like low fences. I hope—desperately hope—that she will be all right in spite of me and in spite of everything I have done and everything I do not understand.

She turns and waves to me across the chairs. I wave.

She is such a clever girl. I have a logical mind and I work well as an engineer but I have never been able to make those leaps of creativity that the great ones make. My own ideas are small and dull and unworkable (e.g., the cell phone under the chair) and though I love my work I will never be more than a conscientious and adequate engineer. But Angie seems to have a creative instinct that I lack and if it is nurtured and given room to grow more sophisticated she could become one of those people who have vision: able to see where technology is headed five or ten years ahead of time and place herself squarely in its path. She will see and create the things that no one else imagines possible. She will invent the flying cars and dime-size computers and better mousetraps and sixty-three-way adjustable office chairs and mechanical supercows and/or more: the things my clumsy mind cannot now imagine that will change and improve the way the human race lives its collective and individual lives.

She has disappeared among the chairs. There is a silence. There are so many chairs. I think of all the thousands—possibly millions—of man-hours these chairs represent. Each chair has cradled a man for ten or twelve or fifteen hours a day. Five or six or seven days a week. Years and years. Held that man up to his computer screen. His phone. His endless intractable tasks. I think of my new chair and perhaps I should feel horror at the thought of it but the fact is I want to go back to it. These are still working hours and I should work.

I call: "Angie."

She reappears. I say: "Okay. Let's go back. Time to go back to work." I hope they will not fire me but lingering here will not alter the outcome one way or the other. Right now I need to retrieve my cell phone in order to get on with my job. Because it is all I know to do.

Aeronautics

Hours of sun and jolting travel had reduced George to a state of dazed, turbid pain; nevertheless, when the pulsing clamor of many hard-ridden horses began closing in behind him he straightened his shoulders and looked around. And as the cavalry caught up and then coursed rapidly by, he wondered if at last the battlefield lay near, and if he would finally see the balloon. The cavalrymen—with their carbines shining, the yellow facings of their uniforms bright, their sabers and caparisons clanging counterpoint to the pounding of hooves—wore their hats low and studied the terrain ahead with grave expressions. They surged rapidly by and disappeared around a low hill, and George saw, at the fore of the caravan he traveled with, Professor Lowe on his black charger gathering pace behind them. Only with obvious reluctance did Lowe eventually halt and wait for the others. The procession behind him included half a dozen soldiers on horseback and two heavily laden pack mules, none which necessarily kept to the narrow beaten road, and two peculiar wagons, which did. All the men wore mustaches or full beards, except George who had been clean-shaven for more than seven decades and felt no want to alter the habit for fashion's sake. The two wagons were shaped like large, wheeled, wooden shipping crates with pieces of gleaming steel hardware and pipe issuing from their topsides. George rode beside the driver on the second of these. On the rear of the wagon before him were letters stenciled in black paint:

LOWE
BALLOON GAS GENERATOR
U.S. No. 14

Professor Lowe called out to the wagons to hurry, and the driver beside George muttered imprecations while he lightly slapped the reins. George leaned forward, trying to alleviate the pain in his hips. This journey had been a mistake. He had known it was a mistake as soon as he had agreed to it, and now he dearly felt the error—he had grown too old for such traveling; he was excruciatingly sore all through his body. Only the thought that soon he would see again a manned balloon ascending recalled to him any stirring of joy and relief.

A little farther on there were tents thrown up beside the road in rows or in seemingly random locations and men wearing uniforms weathered to varying shades of blue. They stood or sat, stared into space or cleaned their weapons and talked without looking at one another. They played cards or probed idly into the embers of cooking fires that leaked upwards uncoiling strands of smoke—George saw Professor Lowe gazing along the length of these, looking for signs of wind. The soldiers watched the passing balloon gas generator wagons sometimes balefully but sometimes with a smile or a wave. Along one stretch of the road an entire regiment was arrayed, standing at rest, and these men stared fixedly at the ground. Some wore wound dressings around the thigh or arm or head, and the bandages were shockingly white against the ragged blue uniforms and sun-darkened flesh made darker by accumulations of dust and mud and the oils of human anxiety. A nearby bivouac of hospital tents smelled horribly like an abattoir. Passing along a short stretch of graveled road, the iron rims of the wagon wheels made a sizzling sound, and George, in a state of mild befuddlement, was cast briefly back to his childhood: a few miles from his parents' house was a wide path scattered with stone that included a lot of flint, and George's father had ridden there one night with George and his twin sister, Madeline, to show them how the wagon wheels and the horses' shod hooves threw sparks. Standing with Madeline in the darkness beside the road, George had thought the scene a little frightening, but Madeline watched undaunted, then called, simply, "Like fairy horses, Pa."

Now, however, the sun was high and hot and it stared down on George with one-eyed murderous intent. They came to a caravan of artillery and caissons stopped in the middle of the road, apparently abandoned by men and horses alike, the cannons angled repentantly toward the earth. To bypass them Lowe's wagons were laboriously dragged off the road. George realized suddenly that he could hear and feel in his flesh the distant thrum of artillery, that he had in fact been feeling it for some time now without recognition. The horses were lathered with sweat, but Lowe urged the drivers on, scanned alertly, spurred his own horse ahead. He cut a striking figure in his black coat, black trousers, and tall black hat.

George had first met him the evening before—a servant boy had arrived at George's house with a message for George, asking if he could ride out to see Smith, who was an old friend of George's, and meet some guests. The servant boy said he didn't know who the guests were, but some were soldiers.

They had ridden together to Smith's. The servant boy took the horses to the stables while George stood alone in front of the house, trying to get his legs to straighten properly, trying to pull his spine upright. The two strange gas generator wagons stood here, and George studied them a minute before easing himself, step by step, up the stairs to the porch. A servant took his hat and conducted him to the parlor, where George hesitated in the doorway. His friend Smith and a half dozen other men were seated in a loose circle, and one of the guests was engaged in a story that had the rapt attention of the others.

"—I cast off a bag of sand ballast," he was saying, "and began to rise away again. And one of those on the ground—there was quite a crowd by now—called up, 'Halloo stranger! Come back,

I reckon you've lost your luggage!'" The gathered men laughed and the speaker sat back, crossing his legs with satisfaction.

George shuffled forward slightly. The men sat around a large, marble-topped center table on which stood a kerosene lamp and a thick Bible. In the shadows behind them could be seen the fireplace and mantel clock, several bookcases and a cluttered whatnot, various end tables and corner tables and vases. Smith stood, smiling at George. "Here's the aeronaut!" he cried.

Embarrassed, George stepped into the lamplight and nodded to the men. "Aeronaut—that's Smith's old joke," he explained. "I've never actually been in a balloon."

"George," Smith said. "I would like to introduce you to a real aeronaut." He touched the shoulder of the gentleman who had just finished speaking. "Professor Lowe is the commander of the United States Aeronautical Corps."

Lowe had a thick handlebar mustache under deep-set eyes and curved, hawkish eyebrows, and even as he smiled these features lent him an expression of concentrated intensity. "It's a pleasure," he said. "I understand you were at Blanchard's 1793 flight."

"Yes," said George. "I was just a boy."

"I would very much like to hear about it."

"That's why I asked you over, George," said Smith. "I thought you should tell the story yourself. And Professor Lowe and his men will be continuing on their way tomorrow, to rejoin the Army of the Potomac." Smith introduced George to the other men—a captain, a sergeant, several privates in blue uniforms, and two civilian employees of Lowe's. Several were smoking pipes, and the room was filled with a pungent tobacco fog. Each man held a glass of bourbon, and after George sat, the servant appeared with a glass for him as well.

Smith said to George, "The professor was just telling us about a balloon he landed in the Carolinas."

George's fingers trembled, so he held his bourbon with both hands while he sipped at it and felt its warmth spreading through him, calming. He listened without comment to the talking of the other men. He noticed a general deferment to Professor Lowe and his opinions; everyone stopped to listen when he spoke. Lowe's landing in the Carolinas had evidently occurred just days after the Confederates opened fire on Fort Sumter, and Lowe hadn't realized the entire gravity of the political situation at the time, but he also had not intended to land in the South, had been flying from Cincinnati to test upper atmospheric winds against his belief that those winds might be used to carry an aeronaut eastward all the way across the Atlantic. But he was carried as much south as east. After being variously shot at, run from, and mistaken for a demon, he finally put his balloon down among some people who carted him away to jail for spying. Someone of learning in town recognized him from newspaper accounts of his aeronautical exploits and got him released, but he was jailed a couple more times during his slow progress northward. Shortly after he had finally returned to Union territory, he traveled to the War Department to propose the formation of an Army Aeronautical Corps. "I am sure," Lowe said to Smith and the others, "that if the Confederates had known I would begin flying balloons for the United States, they never would have let me out of their jails. They waste endless volleys of bullets and cannon in my direction every time we go up. But they've not hit us yet—we begin well behind lines, and then we're up too high." Lowe smiled. He gestured vaguely southward with his bourbon. "They'll have to try another tack if they are to remove my balloons from overlooking them."

Smith nudged George. "Why don't you tell us about Blanchard?"

So George told the story. He had never been one to talk a lot, but there were certain stories he had told aloud many times over the years and many more times inside his head, and this was one of those stories. Blanchard's had been the first manned balloon flight in the United States, and George described it slowly and in detail. Lowe, leaning forward with his hands on his knees, interrupted to ask about technical details—the size of the gondola, the form of the netting over the balloon, the apparatus Blanchard used to generate the gas that filled his balloon—and when George had finished, Lowe exclaimed, "Come with us tomorrow! Come see our balloon launched! It would be an honor for me, to be connected in a way with the famous Blanchard." And George, moved by Lowe's enthusiasm and the idea of the balloon, had agreed.

That night, however, he slept only fitfully, doubting himself and fretting. And the next morning Lowe also seemed to be having second thoughts. "I should warn you," he said, "this isn't some balloon novelty flight. There's a war on, and when that balloon goes up all the enemy artillery aims for us. We've only been lucky so far. Our cookshack was hit not long ago, and recently a shell exploded in a nearby cesspool. One of our sentries was completely coated with filth."

George, however, felt he had already committed himself Quietly he said, "I'm not worried about shelling."

"That sentry couldn't eat for days afterward."

"I'll stay out of your way," George said. He smiled to reassure Lowe. "I'll be gone the next morning."

They left when the black sky was just lightening to a Prussian blue in the east, tinged faintly green at the horizon. George had ridden until about noon on his horse before the extraordinary pain in his back and hips forced him to stable the animal at an inn and take a seat on one of the wagons.

Now the sun was moving west and down the sky. They followed a two-track dirt path past a small farm and through a wood where the arms of the trees met above them. There were no soldiers. Then they emerged again into the sun, and suddenly the little convoy halted. They were in a small meadow protected by a wooded hill. Two tall wooden poles stood in the center of the meadow with a rope running from the top of one to the other, and, some distance away, several tents were spread in a semicircle. Perhaps two dozen men in blue uniforms and kepi hats were here, standing around or sitting on empty hardtack boxes. The rumbling of cannon fire and the riffling of musket shots sounded in the distance, and a boiling gray-white smoke obscured the sky in that direction. Several men rose and came over to meet the wagons, but they did not move with urgency and, conspicuously, no balloon was to be seen. George might have thought it was only packed away somewhere, but Professor Lowe was already trotting from man to man and tent to tent, demanding explanations.

For the moment, George did not care. The pain in his back had become like the probing of a long, thick knife, the joints of his hands were inflamed, and his hips were grinding like emery paper. His teeth, which ached all the time now anyway, were flaring hotly in several places. He managed to lower himself from the high seat of the wagon to the ground, but then he nearly collapsed face-first. He stood gripping the wagon wheel for a minute, gathering his strength before he let go, moved off several paces, and lowered himself to the grass. He put his head in his hands, closed his eyes, and focused on the pain in his back, in his knees, his hips, his fingers, his teeth, sank into the hurt until the hurting seemed merely a kind of warmth from within to counterbalance the warmth of the sun overhead. He leaned back and stretched lengthwise in the grass, which seemed wonderfully cool. He could feel distinctly the heavy, deep sound of cannon reports moving through the ground. Covering his face with his hat, he willed himself to sleep or at least to rest without thinking. He lay for what seemed a long time, moving on the currents of pain, floating between these and the sun as if on a salty sea.

Then he felt a shadow upon him and he pushed back his hat. Directly above, looking down, was a young man with a downy blond beard, a serious expression, and a bulky knapsack slung over his shoulder. "Good day, sir," said the young man. "Please, can I offer you something from among my fine selection of wares?"

George's mouth was dry. His flesh felt dusty and scorched. The peddler suddenly smiled broadly, revealing a pair of black gaps in his teeth. "Maybe," George said, softly, "a little water?"

The peddler nodded and went away. With a great effort, George sat up. He pulled his hat firmly down on his head and looked around. Professor Lowe had dismounted, but he was still angrily stalking about. Several men were opening the bags on the pack mules and exclaiming to one another. On the road, a few dozen loosely assembled soldiers sauntered by. George loosened the cravat at his neck. He saw the peddler returning with a dipper of water, limping badly. He wore brown wool trousers, vest, and coat, all loose-fitting and besmirched by dust and stains of various shades. He also wore a kepi hat such as the soldiers wore, but his was more thoroughly battered, as if it had been discarded and trampled by horses and infantry alike before the peddler claimed it. He offered the dipper full of water to George. "For this," he said, "no charge."

George took the dipper and drank. His hand trembled and water slopped onto his coat and trousers. "Are you all right?" the peddler asked gently. "You seem fatigued."

"I'll be fine," George said. "Thank you for the water. I only need a little rest."

The peddler nodded. He remained crouched beside George, watching him. After a moment he offered his hand. "My name is Nathan."

"Mine is George." Nathan had a firm handshake. George hoped the tremor of his own hand was not too apparent.

"George," said Nathan, "I may have the remedy you need." He swung around his knapsack and extracted a small glass bottle. He shook it. "Rush's Pills," he said, then chanted in a singsong rhythm:

> *What Rush's Pills alone can do,*
> *Man testifies, and woman too.*
> *For thousands say with eager breath,*
> *They saved me from disease and death!*
> *All ye ailing, give me heed,*
> *'Tis Rush's Pills your system need!*

George shook his head. "No pills, thank you." He had spotted Professor Lowe striding across the clearing toward him. He struggled to rise, but his legs were flaccid and would not obey. Nathan, with a last, rueful shake of the pills, put the bottle away, then saw him struggling and slid a hand under his shoulder to help him up. "Thank you," George said.

Lowe hardly glanced at the peddler. To George he said, "I am terribly sorry about this." He lifted his hat and wiped at his brow with his sleeve. "The balloon has not arrived. It's inexcusable, but there's nothing to be done but to wait."

George nodded. "It's all right. I can wait."

Lowe wagged his head in a care-worn fashion. "The truth is, many of the army's officers view my Aeronautical Corps with disdain. They cannot see that these balloons represent the future of warfare, and the Aeronautical Corps seems to them nothing but a distraction of resources and materials. Sometimes I have to go up the entire chain of command and back down again in order to requisition something as simple as a wagon."

"I'm sorry," George said. He felt strangely constrained and formal with Lowe: the man unnerved him with his intense single-mindedness. "I suppose in a venture like this there must always be new obstacles."

"Yes, yes, that's exactly it. That has been the entire history of aeronautics. It makes me chafe, nothing to do but stand around here confabulating." Then, suddenly, Lowe's attention shifted—a man stood at one of the gas generator wagons with a hatch door open, and whatever he was doing was apparently suspicious or incorrect, because Lowe barked at him and hurried over. George turned and discovered that the peddler, Nathan, had moved on as well—he was headed toward the men at the tents. He favored his left leg, and with each awkward step the contents of his knapsack rattled. Something about talking with him had reminded George of Madeline, his twin sister, who had died many years before.

George found a seat on a horsehair trunk that had been abandoned a short distance from the camp. In the south, erratic white puffs of smoke rose until they reached a certain altitude where the wind shredded them. The noise of muskets quarreling was so far away and small it seemed deceptively trivial.

Presently Nathan returned. He set his knapsack on the ground and sat beside George. His shoes, though polished, were indisputably battered; the soles appeared worn to the thinness of a pig's ear. They sat in a comfortable silence for two or three minutes before Nathan asked, "Maybe you would like to purchase some tobacco?"

"I have a plug with me."

Nathan nodded. He glanced around, then looked at George and offered his gap-toothed smile again. "Well," he said, "perhaps you need matches? Or a candlestick? A pencil? Needles or buttons? Handkerchiefs? I have handkerchiefs of the best quality silk. Whiskey?"

"No whiskey. Why would I want any of those things?"

"Maybe something else? Sardines? Blacking, violin string—"

"You carry all that in that bag."

"It is a little heavy. I thought bringing a great variety of things, one or two each, would be wise." Nathan shook his head wearily. "Now I wish I had brought nothing but canned milk. It's all they want, canned milk."

"And, surely, coffee, tobacco, and whiskey."

"Yes, but it's the canned milk that's truly rare. I can hardly take a profit on the tobacco and whiskey. Canned milk is the thing. If I had brought nothing but canned milk, they would have hailed me for a hero. And, I would be rich."

"Well, next time you can bring canned milk."

"Next time?" Nathan hesitated on this. "I don't know. Probably by then someone else will have brought the canned milk, and they will want sauerkraut or some such thing."

A sudden, shrieking scream was followed by an enormous crashing noise in the woods. George jumped, and everyone in the camp stopped what they were doing. Dozens of birds scattered up into the sky, calling loudly. A stray artillery shot, George realized. No more followed, but he needed a minute for his nerves and heart to settle again. Nathan, like the others, looked at the place where a worm of gray smoke emerged from the trees, but he rubbed his fingers through his beard in a sleepy, unconcerned way.

Partly to distract himself, George renewed the conversation. "Well," he said, "I am seventy-eight years old. I remember a time before anyone discovered how to preserve food in bottles and jars. We certainly didn't have anything like canned milk."

Nathan opened his bag and extracted from it an odd, vaguely threatening metal object. He said, "Have you seen one of these before?"

George took it. It had a knifelike handle, but at the other end was a strange arrangement: a short, sharp point with a pivoting length of metal pinned to it, and beside this a longer, curved blade. George said, "It looks like an apparatus for skinning rats."

"Not at all."

"Well then?"

"This is a device for opening cans. See, you puncture the top with the short point. This guard swivels and prevents it from going too far inside. Then you work around with the longer blade. It keeps the contents of the can from going all over when you break it open."

"A contrivance for opening cans," George said. He handed it back. "What a funny idea."

"Would you like to buy it?"

"We don't need a special tool. My daughter-in-law already has her own means for opening cans, with a hammer and chisel. She's very good at it."

"Everyone says that. I thought it was quite clever."

"It is clever. But I don't think that means anyone needs it."

Nathan put the tool away. Behind him, a soldier was hanging laundry on a line strung between tents. Professor Lowe's head and shoulders had disappeared into the interior of a gas generator wagon. A pair of sparrows perched on the rope between the two poles in the center of the clearing. In the distance, beyond the trees, sheets of brown haze squirreled upward while elsewhere runnels of ink-black smoke scored the horizon. From this position the war might have been mistaken for the hissing, spitting, and steaming effects of some vast soup cauldron boiling over.

Nathan said, "Why did you come here? Forgive me, but you don't look like a soldier."

"Oh—" George laughed. "I came because Professor Lowe asked me to, and I said yes. The moment I did I knew it was a mistake, at my age, but—pride, you understand. But now I am glad I'm here. I look forward to seeing the balloon. It will mean a great deal to me to see the balloon."

"Professor Lowe is very famous."

"He is. I think he would rather be flying a balloon across the Atlantic right now, if the war had not intervened."

"It would be nice to be able to fly away from this, wouldn't it?" Nathan looked at George and smiled. "If it were me going up to take a look at the rebels, I would cut the rope. Just drift away on the wind."

George liked this boy. "Yes," he said. "I think I might be tempted by that as well." An artillery battery somewhere not far behind them could be heard cannonading in a hopeful, methodical rhythm. George said, "I saw your limp. How did it happen?"

"Wounded at the beginning of it, at Bull Run." Nathan took off his bruised hat, looked at it, then replaced it to his head. "I swear to you, for three weeks my parts were swollen up as big as two cantaloupes. But I kept them."

"You're fortunate."

"I am." Nathan nodded. "Now, however, it's difficult for me to be out of the war. Many of these soldiers assume I'm faking my injury, or exaggerating its severity. They tell me the prices for my wares are too high. But I cannot charge what a merchant in a city would charge, because that's where I bought them. I must take a profit. This Balloon Corps doesn't have a commissioned sutler, like the regular regiments do, and I thought they would appreciate a peddler to come around and offer them what they need."

Nathan looked at the ground and seemed to dwell on this. He was fair-haired like Madeline, and possibly there was a similarity around the eyes. But, more strikingly, it was his habit of suddenly smiling that reminded George of Madeline, and also something in the calm, languorous dignity of how he presented himself. George said, "I wonder if you have any family from Philadelphia? What is your family name?"

Nathan deliberated. After a moment he said, "No, I don't believe I have any family from Philadelphia."

"Your family name?"

"Stiles."

"I'm sorry. I don't mean to pry. You remind me of my sister, and I wondered if there might be some relationship between us. Probably it is only coincidence."

Nathan nodded. Behind him, the sounds of fighting seemed to have slowed somewhat. The sun was sagging in the sky and the men were lighting cooking fires. Nathan picked up his sack and stood. He said, "I had best try to sell something." He limped away.

George watched him moving among the soldiers. Despite his tattered appearance he approached the men quietly, very much erect and without apparent servility or shame. Perhaps this was the reason the men disliked him—at the bottom of the army hierarchy, they wanted at least to be able to look down on this peddler mongering tobacco and buttons.

George joined a couple of soldiers at their fire. They greeted him, then fell to talking between themselves again. They cooked potatoes on the ends of their bayonets and roasted green coffee beans in a kettle over the fire until the beans began to smoke, then set the kettle on the ground and smashed the beans with the butt of a rifle. The fragments were boiled with water in a tin can, and they crumbled hardtack into the steaming black liquid. The weevils that floated to the surface were skimmed off with a spoon. They offered a cup of this concoction to George. It tasted like hot turpentine, and most of it he poured into the grass behind him. He had a little salted meat and some hard biscuits in his pockets, and he nibbled on the meat, but the day's journey seemed to have beaten hunger out of him.

A few clouds had arrived in the sky and these were patterned with sunset's orange, gold, and crimson. George stood and walked to where Nathan sat by himself on the grass, gazing at the gas generator wagons. George leaned over and said, "What are you thinking of?"

Nathan jerked and glanced around. "Oh," he said. He hesitated, then smiled. "I guess I wonder about all this." With a circling gesture he indicated the tents and wagons. "Why weren't we born birds? Blackbirds or sparrows, maybe—I mean, if we are to fly."

George laughed and clapped Nathan on the shoulder. He saw Professor Lowe at his tent, beckoning to him. He nodded in that direction. "I had better go speak to the great aeronaut."

Lowe shook George's hand. He said, again, what a tremendous honor and pleasure it was for him to meet a man who had been witness to the first manned flight, the very inception of aeronautics, in the United States. He added, "I am sorry about this. The balloon we need has been in New York for repairs. It should have arrived here before us, but it was to be moved by a military train, transferred to a second train, then moved by an army wagon, and it could be stuck anywhere along that route. I only hope there hasn't been some accidental injury to the balloon. We have no funds to build more. In any event, it will be a full moon tonight. With luck, the balloon will continue to travel after sunset and reach us before sunrise."

A couple of the army officers were sitting with Lowe, and George sat with them. While it grew dark they smoked pipes and disputed over the facts and rumors of the day's fighting. George, unfamiliar with the terrain and the units mentioned, had trouble following the conversation. Soon he gave up.

He observed that the men in the camp did not gather together but instead sat at their small fires alone or in pairs, some in somber trios, but no groups larger than that. Well, George thought, it remained a war—even if your task in it was to launch a balloon. Nathan, the peddler, seemed to have disappeared. Where did someone like that go at night? Perhaps he just wrapped himself in a blanket on the open ground somewhere. He might wake with dew on his nose, but the weather looked clear. As Lowe had predicted, the rising moon was large and bright in the sky.

Arrangements were made for George to go back down along the road with one of the horses and sleep in the barn there. He borrowed a wool blanket and a soldier accompanied him through the darkling woods to the barn, stabled the horse, then left him alone with the animals. An enormous pile of hay in one corner offered a better bed than any of the soldiers were likely to rest on tonight. And indeed, when he took off his hat and lay down, the hay engulfed him in a pleasant softness. Yet he discovered he could not sleep. He had felt utterly exhausted while the men talked outside Lowe's tent, had fought the sinking of his eyelids, but now he lay awake, carried up from sleep by memories as if by a rising tide. He crossed his hands over his chest and thought of Madeline. The horses shuffled in their stalls, a breeze pressed and soughed against the side of the barn. Small, faraway events of sporadic musketry could be heard.

His first sight of the balloon had come as he entered the prison yard with his father. Madeline—his dear sister, his twin—was being towed along behind them in a little wooden wagon his father had built to carry her during her illness. George could just see the top of the balloon over the heads of the well-dressed ladies and gentlemen milling about. Hung from a rope suspended between two tall wooden poles, yellow and waxy, only partially inflated and draped with a net of rope, it dangled like some queer exotic beast gutted and strung up for public examination.

It was January 9, 1793, and unseasonably warm. Earlier in the morning, as they ate breakfast by the light of three fat-oil lamps on the dining table, George's father had said that this was a day George would eventually describe to his own children and grandchildren. George had stared hard into the lamp flames trying to get his imagination around that idea—his own children and grandchildren. As they walked through town to the Walnut Street Prison there were thousands already out, claiming places on roofs, in trees, in windows and balconies, on the grass of Potter's Field. His father said the hotels were full of visitors from New York, Baltimore, and parts even more distant. He pulled the wagon with one hand and held several of George's fingers in the other. At a side gate into the prison yard a man took their tickets. George's father was a man of significant girth and breadth and once they had entered the prison yard he shouldered his way into the crowd, excusing himself, calling out, "This little girl is ill! Please make way for her to see the balloon and Monsieur Blanchard!" The ladies in their swishing flounced skirts and their starched fichus upon the shoulders, and the gentlemen in their high, stiff hats and woolen coats with buttons of bright brass glanced severely at George's father, but when they saw the pale blond girl in the wagon they parted quietly before the small family.

Madeline held in her arms a little black lapdog, and she ignored the adults around her, attentive only to the dog, petting him, cooing in his ear. The dog rested his head contentedly on her shoulder. There were actually only about a hundred people altogether here in the prison yard, and the noise of the multitude in the streets, shouting to one another and laughing, created a collective roar that welled over the gray stone walls of the prison yard and obscured the more sober conversations between those here who had paid for tickets. A battery of artillery had been assembled across from the prison in Potter's Field and since six in the morning a pair of cannons had fired every quarter hour. George was counting, so he always knew the time. Just before they arrived at the prison the nine o'clock firing had gone off—a smear of white smoke still wallowed in the dead air. The balloon was to launch at ten.

The tickets had been expensive, five dollars for George's father, two dollars each for the children. But Madeline, on hearing of the planned balloon flight, had only to ask in passing and George's father had gone that very day to Oeller's Hotel and purchased the tickets from Blanchard's secretary. This unsettled George more than any other sign of his twin sister's deteriorating condition. His father did not spend such money without good reason, and George doubted the tickets would have been purchased if his father thought Madeline would be well soon. The dog—Madeline had named him Tad—had been another indulgence, purchased for her a couple of weeks ago. Tad was all black with large glossy black eyes, a quiet, seemingly imperturbable puppy. Sometimes when distressed he made gentle yips of sound in his throat, but no one had yet heard him utter a proper bark. He rarely left Madeline's arms.

A few rows of benches had been laid out, but everyone stood. A nauseating, sulfurous odor permeated the air. A small brass band to one side played patriotic music. The gaunt faces of prisoners could be seen gazing from the barred windows of the prison. The walls of the yard were a gray stone irregularly stained by the spoiled food thrown and chamber pots emptied upon them. George's mother had thought it scandalous that such a historic event was to be held in the prison, but his father had laughed and said no, it wasn't scandalous, it was ironic. And, as a practical matter, the prison yard provided the only available space with both an adequate area for Blanchard's equipment and walls to exclude those without tickets. But, he noted, everyone would be able to see the balloon as soon as it rose over the walls—assuming it did so—which was probably the reason that the number of participants in Blanchard's subscription had been quite disappointing.

From the front of the crowd George could see the full height of the balloon and the little French aeronaut Blanchard below, reaching up to adjust the net of ropes that hung over the balloon. He wore blue knee breeches, a blue waistcoat, and a hat with a long white plume that bobbed gaily as he moved about. A boat-shaped gondola sat to one side, painted blue with white spangles. And all around were barrels, roughly arranged into two large clusters of a dozen each. At the center of each cluster stood an oversized, sealed tub which was joined, octopus-like, by metal pipes to the multiple surrounding barrels, while from the top of each tub ran a thick hose that fed into the neck of the balloon. One of these two clusters lay just a few feet from George and the stink rising from it burned in his nostrils. A young man moved from barrel to barrel with a long stave, opening a plug in the top of each barrel and inserting the stave to stir the mysterious contents with a motion that reminded George of churning butter.

His father stooped and picked a stone off the ground. "Do you know what this is?" he said, presenting it between his thumb and forefinger for George and Madeline to see. It was smooth and round, the size of a musket ball.

"It's a rock," George said. "A little one."

"I can't see," Madeline said. She took it and scrutinized it, then handed it back. "It's granite."

"You're both wrong," their father said, grinning. He bounced the stone in his palm. "This is a precisely calibrated apparatus of scientific inquiry—" he held the stone at arm's length "—a device for the detection of the force of gravity." He let go and the stone fell to earth, bounced once. "The device appears to verify normal gravity force."

Madeline rolled her eyes, but giggled. George crouched and found the stone. It was gray with flecks of black, irregularly shaped but silky under his fingers. It seemed to warm as he held it in his pocket.

"They're manufacturing flammable gas," his father said, indicating the barrels and tubs. "They fill the balloon with flammable gas so it will float on the air, like cork on water."

George examined the equipment for several minutes before growing bored. The concussion of the 9:15 cannonade sounded beyond the wall. A friend of George's father's came up and began speaking to him, and George was given charge of the rope handle that pulled Madeline's wagon. Although George's father now worked a busy trade in the woolens, cottons, silks, and furs that moved over Philadelphia's docks, in his youth he had apprenticed to a spinning wheel maker and he was still an adept woodworker. He had done all he could to make Madeline's wagon comfortable, padding it thickly and putting on large wheels. It still did not ride very smoothly in the deeply rutted streets, but Madeline was too big now to be carried in the arms like a babe and too weak to walk very far. George pointed out to her the oars and the four-fluked anchor that hung over the side of the balloon's gondola. She nodded. She stroked Tad absently between the ears and watched the aeronaut, who was talking to people in French, which George did not understand.

When George glanced at Madeline again, she was watching him. She said, "Can I go in the balloon?"

"I don't think so," he said. He had overheard others at the gate asking about riding in the balloon. Impossible, they had been told.

Madeline looked up, as if imagining the balloon already overhead. It had been hazy, but now the sky presented a clean field of blue.

By the time the 9:30 cannons fired, the balloon was lemon-shaped and swaying lightly between the two wooden poles. From moment to moment George could see no change in it. He fidgeted. His socks itched.

Madeline had fallen into a doze in her little wagon seat, mouth open, eyes closed, head crooked sideways against her shoulder. Tad looked around curiously from his position within her arms. Adults conversing nearby paused to look at her. She seemed pale. Without waking her, George touched her hair, felt gently between his fingers the thin light silken strands. Realizing he was for the moment her protector, her guard, on duty, he put his feet together, locked his knees, and stiffened his shoulders. All his earliest memories involved Madeline, and among their several siblings the two of them, the twins, had always been closest. When he had fallen ill with scarlet fever a year before, Madeline had been the one at his bedside every day, the face he saw when he woke from the hot fearful dreams. He was determined to be equally as good to her now.

At 9:45 a tremendous crash and roar of cannon fire sounded from Potter's Field—they had fired more than two guns this time, perhaps a dozen—and Madeline started slightly then looked blearily around. George took her hand. A cheering rose from the streets just beyond the wall and gained volume, passion. George's father appeared beside him. "That will be your namesake," he said.

Two soldiers entered bearing long-barreled muskets made longer by gleaming bayonets; President George Washington followed, carrying himself with military bearing. He wore a black velvet coat with knee-length tails, and the buckles on his knee breeches and shoes shone in the sun. The brass band sounded a fanfare and the crowd parted before the president and the entourage of diplomats and adjutants that trailed behind him. George had seen the president before, riding the streets in his white carriage, but the sight of him now thrilled a certain nerve. It made him want to laugh although he knew this was inappropriate. When he looked at Madeline, however, he saw that she seemed not to notice or recognize the president—her attention was fixed on the swelling yellow balloon.

"I want to go in the balloon," she said to George. He shook his head.

Blanchard came forward and bowed before the American president. Next to the president the French aeronaut looked small and awkward—his head and his joints were too large, his eyes and forehead bulged, his nose protruded, his chin was weak. George wondered if all the men in France looked like this. He wondered if all aeronauts must be small men.

President Washington drew forth a parchment scroll. He turned to the assembled crowd and announced it was a passport for safe passage wherever Monsieur Blanchard's balloon might carry him in the United States of America. Madeline tugged the hem of their father's coat. "Can I go in the balloon?" Their father shook his head at her, put his finger to his lips. Washington was reading from the parchment: "—receive and aid him with that humanity and goodwill which may render honor to their country and to an individual so distinguished by his efforts to establish and advance an art, in order to make it useful to mankind in general." Blanchard accepted the passport with another bow, then hurried away. He ordered the gondola moved into position beneath the balloon, which buoyed with force now against its tethers. "Why?" Madeline insisted, looking vexedly up from her wagon seat.

"Dear child, I'm sorry, it's impossible," their father said, his voice now low and pleading. "We'll get you some sweets when we get home." Around the aerostat things were happening quickly: ropes were tied, knots were checked and checked again, the two large hoses were extracted from the neck of the balloon. A couple of tethers were released and the balloon rose, then jerked to a stop. A lady in the crowd swooned, causing a minor uproar as a dozen gentlemen gathered around her to offer help. The ropes between the balloon and the gondola were taut. There seemed to be no wind at all. Madeline pressed her face into Tad's fur and began to cry. Their father sighed and knelt beside her. George felt miserable watching them.

Blanchard held up a barometer and a lodestone, put these into the gondola. He checked several knots again. Two cannons in Potter's Field fired ten o'clock and the crowds in the street grew noisy, calling for the balloon. Some began to hiss. George's father held Madeline by the shoulders and whispered to her, but she was shaking her head, and George's father looked near tears himself. Madeline said again, half choking,

"I want to go in the balloon!" George put a hand out, but did not quite touch her, wishing he could do something, but it seemed nothing could be done. Blanchard came forward to address the crowd. He spoke in French and the language sounded peculiar and impenetrable to George. Why, George wondered, couldn't she ride in the balloon? Why should this ugly little Frenchman, of all people, get to go into the sky? But such things were decided by adults.

Blanchard finished his speech and the crowd cheered and he waved his hat. Suddenly an idea struck George and without thinking further he seized Tad from his sister—who stared at him in surprise—and he darted away. As he pushed through the crowd the little dog in his arms twisted to peer back over his shoulder. He heard his father calling behind him but did not catch the words. He escaped the crowd, ran straight to Blanchard, and thrust—nearly threw—Tad toward him, so Blanchard had no choice but to take the dog or let it fall. Blanchard, gaping, held the dog awkwardly and blinked at it, then looked up at George. But George had already ducked into the crowd and disappeared behind a lady's broad hoop skirt. The Frenchman called after him, but the crowd was laughing and many of them cheered jubilantly for the dog. Some called out encouragements in French. The brass band played. When George looked back again he saw Blanchard setting the dog gently in the gondola. Then the Frenchman tipped his hat to the crowd and clambered in himself.

George circled around to rejoin his sister. His father examined him narrowly, as if he suspected his son had been replaced by some other boy, and Madeline stared at him with a blank, cool anger that struck George with horror. Suddenly, however, she laughed and seized his hand.

Blanchard waved. The brass band sounded a flamboyant fanfare. As the last three tethers were loosed, George felt he could not have breathed had he wanted to, and although Madeline was smiling she gripped his hand fiercely. With ropes dangling the balloon hovered, motionless, and it seemed this was all it could do. But then, very slowly, it began to move upward, and the hundred or so spectators in the prison yard released a loud *hurrah!* As the balloon lifted itself over the prison walls, a thunderous volley of the artillery on Potter's Field greeted its appearance and cheers and screams spread rapidly in the streets until a great clamor and tumult of noise resounded from every road and building and the bells rang in all the steeples—to George the extraordinary, reverberating pandemonium seemed like the swollen noise of his own soaring elation, his sense of a broadening, of wonder, of worlds unfolding. The balloon shook faintly in the sky, an effect that startled and worried George until he discovered it was caused by the trembling of his own excitement. Madeline let go of his hand to applaud, and when he glanced at her, she seemed perfectly radiant with joy. Blanchard waved a flag displaying the French tricolor on one side and the American ensign on the other while in the crook of his arm he held Tad, who appeared quite calm in his ascendancy. The balloon continued straight upward, rising precisely like an element from myth or dream, until Tad could no longer be made out, and soon Blanchard himself was a mere dot beneath the orb of the balloon, which looked like an amber moon in the daytime sky. Its position in the firmament was so peculiar that it seemed to mark an extraordinary disjunction, a topsy-turvy world. The hard shell of the impossible had been cracked, and who could say what might appear next?

Soon, however, the aerostat wafted to the southeast, then drifted out of sight behind the roof of a building. Everyone in the prison yard looked there a moment longer before, with sighs, they turned their attention back to earthly concerns. A man was rubbing his neck, and George realized his hurt too.

At some point during the launch President Washington and his entourage had slipped away. Now others began to leave. The young man who had been stirring the contents of the barrels gathered the hoses and disassembled the gas-making equipment. The brass band broke apart. George's father said a few words to some friends, then took the rope of Madeline's wagon in one hand, George's fingers in the other, and pulled them toward the street. "I hope," he said, squeezing George's fingers hard, "that Tad will make it back to us. Madeline would be heartbroken."

George felt a chill of panic. He had not even thought the dog might not somehow return. But Madeline's happy smile and lack of concern was contagious. Either the dog would return, or he would lift onward directly into the heavens: nothing evil could happen to that balloon.

The roads were still crowded with hordes calling and cheering, and now drinking too. His father added, "I must say, I have never seen anything of the sort. So many thousands concentrating their eyes and thoughts at the same instant upon the same object, and all of them made happy by it." He laughed. "To think, Tad, the aero-dog." Then he exclaimed, "A flying man! A flying dog!"

But by the time Tad had been returned, several days later, Madeline was dead, and when she died a knot of sorrow had tied itself inside George's chest. All through the years since that knot had remained. He could feel it still, a small hard point of agony and mourning which would live as long as he did. The entire world had changed—the railroads, the paved and gaslit streets, the cans, the factories, the steamboats, the telegraph—and yet, George wondered, will not a thing leave a man during an entire lifetime? Can nothing ever be put behind? Must the past always be before his eyes?

The eldritch odor. The muted hubbub of the crowd on the other side of the prison wall. The brush of his hands against Blanchard's as he gave him Tad. The light feel of Madeline's hair in his fingers. Her luminous expression as the balloon ascended—he was the only person still alive who remembered her.

Now his feet ached dully with gout. Everyone he had once known was dead—his parents, his siblings, his wife. Why of all these dead did he return now to Madeline? He felt a pulse of guilt. But the others had lived lives and had children, created their legacies and made their mistakes, while Madeline had none of that, had died while still, in a sense, perfect. Also, she was his twin and closest to him in profound ways. He had loved her with a strange instinct.

The blue light of the moon pressed into cracks between the planks of the barn walls. George lay with things coursing invisibly in him, like winds, shifting. He moved through memories and perhaps dreams as well. He thought of Mme Blanchard, Monsieur Blanchard's second wife, who continued ballooning for many years after his death and became a favorite of Napoleon's. She said the only place she could sleep well was aloft at night in the peace of the sky, curled in a gently swaying gondola, a stone's throw from the stars. George had read of her and had imagined Madeline dreaming and sleeping in the sky. He thought of Madeline and again of the peddler, Nathan, who reminded him of Madeline, and he thought how strange it was, how people he thought were gone could resurface, altered but recognizable.

Madeline had been his twin—and it occurred now to George that Nathan perhaps also reminded him a little of himself, when he had been young, a great many years ago.

Somewhere a rooster began to crow, and in answer a dog howled. The horses stirred and stamped their hooves. Something, probably mice, rustled in the hay. A distant bugle sounded reveille. Already muskets were snapping peevishly back and forth.

George thought perhaps he had lived too long. He was not eager for death, could not find that in himself, but neither would he regret or fear it when it came. He wished his last years, for likely these were his last, had not coincided with this war and its confusion and ubiquitous tragedy. He was now the only man in a house of women, all the other men dead or gone west or to the war. And, however he felt about the war, to be left behind was shameful and piercing and hard to a degree he had not expected. Those who went to war might find their lives stupidly bullied about and wasted upon the bullet-sown fields, but at least they had lives to be wasted.

When George stepped outside the barn, his eyes watered in the chill of the air, and it took several minutes for them to clear so he could see again. He brushed the hay off his coat. The sky of this new day was built in shades from black to blue to violet to a rose blush. It was perfectly clear and vast beyond human comprehension: to go up into it seemed a giddy madness.

He walked alone to the grassy sward of the balloon launch site. Some of the men held blankets around themselves against the morning chill. Others stood rocking from foot to foot and smoking. It appeared the balloon still had not arrived. The fires had been revived and were generating odors of coffee and of frying potatoes and onions and emitting lines of smoke that rose long and straight, like pillars upholding the firmament. Soon, in the east, an artillery gun began firing, followed shortly by another, and everyone stopped to listen. Then the rebel retorts could be heard, and as if this were a signal that all things were well, the soldiers began to move again, perhaps more hastily now, consuming their hardtack, potatoes, and canned milk, their tobacco and coffee. Between the wheel spokes of the gas generator wagons stretched spiderwebs glinting with dew. Breath could be seen clouding very faintly. George's hands and feet were cold, but he was so used to this sensation that he hardly noticed. The aching of his body had subsided, and he felt a renewed enthusiasm at the idea of seeing the balloon, and he fretted over the possibility that it had somehow been damaged or indefinitely delayed. He saw Lowe glowering at his pocket watch. Some of the men were already sipping whiskey. The moon was still in the sky, looking wan. In front of Lowe was a crude table, assembled from logs and a few boards, across which several maps were spread, weighted down by a couple of stones, an inkwell, and a Colt revolver. George spotted Nathan standing off to one side and walked over to him. "Good morning," he said.

Nathan nodded. "Morning."

"Tell you what," he said. "I'll buy that can tool from you."

"You will?" Nathan looked as if he thought George might be joking. "Why?"

"It will be a gift to my daughter-in-law. A souvenir of the trip."

"All right. Let me find it."

George gave him three dollars for it without haggling. He took the thing and chuckled at it, flipped the swiveling metal bit, and dropped it into his pocket. Nathan said, "I'm sure your daughter-in-law will find it a real improvement on her hammer and chisel. Better than—"

He stopped, his attention drawn to a noise over George's shoulder. Someone was shouting wildly and incomprehensibly. George turned and saw a rapidly approaching wagon pulled by two galloping horses. With cries and shouts and the noise of hooves it rolled into the middle of the field and halted. All around men shoved the last of their breakfasts into their mouths and kicked dirt or threw water over their cooking fires. Professor Lowe was yelling to get the gas generators and tether lines into position. Soon the balloon had been laid out on the ground, then attached in its netting to the rope suspended between the two tall poles. The soldiers worked in coordinated, practiced fashion to set up the wagons and feed them with chemicals, to connect the balloon to hoses from the gas generators, to lay out various tether lines and windlasses. A man moved between the fire pits with a bucket of water, dousing thoroughly to ensure every ember was extinguished. George began circling round the balloon. He felt extraordinarily youthful and jubilant.

Slowly the balloon began to inflate. It was an autumnal shade of orange, and its name hung within the netting in large letters: CONSTITUTION. The men now stood around in clusters and paused in their conversations every so often to look at the balloon. George felt a warm pleasure—he seemed almost to rise off the earth himself, as if the balloon's mere presence made all things lighter. Not far away Nathan sat on a log with a piece of paper on an overturned iron skillet balanced on his knees, sketching with rapid strokes, glancing up occasionally at the balloon.

This too reminded George of Madeline. Even at her very young age, Madeline had shown skill, did ink studies of plants and human figures with a breezy, precocious confidence. At the time George had resented her talent—the memory of that resentment now slid into him like a blade.

After some minutes Lowe strode over to George. "Come," he said, taking George by the elbow. George gently pulled himself out of his grip while they walked across the clearing toward the balloon. Lowe pushed his hand into the side of it, testing the pressure. He said, "This one carries twenty-five thousand cubic feet of gas. The *Great Western,* the balloon I intended to ride across the Atlantic, before the war upset all plans, had a capacity of over seven hundred thousand cubic feet." He shook his head sadly. "The *Constitution* is a fine craft, but the *Great Western* was a glorious one."

George tried to imagine a balloon of that size, nearly thirty times larger than this, but his mind failed him. He put his hand out and felt the waxy fabric. It smelled of linseed oil. Beside them stood the balloon's gondola, a large basket wrapped in a pattern of stars and stripes. It had no oars or anchor. George looked at it for a moment, considering. Then he pulled a pouch out of his pocket and removed from it a small gray black-flecked stone. It fell—gravity normal, George noted—and landed in the basket with a soft pat of sound.

George returned to his seat and watched the balloon gently swell. It gained volume more quickly than Blanchard's had, but still the process was slow. Artillery shells seemed to be landing not far away now on the other side of the hill. Several crows were roosted in a tree across the road and calling loudly, as if they desired to compete with the noise of the battle. Nathan wandered nearby. He had put his drawing away, and he appeared fidgety, perhaps unsettled by the shelling—he rubbed the back of his neck; he yawned; he took out a small knife and used it to work at his nails. George said to him, "It's quite a thing, isn't it?"

Nathan only glanced at him, nodded.

As the balloon began to near its full shape, Professor Lowe suddenly decided the windlasses were positioned too near the balloon, and a spasm of activity followed. Then everyone stood around again. George sat in the grass. Beside him, Nathan stood packing a pipe. He set it in the corner of his mouth and reached into his trousers for a match. George, preoccupied with his own thoughts, watched these gestures without concern, but a thick, bearded sergeant strode over in two paces, seized the peddler by the neck with one hand and with the other wrenched the pipe from his mouth. "You fool," he said. "Do you want to fire the hydrogen?" He threw the pipe on the ground and shook Nathan by the neck.

A few of the men laughed. Nathan, released, stumbled back and gasped. "I'm sorry," he said. His features were slack and pale.

Someone called, "Let's fill *him* with gas and drop a match in!"

Nathan stooped to pick his pipe out of the grass. Hurriedly he stuffed it into his pocket and limped backward a few steps. The sergeant glared after him, then spit on the ground. "Get out of here," he said. Nathan sighed, picked up his knapsack and began limping away. George felt sorry for him.

Confederate artillery shells suddenly seemed to be landing in great, simultaneous numbers just on the other side of the hill. The men either stared agape in that direction or ignored it entirely. Long ash-gray clouds expanded over the trees. Then, suddenly, the barrage ended and into this abrupt silence came the noise of Union cannons replying at a pace of redoubled irritation. The balloon tugged impatiently at its tethers.

George looked around and saw Nathan hobbling with his knapsack near the tree line some distance off. Then he swerved and disappeared into the trees, and suddenly, with a sharp skip of the heart, George apprehended what Nathan had been trying to do. He had not seen the youth smoke today or yesterday but only just now, beside the inflating balloon. George got up, looked a moment at the place in the trees where Nathan had disappeared, then went after him, moving as fast as he could.

He pushed ahead through the underbrush and between the trees. After a short distance he found the knapsack, abandoned under a bush. A minute later he saw Nathan ahead, moving through a copse of pine, with quiet, cautious steps and quite without any sign of a limp. George ran a few paces and called, "Nathan, wait! I'd like to talk to you!"

Nathan stopped, his back and shoulders tense. He glanced once, quickly, at George, then looked ahead again as if judging his distance to the top of the hill.

George continued toward him. "Nathan, I just want to talk with you."

"My name is not Nathan, old man," the Confederate called without looking back. He crouched on one knee to do something George could not see.

"I don't care what you've done, or where you go," George said.

"What do you want, George?" The Confederate stood now with a knife in his hand, and started down the hill toward George. He moved slowly, cautiously.

George extended his hands in a gesture of appeal and felt them shaking badly. "I thought—" He nearly said, *I thought we were friends,* but the words seemed idiotic, the notion of a child. He said, "Maybe I can help you."

"How?"

George looked around at the trees. "I don't know, but—" He looked at Nathan. No, not Nathan. "What is your name?"

"I like you, old man, but you're a ridiculous idiot. You shouldn't have followed me. Now, if I let you go, I don't know what you'll do."

It was awful, how he still seemed so terribly familiar, this man. Something in George badly wanted to be sympathetic to him. Why had he come here? Had he hoped to stop this spy, to aid him? He found nothing to say.

The Confederate said, "You want to help me, go throw a match on that balloon."

"Oh. Oh, no."

"That balloon is a weapon. Sure as a musket or a cannon. It kills men. I hate it. As surely as I am locked to the face of this earth, I hate it."

The Confederate was nearing, his face livid, his gaze steady and cold. George began to back away but his foot caught on something and he stumbled. "I don't understand," he said. For a moment he hoped the Confederate would break suddenly into his smile, or laughter: it was a misunderstanding, a joke.

Instead, from the young man came a small, tortured, animal-like sound. He stepped closer and said, his voice low, "You think it's just some trifle up there in the sky, don't you? Can you imagine what it is to look up toward heaven and see there your hated enemy gazing down on you? Anywhere you go, still he's up there, peering at you. Can you imagine how naked it feels, how helpless? This thing like—like the eye of God himself, seeing everything. But Union soldiers are not God! They're men, only men, like ourselves. Why should they have this?"

The Confederate crossed the last distance between them with sudden fluid speed and gripped George roughly by the shirt. George, his hand tremoring badly, felt in his pocket for a weapon and drew out the can tool. He was holding it awkwardly, and as he fumbled, the Confederate saw it and laughed; his breath was hot. He shook his head as if bemused by his own foolishness, then smiled and, in a single, flashing movement, raised his knife and brought it down.

Mme. Blanchard, the lady who slept peacefully aloft among the clouds and stars, was killed, famously, in 1819 during a nighttime flight over Paris when the hydrogen of her aerostat was ignited by the explosions and spraying stars of a fireworks display. George was there with her now, cowering beside her at the bottom of a boat-shaped crashing gondola, surrounded by thundering noise on all sides, the balloon burning hot above him, until reason told him he could not be over Paris and it was not fireworks that were exploding. Instead it seemed to be the arrival of an Armageddon that beat overhead and trembled him even as he struggled to return from a clinging darkness into consciousness. He lay on his back and above him the trees were frantically shattering and splintering, shedding leaves and branches in a rain of foliage that dropped all around him. Nearby explosions vibrated in the earth and were followed by the patter of falling dirt. An artillery barrage, George realized. Grapeshot embedded itself into trees with a sound like the pounding of scattered hammers. Boughs broke suddenly and swung to point downward.

George felt like he had been seared above the left ear with a hot iron. It took some moments to separate the pain from the noise and havoc. He pushed himself up, then touched the wound on his head and in doing so drove needles there. He caught his breath and, more carefully, tested it again. There was some swelling, a little blood—the Confederate spy must have struck him with the butt of the knife. The man was gone now. Meanwhile the clamor and chaos continued, fracturing George's already dazed thoughts. He stood for a minute and collected himself. He felt a great anger which quickly centered on himself and became a humiliation. He could not blame the Confederate—indeed, he had been a fool to chase after a spy that way. He could not see why he had not been killed outright. Pity on an old man, perhaps. Or maybe it seemed George could do no harm even if he wanted to. He was feeble and he was absurd. He picked his hat off the earth and placed it gently on his head. He left the can tool lying there. He started downhill, staggering through the trees.

As he came to the clearing, he saw the crew on the ground working frantically to let rope off the windlasses. The balloon was now well aloft. He stared up at it and his head throbbed

and drove pulses of red and black before his eyes. A few soldiers simply stood around, also looking up at the balloon,
none of them apparently concerned for their safety even as
the Confederate barrage raged on. George wandered toward
them. So many artillery rounds screamed through the air that
it seemed impossible the balloon would not be immediately
destroyed, but nothing touched it. It hung like a large mocking orange over the battle, over the explosions and shrapnel
and the shuddering of suddenly riven earth and the tearing
apart of trees, of men—George recalled the bandaged men
along the road yesterday, the sick, sweet odor of the hospital
tent. Young men were dying, now, by the thousands, on the
hillsides and meadows and among the forests, lives cut short
and littered about. He saw the raw fury of shot and shell directed toward the balloon and realized that until now he had
never truly envisioned this object within the context of war.
What would Blanchard, with his plumed hat and his flag and
his scientific instruments, have thought?

What would Madeline have thought?

No. It was very similar to that balloon he had seen as a
boy, and yet it resembled that wondrous balloon not at all.
Everything had been reordered. Each roar of explosion struck
George with the power of the rebels' hatred. The balloon would
try to call death down upon them and seeing it they saw a
species of aerial demon, picking without emotion or mercy
those who should die this day. Of course they hated it. It was
a terrible thing.

The sky turned slowly around the balloon like a wheel
around its hub. Dizziness, George told himself, just dizziness.
He looked down, blinking. Someone dressed in black had
come up beside him. Lowe. George stared at him. Lowe held
his hat between his two hands, peering at the balloon. George
said, "I thought you were on the balloon."

Lowe shook his head. "Not today. One of my men is guid-
ing the balloon, and General McClellan sent a junior lieu-
tenant from his staff to go up and make sketches of the enemy

deployment. The army has cavalry waiting in reserve. If we can detect a point of weakness, they'll be able to go in and maul them."

After a moment George said, "I ought to go home."

"Isn't it beautiful?" Lowe said.

The balloon had apparently risen out of range of the Confederates—their fire suddenly dropped away to the intermittent sibilance of a high, passing shell, the report of its landing far off and seemingly harmless. Then the artillery barrage ceased altogether. George would not look at the balloon. He looked at the windlasses. He might somehow cut one of the tether ropes, but he could not conceivably cut all three before they would stop him. He asked quietly, "How can you do this?"

"It's less dangerous than it seems," Lowe said, misunderstanding. "Ours is a relatively small target at a relatively great distance from the enemy. These balloons probably pay for themselves just in the ammunition that the Confederates waste upon them."

It occurred to George that Lowe had never imagined himself on the Confederate side, looking up at that baleful, invincible object—except perhaps to consider such matters as how the rebels would attempt to disguise their artillery and mask their troop movements. Nor had Lowe stood beside Madeline watching little Tad lift away under a magnificent yellow orb.

But, George realized—while a single cannon somewhere near began thundering mechanically, like a hall clock marking the hour—such sentimentality had no place here. George had no place here. A war was a place for practical men like Lowe, for men not yet overwhelmed by the relentless accumulation of years and memory. Of course it had been a mistake for George to come here. He should have understood that from the first. They did not send old men to war for reasons quite beyond the obvious ones.

Lowe said, "If you'll wait a little, I'll find a supply wagon that's going back. You could ride with them some of the distance."

"No," George said. "I'll walk."

"You'll walk?" Lowe studied him. Then he shrugged. "Tighten that line!" he bellowed to the men at the nearest windlass.

Without conscious intention George's gaze followed that line, curved like a sagging strand of spider silk, up to the balloon. A lone bugle somewhere proclaimed itself, but otherwise the battle now stilled, as though all the combatants, like George, found their attention drawn skyward, as though the balloon made children of everyone. It appeared so small, so precarious and forlorn in all that sky, as unmistakably human as a ship at the horizon's edge of the sea.

The ground crew were still paying out line, and the orange balloon still grew smaller and smaller in the blue all around. George removed his hat and touched his head: the bleeding had stopped. He started up the road. This evening there would again be a round, nearly full moon in the darkened sky, and he resolved that he would walk until he could not anymore. But then suddenly he wheeled around to look again at the balloon.

The Accident

We met in a kind of accident. Maybe call it an instance of happenstance. Outside a supermarket. The sky had dimmed, milky overhead lights illuminated the parking lot, and cars crept up and down the aisles looking for open spots. I came out of the store laden with bags, one of them filled with fresh corn on the cob, and as I opened my car's trunk that bag split and a dozen ears fell and rolled. I first saw her as she bent to the pavement, helping. I protested, but she kept at it, and when the corn had been collected and secured she told me she was Kathy.

Sometimes I grow furious, or hysterical, thinking of it. Of how it began, with her kindness. The beginning of a long mistake.

I mean, I'm still trying to figure this out.

I arrived with flowers and refrigerator magnets. When she saw the flowers, she hesitated. When she saw the magnets she—fleetingly, but distinctly—winced. Certain hesitations in her voice on the phone earlier came back to me.

This was ten months and eighteen days after our meeting in the parking lot.

The magnets featured small plastic corncobs, with green leaves and bright yellow kernels. Kathy flattened her expression, and then she even crafted a semblance of pleasure. "You're very thoughtful," she said. She was always and mercilessly kind.

And I recited the lines that I had composed when I bought the things. "I have some for my fridge, too. I thought it would be fun to knock them off and help each other pick them up."

She smiled a little more. To stop her from conjuring a phrase or joke that would somehow simultaneously satisfy her standards for kindness and honesty—I didn't care to know how it could be done—I said, "Come on. We'll be late."

Wearing loose brown pants, small silver earrings, and a white, white blouse, she walked to the car, her stride a little stiffened. We traveled into the small, stark, varying world the headlamps lit and stopped at one red sign, then another, turned at a flashing yellow light, and moved along a broad street lined with chain restaurants and parking lots lit sickly orange. Kathy broke open the package of magnets and examined them in the fluctuating light of the streetlamps.

In the months after we met I had cooked dinners for her that ended with flaming desserts, had let her pull me onto dance floors, had tiled her shower for her. She taught me how to shave her legs, and sometimes, digging in my pockets for keys or change, I found tightly folded tiny pieces of paper, each with a word in her handwriting. "Lover." "XOXO." We were giddy with ourselves, I suppose, and we both knew how to act giddy. But giddiness is transitory, and as it wore away, I began to find holes opening in our conversations that Kathy waited for me to fill, and I had no idea how. At the time I felt only confused, but in retrospect I can say that the essence of it was that I didn't know myself well enough to know what I wanted to talk about, and the things she wanted to talk about I found uninteresting. She believed I didn't understand people, and I believed she made decisions with too much sentimentality, and we had no knack for saying things like these—which were true enough—to each other.

But I didn't see any of that clearly at the time. That night, as I recalled how she had winced at my gift, I only felt sure that she believed our relationship had reached a tepid finish, and though I knew that there were gaps between us, in the silence in the car I began to think that I could love her, did love her, that she would be wrong to bring it to an end—ludicrous thoughts.

She said something about work while we drove, about the weather as we stood in the line marked by the velvet ropes. Then we entered the darkness and sat below the great glowing screen, and mercifully we didn't have to try to talk.

It's too long ago now, I don't remember the name of the movie, or even the stars, only that it displayed all the glories of Hollywood in summer—actors and plot the backdrop to a choreography of violence and explosions, of hurtling forms, of damage composed in obsessive detail. I appreciated the fact that such stuff required a craft of its own, and I welcomed the diversion of the imagery of blossoming flames and trembling weaponry. In the seat beside me Kathy moved her soda from hand to hand, crossed and uncrossed her legs, and when I glanced at her she seemed especially beautiful in the reflected light of the screen. Vehicles smashed, men beat each other with blunt objects, skyscrapers buckled and fell, while she—I guessed—rehearsed ways to tell me that we were done with each other. She would surely be relieved when this was over, the deeply unpleasant but finally necessary murder of something small and out of place, a spider or a mouse. Kind of her, I thought, to be anxious about it. She might have just stopped returning my calls. She was too kind even to go into it before this movie, which I had told her I was looking forward to. She really was kind.

In the car, in a terror of silence, I talked in a long superficial stream about the movie, about other movies, about TV shows, about the physics of the cathode ray tube. In my thoughts, I cowered. Kathy nodded. She only interrupted to ask, "Where are you going?"

I had no idea. I saw that I was driving in a direction that would take neither of us home, surging and stopping on a broad multilane street with a series of stoplights that had allowed me to keep talking without going very far. I said, "I thought we would go get a drink."

She yawned. She had that habit, when she wanted a moment to think about a question. She let another few seconds pass, then she began to tell me she thought our relationship was not working.

I shouted. I slapped the armrest between our seats. I shouted and cursed.

I suppose I believed the appropriate response to be something dramatic. When I had finished flailing and cussing, we were both silent. At a stoplight I turned toward the interstate.

"I'm sorry," she said.

I saw her eyes filling wet. "Kathy," I said.

"It was just dating, Aaron," she said. "We were dating for a year, we had fun, and now I think we should move on."

So she took the reasonable position, and I, too wretched to think past opposing, took the unreasonable. "You're not breaking up with me," I said. I turned onto a ramp and merged into the interstate's lanes.

"Just take me home, OK?" She watched the lights and the dark a moment. "If you want, we can talk when you're calm."

A couple of miles ticked by. I passed a semi. She said, "Where are we going?"

I didn't know exactly why I had turned onto the interstate. I couldn't articulate myself. All I had were the dregs of my stupid urge for drama. "I don't know," I said. "I just want to drive."

"You're not taking me home."

"I'm driving."

"Stop."

"To clear my head."

"Pull over and let me out, OK? Then whatever. Drive."

"I'd rather not."

"No?"

"No."

"This is kidnapping," she said. Another mile went by. There was little traffic. "Aaron," she said, "this is a little pathetic, you know?"

I said, in misery, "You look lovely tonight."

The interstate dropped gradually downward, high concrete walls rose on either side, we entered a manmade canyon. "Please," she said.

When I looked at her again, the wetness in the eyes was gone. She had a slightly horsey face and long straight hair. On her lap lay a tiny black vinyl purse, the size of a can of tuna. She carried in it, I knew, lipstick, a couple of keys, and a credit card.

"Your purse is stupid," I said. "Barbie has a more practical purse."

She said, immediately, as if she had been awaiting this opportunity, "I hate your pants. All your pants with the ridiculous cargo pockets at the knees. What is that? You're not a Marine."

"They're good for carrying stuff. Unlike the purse."

"I like this purse. Would you like to insult any of my other accessories?"

"You sometimes wear too much eyeliner."

"OK."

"That's all I can think of right now."

"Fine," she said. "And your belt doesn't match your shoes."

"It's supposed to?"

"Your shoes are never polished."

"OK. Guilty."

"They look disgusting."

"OK."

"Your fridge has nothing in it but condiments."

"No fair," I said. "I thought we were only going after appearances."

"Your socks have holes."

I laughed. "No one sees that."

"I do."

"You're not being very nice."

She crumpled a little.

"We've not broken up," I said. "Have we? We haven't."

She sighed. "You'll take me home?"

Surely I could love her, I thought. Yes. I said, "Yes."

"If you want me to say we haven't broken up," she said, "I'll say we haven't broken up."

But we had, of course, and a line of fire speared my chest.

"Aaron," she said.

I shook my head.

"Aaron, can't you—"

A rising engine noise interrupted her. She leaned to look in the mirror on her side of the car. The noise was a distraction, and I recall now that I felt relief.

My speedometer showed seventy, and this car closed on us fast; it must have been going almost a hundred. It was in my lane, and to get away from it I swerved a lane to the right. At the same time, the approaching car lurched sharply toward the left lane, and as it passed us its back end began to come around, like a baseball bat thrown sidearm. It slid through the left lane and entered the median with the rear end still coming around, toward the concrete barrier between the eastbound and westbound lanes.

I looked away, to check my position in my lane. We had come into a dead spot for traffic—a couple of red taillights floated far ahead, but otherwise we were alone. Kathy, watching the car approach the wall, made a faint keening noise.

The car hit the concrete with a crash followed by an oscillating shriek. The noise, however, was actually less than I had braced myself for. I looked over in time to see the front end caroming off the wall, the back end bucked upward and spinning forward, the headlights coming around like the unblinking eyes of a psychopath. "Oh," Kathy said. "No. No." The back corner now struck the wall with another crash and scream of metal and a long dazzle of yellow sparks.

After the second impact it spun back into the traffic lanes. I feared the car would come all the way across, toward us. But when it had gone around a full 360 degrees, and the front end was again pointed forward in the lane, the driver seemed, incredibly, to regain control. The car coasted to a stop in the second lane from the left, the lane where we had been when everything began. I said, meaninglessly, "Careful." I had not yet touched my brakes and in a moment we were speeding past.

I drove not thinking in any coherent, conscious way. Kathy said in a whisper—I'm not sure I actually heard her so much as guessed her meaning—"We have to stop."

All my instincts argued for speed and distance from this thing. But I understood that she had the better, less regrettable instincts, and I moved to the shoulder and clapped down on the brakes so that the wheels skidded on the loose stones and garbage.

We halted more than a hundred yards ahead of the other car. I got out and started running back along the shoulder. Only a single dim headlamp burned on the car out in the lanes. I heard Kathy's footsteps behind me. I knew she had a cell phone, and I shouted, "Call nine-one-one!" A car hurtled by, and it made me slow slightly. If you've ever stood on the edge of an interstate and watched 70 mph traffic go past, you have an idea of how I felt.

But I resolved myself and sprinted out to the damaged car—a little two-door sports coupe—and circled to the driver's window. It was open. I leaned to peer in, and saw a lot of faces. Two men sat in front, and three women crowded the narrow rear seat. They appeared to be in their mid- or late-twenties, and all had straight dark hair, dark eyes, and a familial resemblance, as if they were cousins. "You all right?" I asked. The driver, without looking at me, nodded. "Everyone? OK?" A woman in back vaguely lifted a hand.

I glanced around and saw headlamps approaching in the right lane. "You need to turn on your flashers," I said. "Your emergency lights." Ahead and behind us were street lamps, but we were in a dim spot between. "The flashing lights," I said. No one moved. As the car in the right lane passed by

I felt the thrum of its engine in my chest and its wind wake rocked the coupe. I couldn't understand why the people inside didn't move. I wondered if they could understand English. "You should get out," I said, gesturing.

The driver, with a sudden lurching movement, swung open his door, forcing me away. He wore black jeans and a tight black T-shirt, and his eyes didn't register much. He stood wavering with one hand on the door. "You all right?" I asked. The man muttered a single, incomprehensible syllable. I smelled alcohol. A sense of something, a noise, made me glance back. A pair of headlights were already terrifyingly close and nearing much too quickly. They swerved right at the last moment, tires squealing, and swung by just a couple of feet from the side of the coupe.

The driver took two halting steps past me toward the center median. He didn't seem to understand where he was. I touched him on the shoulder. "You need to get the others out."

He looked at my hand on his shoulder, then turned, walked back to his car, got in, and closed the door. He sat there. I peered into the car again, at the women in the backseat. They all sat there. Placid.

A pickup roared by in the right lane.

I thought I might have more luck on the passenger side. I started around the front of the car. Kathy, on the highway shoulder, talked into her cell phone. Glancing back down the lanes, I saw another vehicle coming up directly behind the stalled coupe. It was too fast and too close, and I saw an inevitable domino action, car into car into me. I looked at Kathy, feeling I badly wanted her to look at me, but she stared at the approaching car, the cell phone limply forgotten out in the air. I thought *I should shut my eyes*, but instead I watched as the closing vehicle turned hard and, tires squealing, got by on the left. Wind spun around me. The driver tapped the horn, more interrogatory than angry.

I was now completely terrified. I trotted to the shoulder and stood before Kathy, wanting very badly to collapse.

"They're not getting out of the car," she said. She had the phone pressed to her ear, and I couldn't tell if she was talking to me or to the person on the phone.

I said, "They won't come out."

She lowered the phone. "What do you mean?"

"They look at me like they're watching TV."

A black SUV flashed by in the leftmost lane. "I saw someone get out."

"He went back in. I think he's drunk. Probably they all are. I don't know if they understand English very well."

"Then we have to drag them out."

"We'll get killed trying to do that."

"Come on," she said. "We'll drag—" And she had taken a step forward when she stopped, and I heard the whisper of a car coming. I glanced over my shoulder in time to see the impact, the explosion.

The explosion was instantaneous; the cars disappeared inside a billowing of light and flame that engulfed both and spread beyond them. The noise and the light seemed to go on and on, as if to fill the world. Then it suddenly collapsed inward to a core that briefly went quiet and dark, then shot a column upward, so huge, loud, and bright that I thought three or four cars had become involved.

When my retinas had cleared away the afterimage, however, there were still only two cars. The rear end of the coupe had been crushed forward to the seats, hunching and twisting the entire vehicle. The other car was a four-door sedan, its front mangled. Both vehicles had spun forward and now pointed at oblique angles. No one could have survived the explosion I had just seen, I was certain. Blue and white flames flickered around the brutalized rear of the coupe. Kathy said, "Aaron."

Fogged by shock, I needed time to recall these syllables represented my name.

The passenger door of the sedan opened and a man stumbled out. Then the driver's door opened, and someone emerged.

The sight of people, alive, coming from that car, confounded me. I know I did not move for several seconds. Then—I don't recall how I got to the coupe. Events become blurry. I remember understanding that Kathy had gone to the men who had climbed out of the sedan, and I went to the coupe. I remember yanking repeatedly on the driver's door, and the driver looking up at me without focus—the door peeled open with a screech and I leaned in to grab the driver under the shoulders. The chemical, searing odor of burning plastics worked shafts of pain upward through my head, and I could feel the slick of the driver's sweating body through his shirt. I recall a skidding sensation of taking actions without framing the decisions to do so. Heat, bodies, blinding smoke. The flames at the rear of the car spread upward and forward. The light was cut with stark shadows from the headlights in the roadway and flickered and flashed with the flames inside the car. Other figures appeared around me. I remember reaching, groping, grasping for flesh, sweaty, dirty, inside the smoke and the hot. Flames flickered and moved over the floor. Kathy came up beside me or behind me, and I leaned against her once, briefly, felt her against my shoulder, or her hand on mine. Others, shadowy figures, took away the people we extracted and shouted or screamed things to me, words I hadn't the energy to interpret. The car's small hell was the only place of significance. Inside was a languid quiet and heat, the shouting outside muffled, a car horn faraway. The flames, however, crackled, moved over the rear seat, into the roof liner. There had been five people in the car and one by one we pulled them free. I don't know how many Kathy pulled out, how many I did, or if we both had a hand on each of them. I remember distinctly only the last, the woman seated in the back on the far passenger side.

She had long dark hair, which was burning, curling in small, delicate yellow flames. She wore a skirt and a tank top that was melting to her skin on her right side, blackening and blistering and smoking. She looked at me steadily.

When I leaned in to grab her, the smoke and the heat hit my face and tunneled into my lungs and exploded. Darkness crowded the edges of my vision. Coughing, I stumbled out of the car. I glanced around at Kathy; she looked at me with a grimace.

I took a deep breath, crawled in again, got a hand on the woman's arm, and dragged her out.

After that, a minute or two passed that I don't remember.

"Where is the ambulance?" Kathy shouted. "Where?" The woman on the ground between us was quietly dying. Sometimes her eyes opened. She never said a word, never screamed or groaned, but each time her eyes opened they appeared less focused, and they no longer found my face. Her left hand gripped at the asphalt of the roadway while her right lay in a blistered, bleeding, frayed end at her side. I could not distinguish how much of the blackening on her abdomen and arms was the melted material of her tank top and how much was the char of direct burns. Within the black ran channels of dark blood, and over the left side of her face lay a sheen of blood, as if exuded from the pores like sweat. Her ruined chest heaved, slowly, but otherwise she appeared entirely, inexplicably calm; it made me strain for calm myself, though my hands shook, and I blinked continually to clear my eyes. I did not know what to do with my hands, hesitated to touch her wounds, and finally put one hand gently on her left leg, which had not been burned. The cloth of her pants was saturated with sweat. Sirens closed on us, but moved slowly, caught in the traffic backed up behind the accident. Perhaps a dozen people milled around and dithered over the injured. The coupe still burned and no one ventured near it. All these useless people. "Please, get out of the way of the ambulance," Kathy said; no one could have heard her but me. Her hair hung in disarray. Black and red smears marked the white of her blouse. Her gaze met mine, then veered off.

The dying woman was looking at me. For a moment we stared at each other. "What is your name?" I asked.

She didn't reply, and when I looked up a paramedic was pulling Kathy away. The woman on the ground didn't appear to be breathing. A paramedic took me by the shoulder and pushed me away. I stumbled off blindly. I feared that she had died. Later I learned that she did not die then, but later, after reaching the hospital.

For some time—I'm unsure how long, perhaps several minutes—I wandered in the milling crowd. I didn't think of Kathy, and it seems strange now but I didn't even think of the woman dying on the pavement. The feeling I had was profound relief. A black hole of relief. The only other time I've ever known anything like it was after a fistfight, at the end, after all that desperate physicality, when nothing more depended on doing anything.

As I began to regain my sense of the world and look around for Kathy, men in a variety of uniforms were swarming the scene with flashing vehicles. But she wasn't at the ambulances. She wasn't with the cops or near the fire trucks.

A screaming ambulance exited down the open road ahead. I turned a circle, then crouched and put my head into my hands. I thought of Kathy, stooped beside me over corn ears in the uncertain light of a nighttime parking lot.

I breathed, regrouped, stood, began to walk. I moved through small gatherings of people, among the cars. Stopped headlights were backed into the distance as far as I could see. If she had wandered out that way I might never find her. I wanted badly to find her. I jogged toward the fire trucks, and I began to recall, dimly, that we had been engaged in an argument before all this began. The conversation came back to me in clumps, a little warped, strangely colored. The way we had talked seemed meaningless now, as if we had been joking in a gobbledygook language. The idea that we could have ended our relationship felt far away. That it might be otherwise for her, however, struck me with terrible, sudden fear.

I remembered my car. Maybe she had gone there. Its position on the shoulder was far ahead of the chaos and lights of the accident; I was surprised how far away. As I ran I tried to spit out the flavor of smoke and fumes. I could see no one in the windows of my car, no human silhouette, nothing.

A single lane of traffic was opened and cars began to trickle past. Another ambulance went screaming off. I opened the door of my car and startled at the sight of a huddled form on the passenger seat, so small and compressed that I thought first: a dog. As if someone had dumped a stray into my car.

But of course it was Kathy, and as I got in, she straightened. "Kathy," I said.

She watched the windshield and her fingers curled and uncurled on her lap. The magnet corns lay in a scatter over the dashboard. They appeared a small, fallen, murdered people. Kathy turned and looked at me, and I reached toward her.

I'd like to be able to say now that that event changed our lives, utterly, for the better. It did in fact startle us out of our narcissism, and we felt again a need to be close, warm, and gentle with each other, to hold together in this dark world where you might get into the backseat of the wrong car and soon be dying, burned on a highway, a stranger asking your name.

And it was all a mistake. Ours was a relationship between two young people that should have ended, but after that accident we clung to it for another seven years, married nearly six of those, in a coupling that seemed to have begun in a state of exhaustion—as sympathetic, as grimly mindful, and as listless as if we had depleted our love over decades.

But the accident wasn't a trap laid just for us, I remind myself at times. One might as well blame the corn that split the bag in the parking lot. Which sometimes I do. At other times, however, in spite of everything since, I still remember— as we sat together on the shoulder of the interstate, as the two smashed cars were trundled away on the backs of a pair of wreckers, the lanes began to clear, and all the backed up traffic accelerated past us into the open darkness, pushing forward with joy, their drivers oblivious, knowing only that for some reason they had been delayed a long while but now everything looked fine, and their lights streamed into the darkness of the open interstate while Kathy and I sat lit in their glow—I remember I was more glad at that moment to be with her than I could have been with anyone else, and wasn't that maybe not an illusion of despair, not an effect of receding adrenaline, not an error of character, not misfortune or hysteria, but simply, in that moment at least, love?

Location

Donald was searching the listings for condos priced mid-threes in the vicinity of downtown when he discovered that Iris's place was on the market. The address and unit number gleamed from the computer screen, and he felt hurt that she hadn't asked him to list her condo, to act as her agent for the sale. But to think she would do so was ridiculous. She was now, apparently, dating a helicopter pilot. Then he thought she might have at least asked him for his advice, his thoughts. But, no, an end was an end.

He was doing research for a new client, a buyer, and Iris's unit met his client's criteria for price, size, and bedroom count. Donald stood and paced through the echoing rooms of his house for some minutes. If he brought her a buyer, surely she would not mind, and while her unit's location in Five Points was a little outside the area his client had requested, the client also had somewhat unrealistic price expectations for the neighborhoods he liked. So Donald decided to go ahead and show him Iris's place.

During a family vacation—an interstate odyssey via Chevrolet Malibu station wagon, with Donald's parents in front, alternating petty arguments with miles of silence, and himself on the hot-in-the-sun vinyl of the backseat, reading or daydreaming or whining—they had stopped in Denver to see a college friend of his mother's. Apparently a woman of some affluence, she lived alone in an enormous red brick Victorian, two stories tall, with a turret at one corner. The woman took them on a tour—outside, through a series of flagstone paths, gesturing to the three-car garage, the flowerbeds, a fountain that trickled glittering water into a goldfish pond, then through a large kitchen to the dining room and parlor, bedroom and foyer, around an ornate newel post and up to the second floor to see more bedrooms and a vast space she said had been a ballroom. Everywhere the ceilings were high and coved; the floors were hardwood. Donald had never been in such an enormous house, nor one with so much exposed wood—in the houses he knew the floors were carpeted, the wood was painted, and he had seen turrets only in picture books. On the second floor, the turret functioned as a sitting area off a bedroom, and from here he saw distant rough peaks, an entire horizon of mountains—they seemed fabulous, hardly credible.

At dinner, while they ate at an old wooden table under a chandelier on a long chain, he watched his mother's friend. She had fascinating skin—tanned as toast with many fine creases feathering her face and arms. She talked a great deal, with languid gestures. When she mentioned she was putting the house up for sale, Donald grew excited. He told his parents they should buy it: the house was marvelous, and it was for sale, and it seemed very simple—he would live in the bedroom with the turret and play in the ballroom while his mother tended to the garden and his father worked on his motorcycles in the garage. The hostess squinted at him, and his parents giggled, then laughed, then guffawed until they grew nearly hysterical—even much later, looking back, he wasn't sure why they laughed so hard. Maybe it was only that his impression of their laughing had exaggerated over time. Especially fixed in memory, however, was his sense of reproach, as if he had betrayed a misunderstanding not only of his parents' range of real estate options but of their very natures. And he spent a great deal of time afterward trying to understand what it was he had not understood.

Years later he drove alone with his possessions piled, wedged, and jammed into an old Buick, traveled westbound on I-80 from Ohio, where he had lived all his life, through

Indiana, Illinois, Iowa, and across the pancake expanses of Nebraska. He was returning to Denver, and he thought about where he was going largely in terms of the turreted house, the view from the turret, his mother's friend's strange skin and strange situation. Why would someone live alone in such vastness? Had she inherited it? Bought it as an investment? When he was only a couple of hours from the city, mountains now on his right, thunderheads appeared ahead and soon lay heaped vast and black all across the plains, so that as he topped a hill and saw at last the towers of downtown, they were trivialized beneath the weather. Fat raindrops struck the car with the noise of a clapping crowd. It was 1998. A friend who had come here two years earlier was now the vice president at an Internet

startup, and he had recruited Donald to work in marketing. Donald was excited about the work, the company, the money— he would make an outlandish salary. The opportunity had come suddenly, and its window was brief; his first home in the city was a motel room with wide cracks where the walls joined the ceiling, loud with the hiss of vehicles on the rain-wet interstate.

Despite his salary, rents seemed high; on his second weekend in the city he signed a lease on an apartment in Capitol Hill with a little balcony that looked out on an alleyway of crumbling asphalt. It had hardwood floors, but in the bedroom the boards were warped with water damage and in the living room the floor had been deformed as the structure settled, so that his furniture sat unevenly and tottered between two legs. He spent little time there. His new work engaged him, was frenetic and thrilling, kept him at the office to late hours and into weekends. It lasted fifteen months before the layoffs began. He survived in the company two months longer, then his friend, the vice president, gave him two week's pay, a few gift certificates to Starbucks, and offered to write a letter of recommendation. Donald realized, as he began revising his résumé, that although the work he had done had kept him busy, he could not articulate clearly what his job had been, or even what the company had done. He spent much of the next several days walking a figure-eight path around the ponds in Washington Park, feeding the mallards crumbs of Starbucks scones, watching unholy boiling sunsets fade over the ragged western range, and contemplating a disorganized retreat to Ohio.

He knew his parents would greet his return with a mild and clammy fussiness, that he would be able to find work, that he would easily reenter old routines with old friends, but he felt a visceral reaction against going back. As he considered this feeling, he came to understand that he had staked a portion of his identity on the move here, that to abandon this place now would be to abandon a part of who he hoped to be. This had an aspect of revelation to him, because he had not previously realized that he had specific ideas about whom he hoped to be, that he might not merely accept the path offered by happenstance or fate. This realization imbued him with an unusual energy. He spent weeks in the library reading books on job hunting, on résumé writing, on interview techniques; he studied the newspapers and internet postings; he spent hours writing and revising cover letters; he submitted dozens of résumés in a score of industries.

But it was a very bad time to be looking for work.

Real estate was a career he had never foreseen for himself. Only in desperation did he get a broker's license, did it with thoughts turning vaguely to the impression the turreted house had made, symbolizing the sum of his real estate experience. At the beginning he knew few people in the city, had no ready-made network to exploit for clients, was clumsy and self-conscious in selling himself and his services to strangers. During the second year, he maxed out three credit cards, his phone line was cut off, and for food money he pawned CDs, books, a camera, and the golf clubs his parents had given him. His radiator stopped working, and he couldn't approach the landlord because he owed rent, so he came home only very late to sleep under a pile of second-hand quilts. But he kept working and grasping. He volunteered to hold open houses for other agents' properties in hopes of meeting clients. He wrote and photocopied neighborhood market analyses and spent days hand delivering them door to door. He rented tables at bridal expos.

Slowly, he began to find clients. When he took buyers out, it was strange at first, examining these past and future homes that were now objects for sale. Some had been emptied by their sellers; others still contained all the possessions of a family. Conventional wisdom held that a place showed better when furnished, but the photos on the wall, the food in the cupboard, and the shoes in the closet gave the eerie impression of an unsettled world, as if a family had been forced to flee by a sudden, secret calamity. He and his clients passed through, touching this and that, assessing, criticizing and, inevitably, smirking. People had strange things in their houses—a Harry Belafonte shrine, a toilet in the center of the bedroom, a pink dungeon.

In time he found he was reasonably good at his work, that in fact he liked it, liked learning about the city, and in a few years he had come to know the streets and neighborhoods, the schools, the little hidden parks, the zoning, the laws pertaining to sidewalk maintenance, how long the wait-lists were for the preschools, the best restaurants for *menudo* or *phò*. When he met someone new and asked where she lived, he was oftentimes able to recall the cross streets, imagine his way along the block, and describe the building—a useful barroom trick, and it occurred to him that he probably knew the city better than most natives. He liked this. And he loved bringing a client to a house the client knew instinctively, just by walking through the door, was fated to be home. This happened more regularly than he might have supposed it would.

Over time it developed that many of his friends were lawyers. He was unsure how this happened, but he liked to
listen to them argue with one another, liked the way they
thought, parsing relevant from irrelevant, distinction from
difference. So he was at a party full of young attorneys and
paralegals when he met Iris, an attorney, and fell into a dis-
cussion with her about the use of the word "home." Iris said
realtors abused it, putting the word into marketing fliers to
describe residences in which no one lived, or in which, anyway, the prospective buyer certainly did not yet live, a cold
deserted structure without soul or possessor or love, so that
the word "home" became mere marketing gloss, an invidious
lie. Surprised, he stood dumb and grinning, not to patron-
ize her—as she accused, laughing—but because listening to
her made him happy. She had a startling laugh—loud, stac-
cato, witch-like. He saw a group of mascara-eyed women
peer over and smirk, as if Iris had belched, and he wanted to
jam needles into these people. As a practical matter, he said,
a word like "house" or "condo" or "duplex" would be overly
restrictive because someone might be interested in any or all
of these, while "dwelling" was clumsy, "abode" was odd, and
"residence" was cold. But, she said, *more precise.* Eventually,
giddy with vodka tonics and an inner trilling, he conceded
that perhaps he occasionally used "home" when he meant
something slightly different.

She lived in a loft-style condo, in a new building in the
Five Points neighborhood. It had ten-foot ceilings and a large
great room and exposed ductwork, but it was loft-*style*, not a
true loft—he pointed out to ding her with some precision—
because the bedroom was walled off, as well as the bathroom
and a couple of closets. It was on the fifth floor, in a corner, and
offered exceptional views—from her south-facing windows
one could see the spread of the city's skyline, while at the
same time, in the western windows, lay the mass of Mount
Evans and all the smaller peaks and ridges that formed its
wide shoulders.

Iris's parents were Chinese immigrants, and she was thin and small—the top of her head came to Donald's shoulders— while Donald's own ancestors were Irish-Greek-Danish-Polish, and his wide build suited the wrestling he had done in high school. To see Iris's uncanny laugh come out of her tiny frame was a bit of a marvel. But after the first evening of talking with her at the party, he rarely thought about the physically odd match between them, unless someone else mentioned it. Before moving to Denver she had spent all her life in Milwaukee, her accent was Midwestern, and her cultural references were the same as his. It took him a few weeks to see that her laugh was a kind of mask on nervousness, and a few more weeks to see that her precision played the same role. The more nervous she was, the more likely she was to delve into droll arguments over exactitude. When she was really pissed, on the other hand, she became merely silent. Then she would do another thing. She maintained her stiff quiet until he was gone, then she would break something. It would be lying around for him to see when he returned. A smashed plate. A dent kicked into the wall.

The plate and the dent appeared when his unpredictable work schedule spoiled things, i.e., the canceled vacation to Puerto Vallarta. But such breakage was rare. On weekend evenings, they boiled bratwursts in beer, mashed avocados into guacamole, and drank stiff margaritas while watching black-and-white monster movies. She enjoyed arguing politics, and when he grew tired of it, she argued with the television. He liked to talk with her about what the real estate developers were up to, about the endless legal vagaries of closing a real estate contract, about the hidden breaches between what his clients thought they wanted in a home and what they actually wanted. He spent most of his days in her loft. She gave him his own closet.

To Donald's mind, the end began with the cat. He and Iris were together for more than two years, making this the longest, most serious relationship of his life. The cat—reportedly still young and sweet-natured, as cats went—belonged to a friend who had taken a new job that involved moving to Nigeria to work in the oil fields. When Iris began to talk about adopting it, Donald was possessed by a sudden, unreasoning desperation, a hate of this unknown cat. He said he was allergic. He thought this might be true; he had had the sniffles once while visiting an aunt who lived with a half-dozen cats.

Iris didn't take in the cat, but not long thereafter she sat with crossed legs on one of the brushed nickel dining-room chairs in her condo and asked Donald what he thought about marriage. Later he saw how obtuse he had been; obviously he should have expected this question would come up. But he was surprised. He stared, then laughed loudly, as if at a moment of unexpected slapstick. As his parents had done years ago. It embarrassed him, but it also seemed to embarrass her. Flustered, she said, "Who wouldn't want to lock into an old ball and chain?"

They laughed too hard. (For the most part he didn't notice the particular sound of her laugh anymore, but now and again it was a like a nail run down the spine.) He said, "My dad used to say, 'I take my wife everywhere, but somehow she keeps finding her way back.'" Iris groaned, began to talk about her family; he stepped into the kitchen to start dinner; one of his clients phoned in a panic about an inspection notice, and it was as if the topic of marriage had been forgotten.

Late that night, however, as he slouched on the sofa with her, weary and vacant-minded, she said that she thought they really needed to have a levelheaded, serious, undistracted conversation on the subject of where their relationship was going.

He sat up. "You mean," he said, pleased to be the one who said the word directly: "marriage."

"Yes," she said. She wanted to get married in the next couple of years; she wanted to start planning that next stage of her life; she wanted to be able to talk seriously about how the two of them could bring into their lives a third life, a child, and while she spoke he watched her dark eyes watching him. She set out her position, he thought, with the precision of a mechanism, or a lawyer. A silence followed. He felt fidgety, sulky, displeased, trapped; he went to the window. The mountains were obscured by clouds. Down on the street a man in a tight white tank top was explosively vacating his stomach into the gutter. She said she was confident they could communicate and work together, find a route through the inevitable compromises that would make them both happy. Or, at least, mostly happy, most of the time. Without looking around, he nodded. He had the sense that she had paraphrased this speech from somewhere, some self-help book or blog. The silence in the room grew long and burdened. Finally he began to talk about his parents' marriage, and the marriages of some of his friends—marriages that had ended in divorce, and he found his way down a conversational path that led away from the original talk of marriage, until once again he was talking about real estate.

He left her condo with a sensation of guilt and conflict. He knew the next time he returned to the loft, he would find a picture frame smashed onto the floor or a serving plate hurled into the wall. It depressed him. And then, in a sudden mental lateral move, he made the decision to look for a house for himself: it had long seemed obvious that he should stop renting and buy, and he had saved enough for a solid down payment. But, while managing a client's expectations and emotions through a process of rational decision-making was a skill that he had developed and refined, shepherding his own expectations and emotions would be something different. That night he began searching the listings. The next day, at Iris's condo, he found that a large potted jade plant no longer sat on the bookshelf but lay in dirt and shards on the hardwood. He apologized and begged for time to sort his thoughts. He spoke with genuine contrition, and she seemed convinced. Then he set out to look at everything anew—adobe-styled houses with tile roofs near Congress Park; converted warehouses with exposed brickwork and high ceilings in LoDo; condo units in the towers of Cheesman Park; fix-and-flip Victorians in Five Points; duplexes among the expensive pop-tops around Washington Park; bungalows and ranch-style houses all over the city. He set showings, and he wandered the rooms, and he felt nothing. Soon he realized that he was waiting for that sudden knowledge—that a place was meant to be his home— to strike upon walking in a door. He began to look at oddities: a house with garage parking for twelve cars and, effectively, no lawn; a house with a two-story rock-climbing wall in the dining room. In the Highlands he found a note written by an eleven-year-old, threatening violence against whoever might buy his home, which endeared Donald to the house, but it was sorely overpriced. He became interested in a Victorian where P. T. Barnum had once lived—when he saw a photo of Barnum on the porch with elephants in the lawn he was certain he would buy it. But that certainty faded as he rolled up to the curb—the house stood along railroad tracks, with a welding shop on one side and a derelict warehouse on the other, and he couldn't convince himself that these could be overlooked. He watched for the Victorian that he had told his parents to buy; over the years he had seen several houses that reminded him of it, but none seemed exactly right, and perhaps nothing was—it could have been scraped to make room for a strip mall, or various owners might have remodeled it beyond recognition. He supposed that he could find it if he really wanted to. Call his mother. But what would he do then? Go look at it? It would become merely another house. Maybe, too, he feared the slight chance of finding his mother's friend: she had presented an open seep of sensuality that attracted and repelled. In his memory she burned, and he would have hated to see her now. Anyway, he didn't like the Victorians he saw, too large for his purposes, too drafty, too dim. The sudden knowledge did not come. His nearest experience to such an irrational trigger was in a bungalow near Berkeley Park, where he descended to the gloomy, half-finished basement and began looking over his shoulder with the feeling of someone crowding behind, as if an angry invisible specter were miming and mocking him. He fled the house gasping.

Finally he abandoned hope of a revelation and bought a small Tudor in the Sunnyside neighborhood. A turret-shaped entryway, cove ceilings, and creaking wooden floors—it reminded him, a little, of the house he had told his parents to buy. When he moved his things from his apartment, they filled less than half of the new house. He didn't love it. It seemed a compromise. He thought perhaps he would learn to love it in time, and, at any rate, it was an area where, he believed, prices could only go upward.

Shortly after he signed the contract, Iris suggested she might move in with him. No, he said. He wanted to keep his own, separate space. She called that evening to say she thought probably they should stop seeing each other. He said, yes, all right.

There was no surprise in this, and the lack of surprise left him curiously dulled, until several days later, when he received in the mail a box filled with several books, DVDs, and clothes. The clothes smelled of her detergent. He began to wonder about the path he had closed off, reserving his freedom from what, to do what? He began to regret. He described the situation to a friend, and the friend, unimpressed, said, "Fear of commitment." He saw that that was exactly it, obviously enough, and the discovery that his psychology was stupid and common enough to be cliché cast his regret into despair, a conviction that he had done the wrong thing, had failed to find the resolve to be who he wanted to be rather than who it was easy to be.

He called her. She mentioned that she was now seeing a man who piloted helicopters for a living. He tried to elicit her laugh, but her solemnity was moat, gate, and high stone wall. When he said he would like to see her, the conversation became broken and confused. When the line clicked and died she had not exactly hung up on him, but it was nearly so.

Several months had passed since then. When Donald took his client to see Iris's place, it was in the middle of a list of addresses that they were touring. He believed time had eroded his feelings about Iris, but as he stepped through her doorway he was struck by the smell of her soaps, her houseplants, and her cooking, an effect so potent that he had to halt in the slate tiled entryway and cough to cover his tears. After a moment he remembered to step aside for his client. A few items of mail lay on the table by the front door. By an exertion of will, he did not look at these. But, moving into the kitchen and then to the great room, he couldn't stop himself from scanning for signs of a boyfriend—a photo, a carton of chocolates, a stray pair of boxers. He saw none of these. He looked into the bathroom: only one toothbrush hung in the holder. In the bedroom she had a bowl on the dresser with a tangle of jewelry inside, and he poked them, looking for the pieces he had given her. In his closet hung several skirts and a dress in dry cleaning bags; he pulled them out one by one, and knew them all.

"Wow," the client said. He was in the great room, at the windows. "This view is incredible."

Donald had forgotten the striking impression made by the space and its views. Iris had furniture with nice, clean lines, and she had painted the walls in earth tones. There were enormous sunflowers in a pitcher on the coffee table and shimmering gold, red, and black art on the walls. Her unit was also, because of the neighborhood, relatively cheap. The client began pacing rapidly, flushed with excitement, and as Donald watched he knew he could not possibly help this man buy this place. Here—where they had spent entire days naked, unwashed, stinking, counting orgasms, where he could still see the dent in the floor where the jade plant had fallen. "You should know that this isn't a great neighborhood. Look."

Donald pointed down through the window. "That's juvie hall. And this building gets tagged all the time. Did you know they use glass etchers on the windows now? Not long ago, a friend of a friend was mugged a couple of blocks from here." He wandered toward the kitchen, hoping to draw the client from the view. "The homeowners' association fees in this building are pretty high, relative to comparable buildings. The stove, unfortunately, is electric."

But the guy returned to the windows. Donald stood behind him, waiting. He cleared his throat and ground the flesh of his cheek with his teeth. She had only been a girlfriend; it wasn't as if they had nursed each other through a cancer. He needed to grow up, move on. He'd thought he had. The client began fussily checking the window shades; Donald recalled lounging with Iris on the couch and watching the storms that gathered above the front range, dropped white eruptions of light, and drifted toward the city while the touch of her fingers tickled the hair above the crack of his ass.

As it happened, later in the day the client fell in love with a unit in one of the new developments along the Platte River, and he forgot Iris's place.

That night, Donald sat up with a lurch, gasping, throwing covers aside, a stark blinding light in the window, a pounding of hellish noise filling his head. For several seconds he stared at the light, and it seemed to return his gaze. Then it rose and turned into the sky, lifting the horrendous noise with it.

He fell back into bed. He had seen and heard police helicopters moving through on other occasions, and they had even cast a spotlight in his windows before, but this one had caught him badly off-guard. The helicopter, surely, was piloted by Iris's boyfriend—or that was the trend of his thoughts, before he recognized it as paranoia. Restless, he clambered out of bed and went to sit in the dark at his dining-room table. He began to think that he had liked this city in part because he had known no one here, and by placing himself here he had cleansed himself of all the confused, entangled relationships back home that he had handled poorly, that had made him awkward. But with time new relationships took their course, and now the only way to disengage fully would be to move on again. He saw before himself the possibility of a lifetime of such moves, and he grew aggrieved toward this version of himself—or, the parts of himself that he saw there.

After a time he dressed, went outside, and took his car from the garage. For half an hour he drove. When he stopped, he was at her building. Her windows were dark, and he didn't see her car in the parking lot. The keypad code at the entryway hadn't changed. He took the elevator up. He stood with his hands against her door, listening.

Presently he knocked. He knocked again, and a third time. Then he opened the lockbox that her realtor had put out with the key.

In the dark entryway he stood listening. Then he went to the bedroom. The door was open. He peered inside, but the bed was empty. Sometimes she preferred to sleep on her couch, but it was empty, too. He wondered if she were spending the night with her boyfriend.

A glass of juice—a quarter full, room temperature—stood on the kitchen counter. She never did finish her drinks. He spent a minute searching the cupboards for the wooden fruit bowl he had given her but finally had to concede it was gone. But he noted, with surprise and a kind of animal hope, that two of the cartoons he had clipped were still on the refrigerator. The experience of being here now was different from when he was here with his client, less desperate and agitating. Was it the nighttime? The solitude? Well, after all, if he had not learned in his work to become comfortable in a stranger's home, what had he learned? He opened the refrigerator and, looking for a bottle of beer, rummaged through juices—she always had four or five different juices, which she mixed in odd combinations—and condiments and cups of yogurt. He located two beer bottles on the bottom shelf toward the back, but then he decided he had better not and closed the refrigerator.

Here in her home. Was it still her home, now that it was also a commodity and strangers wandered through to make price-to-value assessments? What was it at this moment, when she was gone, and he was here? She would have had opinions about such questions.

As he walked, something brushed his shoe. A coffee mug lay on the floor, broken into three large pieces. He crouched and touched the rough, sharp edges. So, maybe the helicopter pilot had broken up with her, or she'd caught the helicopter pilot cheating on her. Or, perhaps she had been thinking of Donald with regret and grew angry. He sat on her couch. To the right, past the suburbs, the mountains were faint black shapes below the sky's midnight blue and stars. To the left shone the downtown's vertical structures of light, and even at this hour a number of cars moved below. He had been sitting here when he mentioned to Iris how frequently his parents argued, and she had said, off-handedly, "Maybe that's why you like attorneys." She probably wouldn't remember it now. It was a theory that had pleased him then, although it seemed like nonsense now.

A tiny noise, a rattle near the floor, came from the far corner. His heart stumbled, then throbbed, and he held himself still. In the corner, behind an armchair set at an angle, was a triangle of open space where a person might hide. "Iris?" he said. He imagined her hearing noises at the door in the middle of the night, waiting for it to go away, and then hiding when the door opened. Well, he thought, at least that would mean the boyfriend doesn't have a key. He talked into the dark. "I'm sorry," he said. "If I could take it all back, I'd ask you to marry me." No one answered. And surely she wasn't a person to hide behind a chair in a corner. Yet, he was certain he had heard something. Before anxiety could paralyze him, he strode over and peered behind the chair. Nothing. He took hold of the armrests and pulled it from the wall. Down at the chair's feet were two krypton-green eyes. A cat. A dark calico.

He laughed. When he reached down, the cat flinched, but he spoke softly to it, and after a few seconds the cat came forward and rubbed against his ankle. He took it in his arms and carried it to the windows to look at the city lights. "I don't want to leave this city," he said, aloud. Yes? Why had he not been struck by love when he was looking for a house? He looked at the lights, the streets, the homes, and thought of his old apartment with the undulating living room floor and tilting furniture. Someone else lived there now, and where he lived now someone else had lived, and the place where he stood would be bought by a stranger. Thinking of it he felt wonder. He was glad he had come here.

The cat stretched its neck, peered at the floor. He ran his fingers into its fur. The claws of its rear feet dug into his arm, and it stared up at him. He put the animal on the floor, and it walked away, strutting.

He wrote the words he had spoken to the cat on the back of a business card and left it on the countertop.

The next morning he faxed over a full price offer.

If Iris was surprised, her agent did not communicate it. A woman with a creaking, oddly modulated voice, she said her client would like to adjust the dates for the inspection resolution and the closing, and, if those changes were satisfactory, they had a deal.They had a deal.

Five days later Donald met his inspector at the condo. The inspector was a heavy, merry man with glasses that exaggerated his eyes. He conducted his inspections with a patter of commentary and anecdotes. Donald liked to send his clients to the guy because he had a reassuring presence and could be counted on to establish clearly which deficiencies were worth fighting over and which weren't. But now, as Donald wandered the condo again in daylight, he desperately wished the man would stop talking about furnace filters, dishwasher hookups, and garbage-disposal motors. Donald said, "Uh-huh." The note he had left had been an irrational, useless gesture. It was hopeless, yet he still had little frog kicks of hope, and he searched for a message. A note. A broken thing underfoot. No, nothing. Still, he looked around the tall open sunlit space, hoping and wanting.

For the closing he wore new clothes. He anticipated an event of grueling embarrassment; still, he wanted to see her. But when he arrived he learned that she had come early, signed her signature lines, and left.

He moved his things into the condo and rented out the Tudor. The condo still looked great, and he remembered the sense of elation he'd felt the night he had come in looking for her. He was glad to be here again, at first. But his happiness soon grew scuffed and bent. Her absence was inescapable. He could not arrange his furniture in a manner that wasn't either an echo or a refutation of her arrangement. When he brought in another woman, everything she did became an exercise in comparison and contrast with Iris's manner of occupying the space.

After twelve months, when the lease on his Tudor was up, he kicked out his tenants and moved back.

He came to believe that sneaking into her condo that night had been an extraordinary mistake, the capstone on a large structure of error, a moment when he thought he had reached some understanding of himself, of the linkages between his sense of self and place. And it had been false. Wrong. It had put him even further from understanding, and he had no place.

But he couldn't live entirely inside an idea like that. He had to put it aside and go on. He went out with a couple of women. He met the third-grade teacher with a long lovely neck and hairy fingers, and after dating for a while they bought a little row house with a view of downtown. He bought a ring and proposed to her at the top of Mount Evans.

Still, when he had to think about the idea of *home*, which in his work he often did, he tended to think of Iris: of her laugh, her loft-style condo, her broken things, an impression that over time gently shifted and distilled and became, mostly, the memory of her cat in his arms.

Armistice Day

1. The Wallet

Peace has come, and in the Manhattan on Larimer Street, where the menu offers steak for 35 cents, a chaotic, exuberant noise rises from the tables. Over the last week the Spanish Flu epidemic has ebbed, and today came word of a signed armistice—soon the boys in France will be coming home! Few still bother to wear the gauze masks that the city mandated to combat the influenza, but a pair seated at a table near the front door wear theirs—white cloths tied back over the ears, covering nose and mouth.

"Someday you'll kill me," the big one says to the little one.

"Sure I will."

"That's what sons do to their fathers."

The boy looks about ten years old. His father has a deep crease fixed into his forehead, as if his mouth, frustrated by the mask, migrated upward. The boy has small, dark eyes, and he is unlikeable. His father is also unlikeable, however, which works out, in a sense. If only one or the other had been unlikeable, they would work at cross-purposes, but as it is they project a peculiar energy together and seem, if unlikeable, also singular.

They cut pieces of steak, lift their masks to put the food into their mouths, let the masks down again to chew.

Their unlikeability has already impressed those at the tables around them. The two talk loudly while watching the door and the celebrating crowds that wander outside. They have a small round table, but sit nearly side-by-side. The father, eating left-handed, jostles his son, right-handed.

"What're you going to kill me for?"

"For picking your nose and a funny look," the boy says. He lifts his chin to speak in a curious, mock-theatrical style.

"You have a very disrespectful manner."

"If there's an apple on the ground, chances are the tree's nearby."

Men, arm-in-arm, pass the door singing. A paperboy casts his voice into an unnerving register, calling the headline, "THE WAR IS OVER."

"You are assuming that you are, in fact, my son."

"I'm hoping I ain't."

"I indulge, but you may provoke me only so far."

"Your patience is legendary."

"You are a little cur."

At the nearest table sit two ladies and two men, all well-dressed. One of the men, particularly wide in shoulders and chest, with a scar across his nose, glances over repeatedly.

"A son of a bitch, then," the boy says.

"I'll put you over my knee right here," the father says.

The boy lifts his mask and places a piece of steak in his mouth.

The waitress comes and looks at them and goes away.

"You should tell her that we can't pay," the boy says.

"I can pay."

The father and son look at each other. The father reaches into his jacket, draws out a wallet, opens it, peers inside.

He curses; the table goes over and crashes as he falls on the boy, knocking over both their chairs; the boy screams. All around the restaurant people stand to look. The father punches his son in the chest.

The man with the scarred nose gets there first and lifts away the father; the boy, still screaming inarticulately, slips out; the father scrambles and writhes, bellowing guttural syllables, while the man with the scar tries to pin him. The boy presses close, livid, and shouts insults.

Suddenly the boy backs away. A half second later the man with the scar stands straight up to feel the pocket of his pants. "You!" He turns to follow the boy, but the boy is gone. The man peers out the door. His wallet has been taken, and when he turns back, the father—the accomplice—has also vanished. The diners begin to chatter again among themselves. The man looks out once more at the passing happy crowds.

2. The Phonograph

In a one-room apartment a floor above the celebration and noise, a woman sings opera while a son lies dying.

A desperate father paces the room. Every so often he goes to the phonograph that stands against the wall and restarts it.

He wishes it had struck himself, let it take him, old, weak, widowed, and alone. But his son, young and strong, is the one who has the Spanish Flu, is the one who lies gasping, bleeding from the nose and ears, hot as a griddle to the touch.

His son owns a jewelry store in Chicago. He attends operas and polo matches, he has a wife and a daughter, he has done well, much better than his father. Still he comes back to Denver every year to visit. He came alone this time; his wife wouldn't travel with their daughter while the Spanish Flu was rampant. He brought the phonograph along instead, as a gift. Entering his father's apartment, he looked around and smirked. "I knew you wouldn't have bought one for yourself."

With a rag daubed in a bucket of water the father wipes his son, who lies naked on the bed. The apartment's two windows admit a cool November breeze, as well as the hullabaloo from the streets, but his son still sweats thickly. Small blood blisters have formed all across his pale skin.

His son set up the machine and showed him how to run it. "Whose voice is that?" he'd asked his son.

"Jeanne Gerville-Réache. I saw her once, on stage. My favorite contralto. A couple of years ago she died in her pregnancy."

"She's dead?"

"This was recorded shortly before she died. A beautiful lady."

Together they sat listening to the voice of a dead woman.

Now, in the street below, a brass band slowly passes, braying a version of "Oh! It's a Lovely War!"

His son had spent the last week sleeping on a cot under the window. When the father went out to work, his son visited old friends or went to see shows at a little theater that had stayed open despite the city's injunctions to combat the influenza. Evenings, the two of them sat drinking from bottles of wine that his son bought and listened to the phonograph, mostly to the contralto. At a certain point he realized that they were both longing for her, this woman who he knew only by a voice, and who no longer lived.

He tries not to think of the telegraph he will have to send to his daughter-in-law and granddaughter, tries to convince himself that, against all evidence, his son might still survive. Tries not to think of solitude. Of his wife who died many years ago, hacking with tuberculosis.

Toward the end of the recording, the singer's voice rises until she strikes against the limits of the machine's capabilities, and there it warbles strangely.

A raw fleshy scent fills the room. He wipes the blood from his son's face. In reality, he knows, all he is doing is all he can do: waiting for the end.

The contralto sings in a language that he doesn't understand, and he can't even guess what it is.

3. *The Photo*

"I wish it weren't already over," says the boy, sixteen. He looks around at the celebrants with dismay. He wears a pressed, new jacket that is too long for him and carries his hands in its front pockets.

"I guess you think you want to go to war." His father walks beside him, carrying a framed photograph.

"Yes!"

"I think I felt that way once, too."

The boy scowls and spits. He has been up, jittery with excitement, ever since the dark early morning hours, when the newspaper companies began setting off a series of explosions to alert the city to the good news, and to sell their special editions. Now, a dozen hours later, the crowds on 16th Street are still chanting, cheering, singing, beating pans, whistling, throwing confetti, waving flags. A car drags clattering pieces of stovepipe. A truck carries a pole with a hanging effigy of the Kaiser.

The boy tugs down his hat, which is also new, identical to the one that Harold Lloyd wore in *Two-Gun Gussie*. He stops to watch a young woman stroll by.

"Here," says his father, beckoning from a storefront: Mile High Photo.

Inside, in the quiet, the photographer fusses with his flash pan. "It will be better," he says, "with one of the backdrops. It will add some style."

The father looks at the photo in his hand. "No backdrop. Just a white wall."

The photographer shrugs, eager to move along. He's been busy all day.

"You kneel there," the father says. "I stand here."

"We can both stand," the boy says.

"No, the point is to make it just the same."

The boy, sighing, kneels. The father puts on his hat, and the boy does, too.

"No, no," the father says, "you hold yours on your knee."

"You're wearing yours."

"Yes, but yours goes on your knee."

"I'll wear it."

The father holds out the framed photo, making little sounds with his lips. "Look here—with my father, I had it on my knee. He wore his."

"Did grandpa tell you to put it on your knee?"

"That's just how it turned out."

"I'll wear mine."

"When you have a son and you take this photo, you can wear the hat."

"I'd let my son wear his hat if he wanted."

"Sirs," the photographer says.

The father lets the boy wear the hat. "Wear it back, so the camera can see your eyes," he adds, to regain some authority. He sets aside the framed photo, and at the last moment he takes off his own hat, thinking there will be a symmetry in that. But after the flash shoots off—and briefly consumes the world with brilliant light—he begins to rue it.

They step outside into the moving crowds and come to 15th Street before he realizes that he's forgotten his framed photo in the photographer's studio. He tells his son to wait while he goes back for it. When he reaches 15th again, his son is smoking a cigarette—where did that come from?—and talking to a young woman in a long coat and a wide straw hat. She's pretty.

From behind her he gestures to his son and goes on alone. He walks looking at the framed photo of himself and his father in their old-fashioned clothes—frock coats and tall bowler hats. It's a photo of a man with a great silly grin standing just behind a boy on one knee, a boy who looks both desperately serious and thrilled just to be there, having his photo taken with his father.

4. *The Leg*

"Now Jack will soon be home."

Ralph has heard Mother say this twice already as she bustles around, bringing in cookies, then tea, and he has noticed that each time she says it, Father shifts his hands a little.

They are sitting in the parlor of his father's Victorian house in the Highlands, in an ornate wooden armchair. Ralph's crutches are propped against his chair back. He gives two cookies to his son, who gravely and silently pockets them. To Ralph this seems strange behavior for a boy, but is it worrying or only amusing? He's not sure. When he returned from France two weeks ago—or, rather, when most of him returned, excepting the left knee, shin, and foot—his son screamed and cried at the sight of him. Ralph thought at first that it was because of the leg. But no, the boy simply had no idea who this man was.

"I wonder if he'll recognize Jack?" Mother says.

But Ralph has no doubt that the boy will. Jack—who could make coins appear out of noses, who could crawl around with his nephew for hours playing with tin soldiers—had been extremely popular.

Again Father's hands twitch.

Finally Mother stops moving, sits at the edge of a chair. She adjusts the plate of cookies and says, "Will you remember your Uncle Jack?"

The boy stares at her. He says, whispering, "Yes."

In the quiet afterward the noises of celebration carries to them. Church bells. School bells. Steam whistles.

Mother says to the boy, "I bet your mama is glad to have your daddy back to get you out of the house, so she can get a thing done."

The boy only stares.

Mother looks around the room, turns to the boy again. "Would you like to see if there's any dough left in the mixing bowl?"

The boy leaps from his seat, and so the two of them exit. Ralph feels inclined to run after them, but he remembers his leg, looks at his father, and sits still.

It'd been a surprise when Jack enlisted. He'd never expressed any interest before, but he'd gone to sign up while his arm was still in a sling, before the general conscription even began; he'd volunteered.

The sling resulted from a beating that Father gave Jack. Ralph had gone with Father in the Studebaker for an afternoon of fly fishing, but Father had stepped on his rod and broke it, so they returned early; then, entering the house, they heard something strange upstairs, and discovered Jack, naked, with another boy, also naked. Ralph had never seen the other boy before or again, only glimpsed him running past, wild blond hair, tanned, penis flapping.

When Ralph dragged Father away, he'd been afraid that Jack might already be dead.

"Do you suppose," Ralph says, "there's any chance at all that Jack could be home for Christmas?"

"When he left," Father says, "he told me that, one way or another, we would never see him again."

In the kitchen, the boy squeals and Mother laughs, the noise of them muffled by the door. Ralph pushes up to go to them, forgetting his leg, and falls.

5. The Dance

Is it the crowds or the crying baby? He contemplates the hysterical noises from the street of people shouting and smashing pans together, and he considers the urgent, remorseless vocal agony of the child. The problem is the baby. He could sleep through a celebration; it has nothing to do with him.

He needs sleep.

He grows angrier and angrier as insufferable minutes pass into an hour, and then another. He cannot sleep, and without sleep he will have no energy for his work. He might lose the job; others will be happy to do it. He cannot lose the job. And he cannot sleep. He cannot sleep because the baby won't be quiet. How can the baby continue like this? It seems inhuman. It seems pure malice, pure hatred, of him, the baby's father.

Finally he scrambles out of bed, throws the door open, and strides into the other room. His wife slouches in a kitchen chair with the baby in her lap, and he falls to a crouch before them and raises his fist over the shrieking creature.

His wife licks her lips. "Stop that," she says.

Her look catches him. "Can't I joke?" he says.

But she stares in a way that twists into him, and suddenly he understands that he will regret the gesture a long time. Already it makes him sad, to think of it, to think of thinking of it.

In repentance, he asks, "Is he sick?"

"It's the noise outside that keeps prodding him. Take him, please. He'll quiet for you. He always does."

He takes the baby to his shoulder. He paces and bounces his step. The trick involves adding movements within the movements, and he thinks of it as dancing very delicately. He has described it to his wife, but she isn't able to do it.

In a minute, the baby quiets.

A few minutes later, the baby curls and sleeps. Then his wife, too, sleeps in her chair.

He continues to circle the room, inhaling the baby's crude human scent. He can put him down—the baby would sleep on—but he keeps the baby on his shoulder.

Acknowledgments

I am grateful to James Michener and the Copernicus Society of America for assistance during the writing of this book.

For their aid in shaping these stories and, especially, for their unwavering support, I want to thank Mary Jean Babic, Ethan Canin, Josh Henkin, Rachel Grace Hultin, Brett Kelly, Valerie Laken, Don Lystra, Jim McPherson, John Pustell, Eric Simonoff, and Steve Zadesky.

Author Biography

Nick Arvin the author of four books of fiction, including the novels *Mad Boy* and *Articles of War*. His work has appeared in *The New Yorker, New York Times*, and *The Wall Street Journal*, and has been honored with awards from the American Academy of Arts and Letters, the American Library Association, and the National Endowment for the Arts. He lives in Denver, where he works as an engineer.